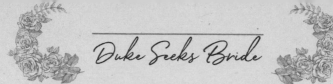

"Did you ever ask her about that night—"

"No," he cut in. "I considered asking but couldn't imagine how to broach the topic."

"'Who was that strange girl in your garden?'" she said in a low imitation of his voice, then smiled.

"And did *you* ever ask?" Alex was shocked how much he wanted to hear that she had.

"No. Why would I?" She shrugged. "I knew it was unlikely we'd ever meet again."

"And yet we have." This time when their gazes met, something in the center of his chest burned, like one of the fireplace embers had planted itself there and sparked to life.

"And yet we have," she repeated.

Never in his life had he felt so immediately drawn to and yet at ease with a lady, especially one who aroused him as she did. And it had all been there from that first moment.

He reached for her, unable to stop himself. Then he hesitated, his fingers hovering near the flushed slope of her cheek.

She tipped her head to close the distance, and he stroked his fingers across her skin. Sliding a silken strand of hair behind her ear, he leaned closer, breathing in her scent—something rich and floral, like the flowers in the garden where he'd first met her.

Her lips parted, and he expected one of them would surely come to their senses.

But she said nothing.

And he wanted nothing so much as to kiss her.

By Christy Carlyle

The Love on Holiday Series
DUKE SEEKS BRIDE
LADY MEETS EARL
DUKE GONE ROGUE

The Duke's Den Series
A DUKE CHANGES EVERYTHING
ANYTHING BUT A DUKE
NOTHING COMPARES TO THE DUKE

Romancing the Rules Series
RULES FOR A ROGUE
A STUDY IN SCOUNDRELS
HOW TO WOO A WALLFLOWER

The Accidental Heirs Series
ONE SCANDALOUS KISS
ONE TEMPTING PROPOSAL
ONE DANGEROUS DESIRE

CHRISTY CARLYLE

DUKE SEEKS BRIDE

A Love on Holiday Novel

AVONBOOKS

An Imprint of HarperCollinsPublishers

DUKE SEEKS BRIDE. Copyright © 2023 by Christy Carlyle. All rights reserved. Printed in the United States of America. No part of this book may be used or reproduced in any manner whatsoever without written permission except in the case of brief quotations embodied in critical articles and reviews. For information, address HarperCollins Publishers, 195 Broadway, New York, NY 10007.

First Avon Books mass market printing: August 2023

Print Edition ISBN: 978-0-06-305451-6
Digital Edition ISBN: 978-0-06-305444-8

Cover design by Amy Halperin
Cover illustration by Judy York
Cover image © James_Fraser/Shutterstock (scenery)
Rose chapter opener art © mikwa59/Shutterstock, Inc.

Avon, Avon & logo, and Avon Books & logo are registered trademarks of HarperCollins Publishers in the United States of America and other countries.

HarperCollins is a registered trademark of HarperCollins Publishers in the United States of America and other countries.

FIRST EDITION

23 24 25 26 27 BVGM 10 9 8 7 6 5 4 3 2 1

To my friend Molly, who I spent summers with riding horses, and to anyone who loves horses or Ireland. Or both.

DUKE SEEKS BRIDE

Chapter One

July 1896
Belgravia, London

Scandal, Alexander Pierpont, Marquess of Kirkham, had learned, leaves a nobleman with two options.

One can retreat into a quiet life beyond society's judgments.

Or one can storm straight back into the center of *good* society with so much *don't give a damn* pomposity that others are forced to give way.

For three years, Alex had chosen the former option. Quiet was his preference, after all. He'd always favored small, intimate gatherings over lavish throngs. Give him excellent coffee and one friend capable of good conversation, and he'd forego the most lauded soiree of the Season.

Hell, he needed no real inducement to avoid the Season. In his opinion, the marriage mart was an antiquated and unfair ritual that favored men more than ladies, and, at least in his mother's case, had led to a marriage so miserable she'd spent much of it living five hundred miles away from Alex's father.

Ireland had been the country of her birth, and it had become home to Alex and his siblings too.

All but poor Edmund. As heir, he'd been kept close by their father. Trained and tutored at the ducal estate in Wiltshire so that he might assume the dukedom, even as their father did his best to bankrupt it.

No one had expected a fever to take him four years past, and Alex had sure as hell never expected to become heir. Afterward, his single year-long attempt at taming his impulses, remembering the rules of etiquette, and living up to his father's expectations had proven why he should never be Duke of Rennick.

He'd ended the year by beating another nobleman bloody.

The infamy that followed had allowed him to go home. Back to Ballymore Castle in Ireland, and there he'd stayed—away from society, away from the hollowed-out ducal estate in Wiltshire, and away from his father's demands.

But he'd always known the reprieve would be temporary. Despite his arrogance and pride, Marcus Pierpont was mortal, and according to his doctors, he didn't have many days left to live.

So Alex had responded to his father's summons to return to London, and tonight he'd acceded to the old man's command that he reenter society and attend one of the most popular soirees of the Season. The hostess was a family friend who had sent Alex a letter of support after the incident that had caused him to leave high society behind for his horses and the soul-feeding beauty of Galway.

He climbed down from his carriage, swept a hand through the overlong hair he hadn't bothered trimming, and clenched the fist that he'd once used to strike a fellow nobleman. At the front door of Lady Waverly's Belgravia town house, he had a moment's hesitation.

Turn back, some last shred of self-preservation screamed from a corner of his mind.

But by then a footman had spotted him, and within moments his name had been ticked off a list, and soon he was wading into the fray of Lady Waverly's famed silver ballroom.

A kaleidoscope of colors and sounds overwhelmed him the minute he crossed the threshold. Peach, plum, fuchsia, and yellow dominated among the ladies' gowns, and a string quartet let out a cacophony in the corner as the musicians warmed their instruments.

Alex accepted a drink from a passing footman's tray, swallowed a sip of tepid lemonade, and planted himself on the edge of the ballroom. The vantage point allowed him to survey the battlefield.

"You look as if you're yearning to bolt."

The feminine voice took him by surprise, but

Alex nodded politely at the lady who'd sidled up next to him.

"Then I've already given too much away. My first ball of the Season," he offered with a tight smile. "The temptation is there, but I don't intend to escape just yet."

"The Season has been underway for some time, my lord."

"I put it off as long as I could." He injected a bit of levity into his tone. The effort felt rusty and inept, but apparently it worked.

The lady let out a low chuckle.

"I am pleased that you chose my ball for your debut this Season."

"Ah, Lady Waverly." Alex turned to face the young, widowed countess. "Thank you for the invitation. And yes," he agreed, "your events are renowned."

The cluster of well-heeled bodies that brought a smile of pride to the countess's face caused an anxious tension to tighten Alex's gut. The same that always overtook him when he was among too many people and too much noise.

"What forced you out of hiding?"

"Necessity." He had no intention of divulging details of his father's failing health, but the countess seemed to know, or at least suspect.

"It's been a while since I've seen your father," she offered quietly. "He was a frequent guest at my soirees, and I have missed him."

The comment was a stark reminder of how quickly circumstances could change. His father had been the bold, brash Duke of Rennick for forty-six years. According to the doctors, that title would be Alex's by month's end.

"I will convey that you asked after him."

"Thank you. I hope we'll see *you* more often."

Alex took another sip of lemonade to stave off the misery that comment sparked.

This was to be his fate. Future duke. Sire to the next duke. With Edmund's death, all other possibilities had been snuffed out.

"Do you know him well?" Alex was curious what drew others to his father. To his family, he'd been controlling, at times cruel. To most, he was charmingly boisterous and convivial.

"We both attended Equestrian Society events."

"Ah yes. He does love horses." Alex wasn't sure that claim was entirely true. If his father treated horses well, it was because they were prized possessions, and being a talented horseman gave him a sense of pride. An appreciation for the beasts was one thing his parents shared in common. The one thing Alex was glad he'd inherited from both of them.

"So he's the only reason you're here?"

Alex sensed Lady Waverly studying him, though he couldn't tell whether it was with carnal interest or mere curiosity.

At the moment, he had no more yearning for a

dalliance than he did for marriage. But he knew that finding a bride was no longer a matter of desire but of duty.

"It is time for me to enter the fray." He couldn't keep the bleakness he felt from his tone. Already, he yearned to return to Ireland.

"There are many here who will be pleased that you have." With her closed fan, she made a sweeping gesture across the ballroom again.

"Are there indeed?" He doubted it. An exiled nobleman with a violent scandal at his back?

And yet Alex noted the feminine glances cast his way. Since he did not attend events during the Season, he suspected some were merely curious about his identity. But he cataloged intrigued gazes too. Even the flare of attraction.

"Dancing commences in a quarter of an hour, Lord Kirkham. I suggest you add your name to a few ladies' dance cards."

"I shall do my best." He nodded and offered a smile. She did the same and then sailed off into the legion of black-suited noblemen and brightly garbed ladies.

His observant hostess was correct. He'd escape now if he could.

But he knew what was required. So he pushed off from the corner and made his way around the perimeter of the room.

The first lady he approached blushed furiously, looked for her chaperone, and then nearly burst into tears when she remembered her dance card was already full. The next penciled him in before he'd barely gotten the request out. He was the first and only name on her card. The third young lady almost demurred until another debutante whispered loudly enough for others to hear.

"He's the future Duke of Rennick."

The moment he stepped forward with his first partner on his arm, tension clawed its way up his middle. The heat of all the gathered bodies hit him as a crescendo of music resounded off the ceiling. Then the dancing commenced.

And he immediately lost count of the steps.

Why the hell had he imagined he could stride into a ballroom after avoiding dancing and large gatherings for years? He felt awkward and uncoordinated next to the fuchsia-clad debutante with her dainty gloved hand on his arm. He stepped one way, then the other, losing count and uncertain in his movements.

The lady sensed his unease and apparently felt the same. Her cheeks flamed crimson, and she could barely meet his gaze.

"Forgive me. I have not danced in a long while," he told her, still trying to count the steps in his head.

"I've danced far too much," she said on a quavery breath.

"Then perhaps I should let you lead."

She giggled at that, which caused her to forget her steps at the same moment he misstepped. She began to pitch sideways, and Alex clutched tighter to keep her from falling. In those few seconds, they'd all but stopped moving, and another couple nearly collided with them.

Without a word, his partner yanked her gloved hand from his and rushed from the ballroom.

Alex stood for a moment, enduring the stares and whispers, before wending his way through the dancing couples. He knew he owed a dance to another lady, but the need to escape tempted him. Staring at the front door, he considered the offense he'd cause. The young lady might be disappointed, but after his performance in the ballroom, she'd be safer with anyone else.

A few steps and he could be in a carriage on the way back to his family's London town house. Instead, he went in the opposite direction, searching for a door out to Lady Waverly's back garden.

Fresh air tended to ease his anxiety, and that was something he needed before facing his other unlucky dance partner.

MISS EVELYN GRAVES closed her eyes and let the images in her mind coalesce, her ink pen perched over the foolscap she'd begun to cover in quickly written lines.

Something about the hero in her story wasn't quite right. He was almost too good, too noble. She mused on what deep, dark secret she might plant in her character's history.

At a round of applause from belowstairs, she opened her eyes, and her concentration scattered.

Evie didn't mind the late nights when her employer hosted balls in her Belgrave Square town house. Lady Waverly was one of the most popular hostesses of the Season. That was why the widowed countess employed Evie as her personal secretary.

And sleepless evenings gave Evie time to write her novel. Her younger sister often teased her about writing for work and then going to her room and doing the same again. But writing speeches and correspondence for Lady Waverly came from a different place than her stories. One required mostly logic, the other unfettered imagination.

Of course, writing wasn't her only duty for Lady Waverly. Organizing, planning, appointment-setting—Evie took part in all aspects of pulling off the countess's events. Usually, she was relieved when her duties for the day ended and she could return to her room to work on a manuscript. Tonight, for some reason, seeing to final details had sparked a foolish wish to attend such a lavish soiree. Just once. Just to know what wearing an elegant evening gown and being whirled around a ballroom felt like.

But she reminded herself that she didn't belong among the nobles downstairs. Though her father had been an earl's third son, marrying her commoner mother had caused a break with the

Graves family. Evie and her sister had been raised in a modest home, and her father had encouraged her to be strong and self-sufficient. It was why she'd been so certain she could support herself and her sister after their father's death. Being employed and having a roof over her head—and one in Belgravia at that—was plenty to be grateful for.

Lady Waverly had been good to her. And, in turn, Evie worked hard. Indeed, the last few days had been a whirlwind of activity as they prepared for a charity event to be hosted at the town house in the coming week. Every detail had to be perfect, since a princess of the realm would be in attendance.

But now, sitting in bed with pages of her writing spread out around her, the music reverberated through the house, and a low buzz of conversing voices hummed in her ears. When the musicians struck up a lively piece, she couldn't resist tapping her fingers.

All hope of concentrating had fled.

One thing that usually helped to focus her mind again was reading. Often, she'd seek out the countess's library when the rest of the household were tucked away in their chambers. Curled up on a sofa with a book, everything in Evie's head would calm.

Unfortunately, the library was off-limits tonight,

since guests from the ball would be using the sitting room next to it as the ladies' retiring room.

But there was always the allure of the garden—another of her favorite solitary havens.

Evie got out of bed and took a peek out onto Lady Waverly's back garden. A pleasant breeze lifted the curtain, and she decided to take a book down to the lantern-lit space near the rose arbor.

Her ladyship had installed wrought iron tables and chairs for her garden-club friends to use during meetings, and there was one little bench hidden away from view but with enough light from the lanterns to make it a perfect reading nook.

Evie slipped out of her nightgown and back into the petticoat and dress she'd worn earlier in the day. Then she scooped up the book on her bedside table and headed downstairs. She used the servants' stairway to avoid any guests, and it deposited her outside the kitchen, which also had a door that led to the back garden.

The music and the shuffling of dozens of bodies were louder on the ground floor, but the first breath of night air soothed her. It was a blessedly clear night, so London's fog hadn't trapped noxious industrial fumes as it often did.

She found her bench and collected a few embroidered cushions from chairs nearby, creating a little pile she could lean against. The moon lit the lovely stretch of neatly clipped grass next to her favorite rosebush. Its blooms were the palest of pinks but with a splash of yellow near the base of each petal. They gave off a heady scent that reminded Evie of the cottage in Hampstead where she and her sister had been raised by their widowed father.

The grass felt so good beneath her slippered feet that Evie changed her mind and threw a few pillows down and settled in as if she was on her own little evening picnic.

Since the ballroom was at the front of the town house, the music and voices were faint, and Evie listened intently to the night sounds—crickets chirping nearby, the clip-clop of hooves as someone drove a carriage into the mews, and leaves rustling in the summer breeze.

The symphony of noises soothed her, and Evie was very tempted to let herself doze right there in the garden. But then another sound caused her to open her eyes.

Someone had burst out the back door and into the garden. The man's footsteps thudded in quick succession on the paving stones as if he was escaping a pursuer. Then they slowed, and he began grumbling to himself under his breath.

Evie heard *fool* and *wretched soiree* and a curse that involved the devil and hell and a word she couldn't quite make out.

Eventually, the footsteps stopped, and she heard no more mumbling. Only frustrated sighs. Then the garden intruder turned, bootheels scraping on the stones. A moment later, he aimed himself in her direction.

Evie froze, uncertain whether to stay and hope he didn't see her or scramble to her feet and make her escape.

Then the man was above her before she had a chance to decide.

A tall, bulky figure cut toward the rosebush and crashed into her. She put her hands up to stop him from tumbling over her, but her efforts were no match for the man's momentum.

The gentleman lost his footing and grabbed for her, tumbling her onto her back as he landed on his knees and caught himself with one palm on the grass near her head, the other near her arm.

He loomed over her in the darkness, and she could make out little but the shape of him—enormous shoulders and wild, dark hair. He blocked the light from the lantern with his bulk.

And then he spoke.

"What the bloody hell are you doing?" The words emerged on a breathy growl as he got to his feet and stared down at her, hands planted on his hips.

"Me?" Evie squeaked, lifted herself onto her elbows, and then pushed down the fabric of her skirt so she could get to her feet too. "*You* crashed into me."

He let out a long-suffering sigh. "You're right. Forgive me. Are you hurt?"

Stepping closer, he stretched out a hand to assist her.

Evie considered ignoring the belated chivalry but then found herself reaching for him.

The moment his large hand enveloped hers, an odd shiver chased along the length of her arm and settled in the center of her chest.

She tipped her head up.

He was staring down at her. Intensely.

A few breaths of time passed, and yet he didn't tug her up. When Evie moved to push herself up, he stayed her with his free hand.

"Careful," he told her quietly. "Don't move too quickly."

Quickly? She'd barely moved at all.

Then he pointed, but not at her. At something that had caught his notice in the rosebush next to her.

"A glowworm," he said in a tone so unlike his bark a moment before, it was as if he'd transformed before her eyes.

And still he held her hand. The heat of him enveloped her from that single point of contact.

"Just there," he added, then lowered himself onto his haunches.

Evie looked over and immediately saw the luminescent flicker. The worm clung to a branch of the bush, and she immediately understood the stranger's awe: such a little creature to give off such an otherworldly glow.

"She's trying to attract a lover," he told Evie quietly, his deep voice rumbling in her chest.

At the words, all the warmth of the July evening and a stranger's touch flamed in her cheeks, chasing up to the very tips of her ears.

A moment later, he seemed to remember himself. He shot to his feet, tugging Evie along with him.

After she'd swept her hands down her dress and reached up to tuck her hair back into loose pins, she faced him. And her lungs chose that moment to fail her.

In the lantern light, she discovered he was handsome. His hair had looked dark in the shadows, but it was blacker than the night sky. His eyes were light. Blue if she had to guess, though perhaps a pale green.

"Forgive my outburst," he said tightly as he studied her while she assessed him. "I didn't—"

"It's my fault."

"No, it's mine. I should have taken more care. Are you injured?"

"I'm well." Her shoulder twinged with pain, but she'd simply landed wrong. Evie didn't think it worth mentioning. She'd been the fool to plant herself on the grass. "And you?"

He released her and glanced down at his trousers. "Perhaps a bit messier than when I entered the countess's home, but I think I'll survive." Lifting his head, he shot her a sheepish smile.

Evie's throat went dry. Then her brain tried to compensate.

"I was going to sit on a bench." Evie pointed to the exact one she'd selected. "It's a warm night, and in the lantern light I can read. Her ladyship installed them quite recently. The benches, that is. And chairs too. And tables. She enjoys garden parties, you see. She's on the board of the Ladies' Gardening Society. They meet out here when the weather is fine." She realized her tongue, regardless of her dry throat, was racing over syllables. Willing herself to stop rambling, she said more succinctly, "In the end, I chose to sit near my favorite roses." She pointed to the flower-strewn bush with the glowworm still flickering in its greenery.

Whether out of guilt for tumbling onto her or a desire to be chivalrous, he dutifully examined both the chair and the rosebush.

"You prefer roses to dancing, I take it."

"Oh, I'm not attending the ball."

Underneath a disheveled fall of inky hair, his brow furrowed.

Usually, Evie thought nothing of admitting her role as a member of Lady Waverly's staff. She was proud to be employed. Many were not so lucky. And yet she resisted admitting the truth to this gorgeous stranger in a moonlit garden.

For a moment, she imagined a different life. The sort of future that lay ahead for the ladies in the countess's ballroom. A future that she'd come to accept she might never have.

A suitor. A husband. A home. A family.

"I see," the tall nobleman said. If he'd been invited, he was most likely an aristocrat.

What if she had been one of the lady attendees? What if, for a moment, she did belong among the bejeweled aristocrats in the silver ballroom? Would he have invited her to dance with him?

To her shock, he took a step closer. "Careful you don't lose this." He gestured toward her neck, and Evie reached for the pendant she'd worn since the day her father had gifted it to her.

The chain was tangled in the hair at her nape, and from the feel of it, the clasp had opened or broken. She tried to untangle the chain, but it clung stubbornly to several strands of her hair.

"Allow me," the nobleman said and then moved to stand behind her.

She held her breath when his fingers brushed hers.

"I've got it," he said quietly. "The hook didn't want to let go."

Evie lowered her hands as he worked gently to free the chain.

Then he stepped in front of her again and offered the necklace coiled in the palm of his hand. Evie took it, clasping her fingers around the warm metal.

"Thank you." When Evie met his gaze, she found she couldn't look away.

And that wasn't at all like her.

Handsome, eligible noblemen passed through

Lady Waverly's drawing room or ballroom all the time. But something about this one intrigued her.

Somehow, she intrigued him too, despite the fact that her hair was mussed, she was wearing a day dress and not a ballgown, and they could only see each other by the low light.

He tipped his head as he looked at her. "Why are you out in the garden?"

The silliest thought slipped through her mind: that it was because she was meant to encounter him.

Then a feminine voice called out, and the wistful spell she'd fallen under broke.

"My lord, we're paired for the next dance."

The words caused his whole body to stiffen, and for the briefest moment he closed his eyes. "Yes, of course," he called without even glancing at the girl. Then he took a breath as if he meant to say something to Evie.

She found herself hopeful. Yearning so fiercely that her heart began thrashing in her chest.

"Forgive me for—" he said quietly.

"No." Mortification had set in. She could see herself as if she was looking down from her window. A spinster imagining she'd been fated to meet her destiny in a moonlit garden like a heroine in her stories.

Evie was grateful for the life she'd made and needed no awkward encounter with a handsome man to change her fate.

"Good evening, my lord," she said and then collected her book, swept past him and his dance partner, and rushed back into Lady Waverly's town house.

Back into the life she had, rather than the one she sometimes let herself imagine.

Chapter Two

October 1896
Three months later
Belgravia, London

*E*vie was rarely at a loss for words.

As secretary to a popular and busy noblewoman, she spent her days crafting letters, invitations, and even speeches the Countess of Waverly gave at various charitable clubs and organizations.

But now she found herself fretting about what her next words should be. Sitting on the edge of an extremely uncomfortable chair in the sumptuous sitting room of London's most fearsome duchess, she sifted possibilities and rued her own foolishness for walking straight into potential disaster.

It had all *seemed* so simple. Lady Waverly had asked her to take an invitation for a charity ball to the Duchess of Vyne. Apparently, Her Grace had requested that it be delivered by hand, and therein was the ploy.

The formidable older duchess had shocked Evie

by insisting they take tea, and now they sat facing one another, the air as tense as if they'd stridden out to meet on a misty dueling field.

The proposition that had just been put to her was a volley she could never have expected.

The Duchess of Vyne wanted to steal her away from her employer—though she offered a position as companion rather than secretary. What did a companion even do? Follow in a noblewoman's wake? That sounded dreadfully boring.

Besides, Lady Waverly had given Evie a job at a desperate time, and that demanded some measure of loyalty. Three years past, she'd been nearly hopeless. She'd just lost her father and found herself the sole means of support for both her own livelihood and that of her younger sister.

Lady Waverly had seen her potential, and though she kept her busy, Evie still had time to work on her stories in the evenings. She wouldn't give that up to be at a duchess's beck and call.

Swallowing hard, she faced the elegant older woman squarely, but the words that came to mind would cause offense. And offending the powerful duchess wouldn't do. That would reflect poorly on Lady Waverly.

The Duchess of Vyne shifted in her chair. Her smile was sharp enough to cut glass, and she offered it without a hint of warmth.

"Word is that you are a clever little thing."

"I am clever, Your Grace." After three years of dealing with noblewomen, Evie had learned that false modesty impressed none of them. "I was provided with an excellent education."

"Hmm." The single murmur felt as if it held half a dozen judgments. "Granddaughter of the Earl of Wexford, are you not?"

"I am, but I hardly knew my grandfather. He and my father fell out."

Evie didn't have time for any of this and snuck a peek at the duchess's elaborate ormolu mantel clock. Lady Waverly's beloved pug, Chester, had accompanied Evie on what she'd expected to be a short walk they could both enjoy. Now he lifted his head as if to say he was ready to go too.

"You do not wish to waste time," the duchess declared loudly, as if Evie was a child who'd been caught lunging for the cookie jar. "An admirable quality for a girl in your position."

The *girl* part grated on Evie. She was four and twenty. Hardly a girl, and she had a good deal to be getting on with. "Lady Waverly will be expecting me. I'm sorry, Your Grace, but I cannot consider—"

"Very well, let us cut to the chase." The duchess set her teacup aside and arched one silver brow. "How much is Katharine paying you?"

The Duchess of Vyne might be at the top of London's social ladder, but Evie's employer wasn't far below. And since Evie's main goal this week was to ask the countess for an increase in wages, she couldn't afford to do anything that might displease her.

"It would be indiscreet for me to say, Your Grace." Evie chose precisely the wrong moment for a sip of the duchess's fragrant jasmine tea. The heat seared the back of her throat. She coughed until her eyes watered and returned the cup to its saucer with so little poise a bit spilled onto her hand.

When she'd composed herself, she found the duchess staring at her with an almost bored expression, as if Evie was now wasting *her* time.

"You're much less biddable than I expected." This time the duchess's grin held something like true amusement in its curves. "But discretion is what I seek in a companion most of all, Miss Graves. So nothing you've said dissuades me. I would like you to join my household. If you agree, I will pay double your current salary."

Evie's jaw dropped, and she gulped before snapping it shut. Her heartbeat sped, her emotions veering wildly from excitement to uncertainty to anger.

How could the duchess praise her—though there was the *girl* thrown in to undercut much of it—and expect her to abandon her employer so easily?

Lady Waverly was kind and had given Evie an opportunity over all the other male applicants. Though Lady Waverly kept Evie busy, she still had time to work on her stories in the evening.

Though the cruel truth was that what she needed most at the moment was income.

"You have a sister, as I understand it. With aspirations to go to medical school."

Good grief, the duchess had done her research well.

Evie's younger sister, Sybil, had taken after their mother and her knack for medicine and healing. She would graduate from finishing school soon and had already been accepted at the London School of Medicine for Women. Since the death of their father, Evie's income had supported both of them, and Evie wanted nothing so much as to see Sybil succeed in her goals.

Yet leaving her employer in this way? Lured away by a noblewoman who everyone spoke of as demanding if not downright unkind? It felt wrong, and Evie had learned to trust her intuition.

"Thank you for the tea, Your Grace, but I must return to Waverly House. There's much to do before the countess's charity ball next week."

Evie risked the faux pas of rising before her hostess. She really had lingered too long. Chester agreed and gave out a snuffling whine as he got to his feet and leaned against the bell of her gown.

Her employer was to return from a luncheon, and Evie was expected to meet with her soon after to discuss the upcoming event. Evie had planned every detail with care, including all the schedules, supply orders, and notes about attendees' preferences that

Lady Waverly appreciated. She hoped that in going over it with her, Evie could make the countess see how worthy she was of a raise.

The duchess thunked her cane on the ground as she stood.

"I see," she said, her tone dripping with disappointment. "Your loyalty only makes me more determined to employ you, Miss Graves."

"I'm happy where I am, but I do appreciate the offer, Your Grace."

"Do give it a good deal of thought, girl. Your employment with Katharine may be in more jeopardy than you know. Word is that she plans to marry again." The Duchess of Vyne thwacked her cane on the thick carpet twice. "Apparently, my dear friend Oona's nephew is considering making her his bride."

Evie frowned, her brows knitted so tight that her head began to hurt. Bride?

Lady Waverly was as fiercely independent as any woman Evie had ever known. During the three years of her employment, there had been gentlemen who showed interest. Though most had been fortune hunters determined to woo her ladyship's wealth into their own pockets. Perhaps this nephew of the duchess's friend was one of those.

Regardless, Lady Waverly had never expressed any inclination to remarry, and she'd never mentioned any specific suitor.

In short, Evie didn't believe the Duchess of Vyne.

"If Lady Waverly is to become a bride again—"

"A duchess, at that."

"If she is to become a duchess, I suspect she'll need a secretary more than ever, Your Grace." Evie wrapped Chester's lead around her hand to keep him near. "I must go. Thank you for tea."

She offered the duchess a curtsy, then turned on her heel.

"I have not been entirely forthright with you, Miss Graves."

That stopped Evie, and she turned back to find the duchess's expression had softened.

"I knew your father, years ago. We were little more than children. My family attended a country-house party the Wexfords hosted, though this one was for families too. Reginald and I got on well." She smiled, and this one was less sharp, more genuine. The lines of her face softened, and her eyes looked momentarily misty. "I do not think what happened to him was fair, if you must know. I was not acquainted with your mother, but banishing one's son is a cruelty I cannot imagine."

"Nor can I." Evie was rarely afforded the opportunity to speak of her parents. Even she and Sybil avoided talking about their father. Three years on and the grief was still heavy. And of their mother, Sybil remembered almost nothing. But Evie did. Their mother had been intelligent, poised, kind—everything Evie wished to be.

"My mother is the one who taught me etiquette,

who taught me to read and made sure my sister and I were well educated. Father's family should have been proud to embrace such a woman."

The duchess held still, saying nothing and merely assessing Evie as she had since inviting her to stay for tea.

"As a companion, Miss Graves, you would have more freedom, and I daresay more respectability than as a secretary. You would be a member of my household more than an employee, and you would attend all the social events I do. A young woman in such a situation might change her stars in a way you would not as a secretary."

"My job is respectable, Your Grace."

The duchess tsked and shook her head. "You willfully misunderstand me, girl. I am offering you a widening of your world. Katharine will find herself another secretary, but you may not receive such an opportunity again."

Something about the way the duchess spoke Lady Waverly's name sounded a warning bell in Evie's mind.

"You don't like her?"

"What a question! I am fond of Katharine. As widows, we navigate society in much the same way." The duchess shrugged. "But my sympathy for you is born of my acquaintance with your father."

Sympathy. Something about the word caused Evie's hackles to rise. Perhaps she was too proud or too defensive of her employer, but she did not want the duchess's sympathy, even if she had known Evie's father. And she did not want to be a lady's companion.

"Forgive me, Your Grace, but I cannot accept your offer, and I cannot be late." Without another word, she turned and headed for the front door. Her breath snagged in her throat until she was on the sidewalk.

"That was not a good experience," she told Chester as she set their course for home. The pug side-eyed her in what she felt certain was understanding. "I have no interest in following a duchess about." The prospect of having to attend the sorts of soirees she planned for Lady Waverly held no appeal. Even if it had one night in July.

Evie stumbled and stopped in her tracks as memories of that night came back—a sweet, fleeting assault on her senses. The warmth of the stranger's touch, the scent of roses, the glimmer of a glowworm.

Chester planted himself next to her, glancing up in confusion.

"Sorry, Chessie. Woolgathering." She started off again and forced her mind back to the matter at hand. "If Lady W plans to marry, she'll just take us with her. I'm sure of it."

The pug let out a heavy breath in reply, and she realized she was walking faster than their usual pace.

"Forgive me, boy. That whole business rattled

me." Evie slowed to a more leisurely pace. Her heartbeat still raced, but she wasn't sure whether it was due to the duchess's presumptuous audacity or fear for her future employment with Lady Waverly.

As they turned the corner, Evie looked ahead and spotted her ladyship's carriage already pulled up to the curb.

"She's early," she murmured to herself as much as to the pug trundling along beside her. "I hope nothing's wrong."

Chessie let out a whine, but it was the dog's typical reaction when he sensed his mistress's presence. Still, Evie gave the pup a look, wondering if he'd sensed that something was amiss.

A moment later, she decided to scoop him up, cradling him in her arms so she could walk faster toward the front door of Waverly House.

Inside, she encountered Mrs. Robards, her ladyship's trusted housekeeper.

"Is anything amiss?"

"Not to my knowledge, Miss Graves." She eyed the pug in Evie's arms. "Is the little man unwell?"

"Not at all." Evie looked at Chessie, and he leaned closer to lick her face. "He's a perfect companion, as usual."

After setting the dog down, Evie removed her coat and made her way into the study, where she usually worked throughout the day.

"Oh, Miss Graves, the countess did ask me to send you up when you returned."

"I didn't expect her so soon."

Mrs. Robards glanced at the longcase clock. "I suppose she is a bit early. But she mentioned something she needs to discuss with you."

Tension tied itself into a knot in Evie's stomach, and a thick constriction formed in her throat. Perhaps the duchess was right. Everything was about to change, and she'd turned down a lucrative post just when Sybil needed funds.

"Are you unwell?" Mrs. Robards approached. "You've gone pale."

"I'm all right." Evie swallowed against the lump in her throat and collected the notebook and pen she brought to every meeting with the countess. She also scooped up the folio that contained all the work she'd completed for the upcoming charity ball.

That and a potential increase in wages were what Evie had planned to discuss with her ladyship, but she tried to prepare herself for whatever the countess wished to say.

Evie took a deep breath and made her way upstairs. As usual, her ladyship's sitting-room door stood open. Through it, Evie could hear the countess murmuring to Chessie, who'd bounded up the stairs the moment they were inside. She knocked lightly and then entered.

"Oh, there you are." Lady Waverly smiled. That boded well. She was usually high-spirited, and despite being six years Evie's senior, she often had more energy.

"Good afternoon, my lady."

"Come and sit by the fire. I have much to discuss with you."

Evie nodded and then noticed that something had changed. The two chairs near the fireplace were where they sometimes sat to conduct their afternoon check-ins, but a tall side table was usually provided, so that they could go over menus, lists, and correspondence together. Today, the two chairs had been turned so that they faced each other, and the side table stood at a distance as if to indicate that it would not be needed.

"Tea?" This was all part of the daily ritual of their meetings.

"Yes, please." Evie took cream and no sugar, and she watched, willing her pulse to settle into a steady rhythm as the countess prepared her a cup.

"Now," Lady Waverly began, "I first want to acknowledge the hard work you've done for me for the last few years. You've been a godsend, to put it plainly. I don't know how I would have managed without you."

"I'm glad to have helped, my lady. And I appreciate the opportunity you gave me three years ago."

"Yes." She gestured toward Evie. "That's it, isn't it? Three years is an awfully long time. And in all that while, you've not yet had a real holiday."

Evie let out a long exhale and took a quick sip of tea before setting her cup aside.

"I did intend to ask about my wages."

"Hmm, did you indeed? Perhaps an increase is in order. Shall we say fifteen per cent?"

The chuckle that flew from Evie's lips wasn't at all ladylike, but it was full of genuine relief and joy, and Lady Waverly smiled in response.

"Excellent. I'm glad you're pleased." The countess clasped her hands together. "And now, I have a bit of a surprise for you."

The countess could have told her that she'd decided to marry two noblemen and Evie would have smiled and nodded. All that mattered was that she was not being sacked and her income would cover Sybil's schooling.

"Have you ever fancied a trip to Ireland?"

Evie had taken up her cup again and stilled midlift toward her lips. "Ireland, my lady?"

The countess offered a tight smile. "I've made a bit of a muck of things, you see. I received a lovely invitation to visit Ireland, to host a charitable event on behalf of the Irish branch of the Equestrian Society."

Evie picked up her notebook and began making notes to herself. "When will you go, my lady?"

"Well, that's just it, Evelyn. I cannot go. I agreed to leave next week."

"Next week?" Evie felt her brows jump on her forehead. But then she reminded herself that she'd pulled plans together on short notice in the past. It wasn't impossible, by any means. "I shall begin preparations. Surely, we must first book passage, secure lodgings—"

"You misunderstand, my dear. Do let me explain, and you'll see."

"Of course." Evie nodded and clasped her notebook in her lap.

"I cannot go to Ireland, but I think you should. Have the holiday that you so richly deserve."

"My lady—"

"You will also be doing me a great service by going. I have agreed to make a donation to the Duke of Rennick for the Irish Equestrian Society. I knew his father, you see. But there is also to be a small charity event that I was asked to organize and speak at. Since I cannot go, someone will need to do that organizing, and there is no one I trust more than you. Rennick can convey the little speech I've prepared."

Evie sat frozen, unsure where to begin. One thing she'd never had reason to divulge to her employer was that she wasn't good at traveling. As a child, her father had taken her and Sybil to Margate for a seaside holiday, and Evie had spent her entire time on the train trying not to cast up her accounts.

But Ireland. She *had* dreamed of visiting that isle. Even as some part of her panicked at the prospect of organizing an event in a household where she knew no one, not to mention navigating interactions with a duke and his family, something deep inside her longed to go. Get out of London. See something new and beautiful, particularly Ireland. The ancient Celts had fascinated her antiquarian father.

She might never have a chance like this again.

The room quieted to the ticking of her ladyship's mantel clock and the snapping of the fire.

"You'll go, yes?" Her ladyship often posed tasks in this way, giving Evie what felt like an option to decline. But she'd never suggested any task that Evie had felt the urge to refuse.

And she couldn't refuse this one, despite her misgivings. The opportunity felt challenging, for certain, but also like one she would always regret if she let her anxieties keep her from it.

"Of course, my lady."

"Wonderful!" Lady Waverly smiled with genuine warmth and not a small amount of relief. "I felt dreadful when I realized I'd overcommitted. But perhaps it was meant to be, in order for you to have this time away." She took a sip of tea and then cast Evie an assessing look. "Now that I think of it, I'll be a bit lost without you."

"I'll prepare everything I can before I depart."

"I have no doubt." She ran her fingers along the seam in the upholstery of her chair.

Evie had learned this indicated that something was brewing in the countess's mind, and she need only wait for her to divulge whatever it was. While she waited, Evie opened her notebook and began making a list of everything she would need to do before she left.

"I have a suspicion about the Duke of Rennick that I feel I must tell you."

The countess's ominous tone sent a familiar skitter down Evie's back. Lady Waverly didn't like complications when planning her events, and she tended to avoid mentioning them until the last minute.

"What suspicion, my lady?"

"I think the family—well, his aunt—may be trying to play matchmaker between myself and Rennick."

Evie's cheeks warmed, and she willed herself not to blush furiously. She didn't intend to tell her employer about the Duchess of Vyne's offer, but the older woman's words rang in her mind now.

"And do you wish to accept his—"

"No, goodness, no, my dear. Not a bit. But his aunt has been unusually friendly via correspondence, and I'm not sure she didn't pen some of the letters I've had from him regarding the charity event." The countess lowered her voice and leaned closer. "Word is that the dukedom has had its challenges since the death of Rennick's father."

"So he's a fortune hunter?" Evie frowned and instantly deflated. The trip to Ireland sounded less appealing by the second.

Lady Waverly was set upon by such men often enough to wave them off and take it all in her stride, but Evie hardly wanted to visit and work with one on a charity event. If he was a scoundrel, he'd probably pocket the donation himself.

Then another thought struck.

"He'll be displeased that I've come instead of you, if that's the case."

"The duke wouldn't have gotten anywhere with me even if I was going myself. And, as I said, I can't be sure how much of this is the family's doing rather than his. Still, I thought it best you know."

"Yes, my lady."

"Do not fret, Evelyn. You have my permission to tell Rennick that I do not intend to remarry."

Evie managed a nod. Surely, the duke would be wildly pleased to hear *that* news from a stranger.

Lady Waverly didn't give much consideration to the duke's disappointment. She beamed the disarming smile that tended to charm everyone and said, "And I intend to send a generous check for the Irish branch of the Equestrian Society. I'll also write to him, insisting that he be agreeable to you. And why wouldn't he? Your entire purpose in going is to assist him."

"And to see Ireland," Evie reminded her employer, though she understood now that Lady Waverly had meant that as an enticement, and the trip would involve much the same duties she performed in London.

"Yes, a working holiday," the countess amended.

Evie could accept that. She'd certainly never expected an opportunity for travel to a place she'd long dreamed of visiting.

Yet she couldn't deny a lingering wariness about Rennick. She couldn't stomach the men who pursued Lady Waverly for her wealth.

Evie wasn't certain when or if she'd marry, but she didn't wish for it to be a cold transaction.

And if this Rennick gave her trouble, she'd simply work around him as best she could to pull off the charity event. She'd ignore the man entirely if necessary. Let him do whatever dukes did while she worked behind the scenes. It was the pattern she'd grown used to with Lady Waverly.

"I do like it when you get that determined look on your face," the countess said as she sipped her tea. "I have no doubt you'll show the duke what a determined lady can accomplish in a week."

Evie intended to do just that.

Chapter Three

Eight days later

Alexander Pierpont, Duke of Rennick, was running out of time.

The clock had begun ticking down the moment he'd inherited his father's dukedom. Who could have guessed a man with mistresses in several counties would insist his heir marry within six months? Not that his father's requirement affected the title itself or any of the entailment. Even a willful duke couldn't play fast and loose with the laws of inheritance in England.

But his father had been skilled at noting others' weaknesses. Alex had watched him charm, finagle, and move others around like chess pieces from the time he was a child. Marcus Pierpont could be frivolous at times, driven by his urges, but he'd also possessed the ability to see into others' hearts and discover that one fragile point at which they'd give way.

It was why Alex had striven all his life to avoid emotion when in his father's presence. What his father could not see he could not use against him.

And yet, somehow, he'd known.

The man's obsession with Alex holding on to the Rennick dukedom—despite the fact that it consisted of little more than acres of field grass and an all but empty country house by the time his father died—meant he'd used that one piece of leverage that would cause his son to bend.

If he failed to marry by the close of February, he would lose Ballymore Castle, the single part of his inheritance that mattered most to him, his aunt, and both of his siblings.

The castle might be a ramshackle heap with a colorful, tragic history, but it had been a place of comfort for Alex and his brother and sister. When their mother brought them to spend summers and holidays at Ballymore, their father had rarely joined them. The castle represented freedom from his overbearing presence and mercurial moods.

Though the aged structure had been a marriage gift from their mother's oil-baron father, it had become Rennick property in his parents' marriage contract. And with his canny insight, Marcus Pierpont knew it would be the most powerful way to influence his heir.

The will decreed that his uncle—their father's brother, a curmudgeon without any sentimental connection to the property—would inherit Ballymore if Alex failed to find a bride.

Not that Alex ever considered shirking his duty. Unlike his brother and sister, he led a scandal-free life. Or at least he had since *the incident*. No mistresses. No drunken brawls. No reckless elopements.

But Alex did like to take his time making choices. Even as a child, he'd driven his siblings mad with how long he took to make a move when they played chess or concocted some mischievous endeavor. He wasn't as quick-witted as others, and when he tried to be, when he gave in to impulse, it invariably landed him in trouble or scandal.

So he'd not yet decided on a bride. He hadn't gone to London or Dublin to attend social events that might put him in the company of eligible ladies. He'd only assembled a list of those he knew, rejected most of them for how incompatible he suspected they'd be, and then turned his attention to the other matter that weighed on him every single day: how to solve the pecuniary mess his father had left for him.

Thus the current crick in his neck and the pile of ledgers, documents, and half-formed plans that he'd been poring over for hours. His objective was to bring the ducal coffers into the black again. Leasing the ducal country house in Wiltshire to a wealthy American and his noblewoman bride had been the first step. Since there were no longer any tenants on Rennick lands, the American's rent payment was Alex's main source of income. But he also dreamed of generating revenue in Ireland. Ballymore Castle was in sore need of repair, and Alex was determined to see that the castle was not just restored but that the family coffers were solvent and then, eventually, that its assets became profitable.

There was also the matter of the promises his mother had made. Born in Ireland and raised partly on the west coast and partly in America before her marriage to an English duke, she'd dreamed of contributing to the local village and community. She'd promised to help fund a hospital in the largest nearby town and had been a benefactor of a local farrier school. Then she'd discovered how spendthrift her estranged husband had been. Alex's father had drained much of what he'd inherited and gambled away the cash included in her dowry.

To honor her, and to be more to the community than an absentee lord of the castle, Alex was determined to fulfill her aspirations and make Ballymore his chief residence. He'd never seen a more beautiful spot than this stretch of land near the Atlantic coast.

And he had a plan. His mother had begun to fill Ballymore's stable with fine specimens, including two thoroughbreds. Alex had ridden since he was a boy; it was one of the methods he often used to settle his mind. But his interest had extended to breeding horses, even treating their diseases. Before Edmund's death, he'd considered making medicine a formal study, and he'd always wished to eventually use those skills to treat animals.

Alex's current plan involved breeding horses, both the Connemara ponies native to Ireland and the sleeker thoroughbreds in Ballymore's stable. Those would fetch a fine price among equestrians across Ireland, and expanding their stables would provide work in the village for the farrier, the blacksmith, and others.

Even now sounds from the stables carried on an ocean breeze through his study window and lured him. He stood and stretched his back. Sunlight flickered between thick, rolling clouds, and he considered heading down to the stables to take his daily ride across the countryside.

Before he could decide, the door to his study flew open, and his aunt burst in, a cat in one hand and a piece of paper in the other.

"She's agreed! My boy, she's on her way already."

Unease started at the back of Alex's neck and worked its way down, knotting the muscles he'd just stretched.

"Who's agreed and to what? And where is she on the way to?" He feared the answers even as he posed the questions.

His family had taken to matchmaking with a zeal that made him dizzy. Not that he didn't understand the urgency. He felt it too, just as his father had wished him to.

His aunt approached, handed him the cat, and held up the letter with both hands.

"Lady Katharine Waverly. She says she will attend

the Equestrian Society event, help organize, and give a speech, just as you suggested."

"I don't remember suggesting anything of the sort." Alex pinched the skin between his brows. "I mentioned her in passing, Aunt Oona. She's a member of the London Equestrian Society, and I attended one of her balls."

An image flashed in his mind at mention of that event—his chief memory from that evening. But it had nothing to do with Lady Waverly. No, what stuck in his mind was a chestnut-haired beauty sprawled on the ground next to a glowworm. The softness of her hand in his. The warmth of the smile she gave him before she'd apparently thought better of their acquaintance and stormed away.

He could still remember her scent—violets and night air and bergamot tea—the ink stains on her fingers and the flicker of gold in her emerald eyes.

"Alexander, are you listening to me?"

"Yes, I hear you." He ran a hand over Persephone, his aunt's sweet, spoiled feline, willing the memories away. "How did mention of Lady Waverly turn into her visiting Ireland and giving a speech?"

His aunt gave an affronted frown. "Do you not wish her to speak at the event? Or help organize? She is reputed to be one of the finest hostesses in London. And her donations are always generous. And why wouldn't she wish to visit Ireland? The beauty of this island is renowned."

Aunt Oona, like her sister, Alex's mother, cherished her Irish heritage and could never bring herself to make a match with an English nobleman, despite their father's urging and her sister's example.

"Lady Waverly is an excellent orator and quite skilled at encouraging benevolence in others," she added emphatically. "The lady has deep pockets."

Aunt Oona could try to make this about Lady Waverly's philanthropy, but Alex understood what she was really emphasizing. The widowed countess was wealthy and would be an excellent match for a duke in need of funds and with a castle on the verge of being lost.

He'd considered her. She'd made his list of eligible noblewomen of his acquaintance. And since they had at least common interests, he'd yet to strike her from the list. But he so loathed the notion of picking a lady from a list as if he was ordering from a restaurant menu that he'd happily set the whole matter aside.

Now the matter was about to show up at his door, and he would have to deal with it as best he could.

Though his late father and now his aunt were determined to maneuver him, he would take time with his choice. He couldn't agree to marrying Lady Waverly, but he could show her hospitality and gratitude for her efforts on behalf of the handful of local riders and horse enthusiasts who made up the west of Ireland's Equestrian Society.

"You're right," he acknowledged. "Her help and donation will be much appreciated, and I'm sure the local members will be pleased to hear from her."

Alex wondered if the poor woman realized their event would be much smaller than any she'd organized in London.

More to the point, he wondered if she suspected his aunt's scheming wasn't simply about horses.

"I knew you'd agree." Aunt Oona beamed and took Persephone back from him. "And judging by the postmark on this letter, she'll be on her way already."

"We'll have to sort out a room in the family wing." Parts of the castle structure weren't safe. Mostly, the family stayed to areas that were added in later centuries, though even some of those rooms hadn't been maintained as they should have been.

"All of that is in progress as we speak," she assured him with a satisfied smile. "I've spoken to the staff, and all will be ready for her arrival." Her gaze wandered to the piles of ledgers and documents scattered atop his desk. "She's still quite young, you know, and famously quite skilled at organizing. She could help you with all that." She gestured vaguely at the stacks on his desk. "And I understand she's quite an attractive woman."

"Aunt Oona . . ." Alex employed a warning tone

without any real threat behind it. "Of course I will welcome her and be hospitable. She was kind when I attended her ball. But I will not promise to woo the woman."

"Alexander, you must woo someone and soon."

"I am aware."

He had but a few months left to find a lady, propose, and get her to the altar.

Of the ladies he'd already considered, none had inspired him to consider a courtship. Courtship took time, and that was something he was running short on. But Lady Waverly was a widow. Perhaps she wouldn't wish for an extended courtship at all.

Perhaps Lady Waverly could be the answer. She'd been kind that single time he'd met her, and they did share a love of horses and charitable endeavors.

"May I see the letter?"

"Oh, you wish to see it?" His aunt's gaze darted down to the piece of paper, up at him, and back down again.

"Yes, if I may." Alex held out his hand and noticed her hesitation.

"Of course, my boy."

Alex scanned the missive and realized immediately why his aunt hadn't volunteered it earlier.

"She has the impression that I personally invited her." He flicked his gaze up, and Aunt Oona's cheeks pinked ever so slightly.

"Well, you must understand that it was more hospitable to extend an invitation from you."

"Hmm."

Nothing in the letter indicated that Lady Waverly understood the matchmaking intent of her journey. She merely mentioned her love for riding and her eagerness to support his local equestrian society's goal of subsidizing local breeders who wished to help preserve Ireland's native Connemara pony.

Thanks to his mother's efforts, Ballymore stabled some of the finest Connemara ponies in the country.

"Very well," he finally said as he folded the letter and handed it back to his aunt. "I'll look forward to welcoming her to Ballymore."

"Wonderful." Aunt Oona waved at the heap on his desk. "I'll leave you to it."

After she'd gone, Alex heard one of the horses whinny in the stable yard and decided to give in to the yearning for an early ride.

But as he headed out of his study, a maid approached at a quick pace, stalling his progress.

"Pardon, Your Grace. There's a gentleman to see you."

"And his name?"

"Mr. Givens, Your Grace." The girl was nervous, her cheeks flushed and eyes wide. "Says he must speak to you urgently."

Oh, this wasn't good. Tension stiffened his jaw,

but Alex tried not to jump to any conclusions until he spoke to his hired man.

"Send him up to my study." Apparently, his morning ride would be an afternoon one after all.

When the maid had gone, his aunt poked her head in again. Apparently, she hadn't gotten far. "Who is Mr. Givens?"

"Someone I hired in London."

"Hired to . . . ?"

"Advise me. He's a good man, Aunt Oona. Don't fret."

She narrowed her gaze at him. He was used to her suspicious nature and her tendency to meddle. But eventually she nodded and took her leave again.

Several minutes later, his employee appeared in the doorway.

"Givens." Alex gestured to the seat in front of his wide oak desk.

"Your Grace." The investigator gave a grim nod, which was his usual greeting. But the hard set of his jaw and pinched lines in his brow indicated something more than the usual update would be forthcoming.

"You've come a long way."

Givens hesitated, glancing out the study's long window at the endless swaths of undulating green fields surrounding the castle.

"Beautiful country. I can see why you love it."

Alex arched one dark brow. Givens wasn't

usually this dour, but nor was he known for complimenting the landscape. His business was noticing people, researching their history. He'd initially engaged the inquiry agent when considering a risky investment scheme that promised too-good-to-be-true dividends. He'd decided to keep the man on retainer for far more personal reasons.

"Stop pacing and give me the bad news first." Alex always asked for the worst before the good, if there was any. "Which of them has caused a scandal this time?"

One of his siblings was due for some outrage or another. Though instinct told him it was his baby brother, Rupert. While his sister, Belinda, had married—a shocking, scandalous match with a dashing newspaper reporter—Rupert was determined to avoid becoming *entrapped in matrimony*, as he put it, for as long as he was able. Both had come to visit Ballymore, so he'd have the chance to address any gossip-inducing mischief with them directly.

"It's neither of your siblings, Your Grace. It's your uncle." Givens looked at him square, dread gradually giving way to sympathy with the dip of his grayed brows. "If my sources are correct, Pierpont is on his way to Ireland."

"When?" Alex stilled, forcing his breathing to slow, taming his emotions. Much as he'd done when in his father's presence.

"He was overheard at his club saying he intended to come see the castle he'd soon inherit."

Alex scoffed. The man never passed up a chance to be a thorn in his side. Uncle George seemed to resent that he'd lived his life in his brother's shadow and could never be heir to the Rennick dukedom.

But he wouldn't inherit Ballymore either. Alex intended to ensure it.

"What will you do?" Givens asked in his usual gruff tone.

"I'll marry and fulfill the terms of my father's will."

"Time runs short, Your Grace."

"I've been reminded of that already today."

"Forgive me." Givens rocked on his heels. "Must be obvious to you more than any."

"A noblewoman has been invited to visit from London. She's arriving soon and may prove to be the perfect duchess for me."

Finally, the detective smiled. "I'm glad to hear it, Your Grace."

"My uncle likes making others uncomfortable, and he knows my family will not welcome him here." For as long as Alex could remember, his uncle had been a blight on their family. Lurking in the corner at family functions, always looking as if he had something to say, and yet holding back from ever explaining himself. He was a constitutionally unhappy man, and as far as Alex could tell, he wished to infect others with his misery.

"But you'll have a duchess soon." Givens couldn't keep the questioning pitch from the statement.

"Indeed I will." Alex turned to gaze out the window, uninterested in glimpsing any doubt in the other man's expression.

When he turned back, Givens shuffled as if anxious to depart.

"I'll take myself off and remain in the village until your uncle has come." Givens gave him a long look and then finally nodded.

"Stay here, if you prefer."

"Thank you, sir." Givens hadn't been hired for his brawn, but he had a knack for collecting information, and Alex preferred someone keeping an eye on his uncle. "But if your uncle is to stay at the inn, that'll allow me to note his movements and suss out his intentions."

"If you change your mind, it's no trouble to have the servants prepare a room."

At the feminine voice, both Alex and Givens snapped their gazes to the doorway of the study. Belinda stood on the threshold.

"May I speak to you?"

"Good day, Your Grace. My lady." Givens took his leave with a nod at each of them.

Belinda closed the door behind him.

"The staff is all aflutter. Apparently a Lady Waverly is arriving soon?"

"I was sure Aunt Oona would have let you in on her scheming."

"Well, she didn't. Not until a few moments ago when I encountered her in the hall." She picked up an old glass paperweight that had belonged to their mother and twisted it in her hands as if it fascinated her. Then she approached his messy desk.

"Are you distracting yourself with your plans again?"

Alex pushed aside the documents regarding his ideas to expand Ballymore's stable. There were even blueprints for horse-breeding and veterinary facilities he hoped to build one day.

"I'm quite aware of where my focus should be." He wouldn't admit how hard it was to quiet his mind long enough to focus, nor how much he'd avoided dealing with the matrimonial requirement of his father's will.

"I know you have aspirations, brother. But will they answer your current dilemma?"

His family thought his ideas were little more than daydreams, and all of them knew he could talk about them for hours given the chance. To Bel's credit, she had listened, though he sensed she had no faith in his ability to bring his goals for Ballymore to fruition.

But she hadn't come to talk about that. His sister wasn't hard to read, and she had something on her mind.

"Out with it, Bel."

"Are you entirely sure about this visit?"

"You mean the visit I only learned about minutes ago? Do I have a choice?"

"Of course you do. Why let Aunt Oona maneuver you into marriage? Wouldn't you rather choose for yourself? Why aren't you in the city meeting marriageable debutantes?"

"I have a great deal to do here." He gestured to the piles on his desk. In truth, there was so much on his shoulders at the moment that he couldn't bear the thought of entering a crowded ballroom, trying to tame his thoughts long enough to make inane small talk, and attempting to choose between a handful of young ladies he didn't have nearly enough time to know.

"I worry that a match made by someone else will not make you happy."

"If it means we keep Ballymore? I suspect it will make all of us happy."

She nodded, her gaze locked on a portrait of their mother. "You do know Mama wanted all of us to marry for love?"

Alex barely stifled a groan. "I adored our mother, as you know, but she was not the most practical woman I've ever known."

"I suppose you think the same of me. An impractical woman. Fanciful even. Ridiculous perhaps?" There was an edge of bitterness in her tone that Alex regretted.

"I've never thought you were ridiculous. I understand why you married Beckham."

She finally faced him as she approached his desk and laid the paperweight on the edge. "Even if you haven't forgiven me for it yet."

"Of course I have. Your happiness matters to me, and the titter about it died down quickly."

Her laughter was full of genuine mirth, but there was still a bit of sadness in her eyes. "You don't read the scandal sheets, apparently. And I suppose that's part of it, isn't it? You marrying someone like this popular, widowed countess is about as far from scandal as you can get."

"I'm done with scandal, Bel. I took the consequences of the choices I made, but I will always regret that they touched you and Rupert too." After he had been banished by London society, his siblings were no longer invited to certain soirees and balls. Eventually, the hubbub blew over, and Bel's and Rupert's own gregarious natures brought them back into good standing within months. But Alex would never forget how his rash choice had affected them.

"I understand." She pursed her lips, and the expression usually indicated that she was biting her tongue or weighing her words. "Yes, we all love Ballymore, but I don't wish to see you miserable. You hardly know this woman."

"How long did you know Mr. Beckham before your elopement?"

"That's not fair. I loved Guy within days. I was mad with loving him. I still am."

Alex resisted pointing out that they'd only been married for a handful of months. "I do not wish to marry anyone who drives me mad. That sounds miserable."

She crossed her arms and shot him the frustrated, pouting expression she'd perfected as a child. "I know you're not as boring as everyone thinks."

Alex let out a chuckle. "Thank you for that."

"What I mean is that I know you"—she lifted one hand and waved it toward him—"think differently. You need time to make your choices. Which is why what Father has done is so cruel."

"Bel—"

"I know after what happened in London, you tried to be perfect."

"I didn't, and I'm hardly that."

"You try to be."

"I endeavor not to cause a scandal. That is all." Alex stalled her with a raised hand. "That was not a commentary on you."

She approached their mother's portrait and ran her finger along the lower edge of the gilt frame. "And Lady Waverly has never caused a scandal either?"

"Not that I'm aware of." Unbidden, his mind went to the lady in the garden again. That night, he could have easily waded into scandal. There'd been moments in the last few months—secret, impulsive moments when the beauty he'd met in the garden came to mind—that he'd wished he had. But, of course, such reckless thoughts had been pushed down.

Belinda turned back to him. "So two staid, scandal-free individuals locked forever in matrimony."

Something about the words *locked forever* made Alex tug at his necktie.

"What about passion, brother? What about love?"

He let out a long sigh. "You know the terms of our father's will. I need to marry in half a year's time or lose Ballymore." He crossed his arms, forcing his mind to practical thoughts. "Lady Waverly might be a good choice."

"And she's astoundingly wealthy."

"She's also fond of charitable endeavors. Carrying on her benevolent donations was also something Mother wanted for each of us."

"Very well." His sister's voice had lowered to a soft whisper. "If she is the right choice, then I hope it's a union that brings you joy."

The nod he offered her was to agree with Lady Waverly possibly being the right choice, not the bit about joy. He wasn't sure he'd ever felt it or even glimpsed it. When he was riding, his worries lifted somewhat. But since inheriting, even that familiar solace rarely came. There was too much he wanted to do. Too many knots his father had left him to untangle.

Joy was for Bel. For Rupert when he won at

his club's gaming table. For Aunt Oona when she worked in her garden. Alex wasn't sure it would ever come to him.

He wasn't even certain his heart worked in such a way.

Chapter Four

Two days later

*E*vie stared eagerly out the window, desperate for a sign that they would soon reach Ballymore. After two days of travel, she was sore, exhausted, and ready to be in a bed she could sleep in for more than one night.

Her past travel sickness only reared its head off and on throughout the journey. Such as when the carriage wheels found a rut in the road or during the crossing from England. Dizziness had been the worst of it.

Considering Lady Waverly's need to be up and moving about, Evie wasn't sure she would have enjoyed the trip any more than Evie had so far. But Ireland, at least what she'd seen of it from the train car—glimpses of green through the fog that clung to the fields—looked beautiful. And not beautiful in the neat, well-manicured style of a London square. Variations of green—from rich lush emerald to pale mossy patches on jagged stones—undulated over fields that stretched as far as her eye could see. Evie spied lots of sheep and a few of the famous ponies her employer was so eager to support.

She stretched her arms, rolled her neck, and longed for nothing so much as a hot bath. Though she would've settled for a basin of warm water.

Clouds filled the sky, but Evie turned her face to the window, hopeful for a flash of sun as the morning stretched on toward noon.

They would arrive today. Soon, by her estimation, and yet the coach trundled on. So long that her eyes slid shut once again.

When she opened them, her watch said an hour had passed. Clouds still hovered in the sky, but the fog had cleared, and the coach ascended what appeared to be less a road than a barely worn path. The carriage began to bounce and sway, and Evie clutched her middle to stem a rush of queasiness.

Soon a structure came into view, and it was not at all what she'd expected. In her mind, the duke's Irish castle would reflect its history: a structure built more for fortification than leisure, and maybe Ballymore had once appeared that way. But the castle before her looked more like one that had befriended a country house and the two had joined in an awkward partnership. The stone tower she expected reached into the clouds, while the broad facade of a multistory house spread toward the drive.

A very busy, bustling drive.

"Oh no." Evie pressed closer to the glass,

rubbed the edge of her hand over the condensation, and let out a groan. "How could he not have received it?"

The countess's note. She would have explained that her secretary was coming in her stead and absolutely did not need the entire staff of maids and footmen assembled in a double row in front of a . . .

Evie's eyes rounded. Was that a runner they'd pulled out into the drive for her to step on as she exited her coach?

No, this wasn't right.

Evie swept her hands through her hair, pinched her cheeks because she suspected she looked as exhausted as she felt. She'd simply explain to the duke. She was good at explaining. What did Lady Waverly say? *Skilled at plain speaking.*

But, of course, Lady Waverly bid her to speak freely. Not all aristocrats would do the same with a young lady of her station. Especially a duke who was expecting her to be someone else entirely. Anxiety rushed in—all the worries about the trip that she'd pushed away each time they'd arisen in her mind.

There were a dozen ways she could muck this up, embarrass her employer, and thereby ruin her chances of continued employment.

The coach slowed to a crawl. The servants stood like sentries on either side of the runner.

Evie closed her eyes and took a deep breath.

The countess had described the new Duke of Rennick as staid and formidable, and that didn't sound like the sort of man who'd find a sliver of humor in being embarrassed in front of his entire Irish staff.

The coach stopped, and Evie opened her eyes.

She could do this. She'd soothed Lady Waverly's wounded pride on occasion. Good grief, she'd stood fast against the pressure of the Duchess of Vyne.

Back straight, tension exhaled, Evie glanced out the coach window with all the ladylike poise she could muster . . . and gasped.

The sun had broken through the morning's clouds, and its warm light made the interior of the carriage glow. Stones on the castle's facade that had looked dank and foreboding a moment before were bathed now in a buttery warmth.

And in front of those caramel stones, the sunlight shone on a man. Tall, dark, and forbidding, just as Evie had expected him to be. Even in the golden glow, he stood like a monolith. He appeared immovable, like a statue planted very inconveniently in front of Ballymore's door.

Then he shifted. A breeze lifted the long black flaps of his overcoat and sifted the dark strands of his hair, and that sparked him into motion. He stepped closer, long strides swallowing up the distance between the two of them.

He looked so regal as he strode toward her that Evie wondered if the runner hadn't been for her but for him to look just this impressive as he approached his potential bride-to-be.

Evie saw the precise moment when he realized she was not at all the lady he was hoping to greet. It was the same moment she recognized him as the man who'd haunted her dreams. Her heart did a strange fluttery dance in her chest, and she felt dizzy. Dreams and reality weren't supposed to clash like this.

His pitch-black brows arched over pale blue eyes as he reached out to open the door for her.

Evie felt a demand in those sharply carved brows, an insistence that she explain.

"Your Grace . . ." Evie began, knowing this was one of those awkward moments that would soon have her tongue rushing headlong into nonsense. But no words came. Only questions filled her mind.

How could it be? How could *he* be the one she'd been sent to meet?

"Welcome to—" He offered his hand and then quieted on an inhale as if the sight of her had stolen his breath.

Evie couldn't decide whether that was a good thing or a very bad one. She was too busy staring like a ninny at his extended hand. Every single bit of sense she possessed scattered like dandelion fluff. Large hand. Long fingers. She'd touched that hand once before. It had enveloped hers.

"You," he breathed, his soot-lashed eyes wide.

"And you," she whispered, desperate to decipher the spark that suddenly lit his stormy gaze.

"Welcome to Ballymore," he said a bit more loudly. A bit gruffer. As if he was biting off the end of every word. "We have been looking forward to your arrival."

Not a statue, after all. But still the tallest man she'd ever seen. And shoulders. Broad shoulders. A jaw like a chiseled edge of marble, hair so black the sunlight offered it no glow of warmth, but it ignited his eyes. They were the only thing light about him—clear and perceptive and staring at the coach where he, no doubt, expected his potential fiancée to emerge and smile appreciatively at the grand reception he'd planned for her.

Evie flung the coach's door open wider. He still held out his hand, now inside the carriage, urging her to take it.

But as she rose from the bench, dizziness took hold.

The duke leaned an inch closer, waiting. Impatiently.

"Take my hand. Step down." The commands came with quiet insistence. And not a small amount of irritation.

Evie could see the heat of it coloring the tips of one ducal ear. The other was obscured behind crow-black waves of hair that the wind continued to riffle.

Evie swallowed back a wave of nausea and took

a step down. But there was no gracefulness in it. No stability either. Her knees felt as solid as warm porridge, and she weaved forward, reaching out to keep herself from falling.

Yet the only thing to reach for was a man she'd thought of so many times she'd lost count. A man she never dared hope she'd meet again.

Her hand brushed the night-black fabric of his cloak, and she gripped a handful.

The ground rushed up, and the bile in her throat wasn't far behind. But then she was enveloped by forest-scented warmth, braced against muscles, pressed against that same black fabric she held onto and the hard body beneath it.

A few of the maids gasped.

Evie decided to worry about mortification later and soak up the heat and strength of the arms that held her.

"Better?"

Evie felt the word rumble from his chest, and there was a shocking hint of tenderness in his tone.

"I think so." Stepping back, she felt much steadier.

The duke held her a moment longer and then stepped away too. But he didn't go far. He held out his hand again.

Evie stared at it and then met his gaze.

In the cool blue depths, she couldn't detect a single emotion. It was as if he wore a mask that was so unlike the gentleman she'd met in Lady Waverly's garden that, for a moment, she wondered if she was imagining the resemblance.

No, he'd recognized her. And she'd never forgotten him.

Minutes passed while they stared at each other.

Then she realized what a fool she was being and took his offered hand. He closed his fingers over hers as if they'd done this dozens of times before. Yet it had just been the once. Next, he expertly slid her hand along his arm and tucked it around his.

Despite the tension she sensed in the muscles of his arm, he guided her up the runner slowly. The pace allowed the staff to get a good look at her. The eyes of a few widened, and several glances were exchanged between housemaids.

She knew she looked a fright and had just tumbled into their master's arms and couldn't blame them for their judgment.

An older man, the butler Evie suspected, offered a slight bow, and then a lady wearing a dark gown with keys hanging at her belt approached from the opposite side of the front door and preceded them into the castle.

Rennick held Evie's hand in place with a firm grip, almost as if he feared she'd run back to the carriage if he let go.

"Your Grace—"

"Wait," he whispered.

Through the castle doors, Evie gaped at the colorful tapestries and soaked in the welcoming crackle of a fire burning in an enormous hearth. The open room was perfect for hosting a large gathering, yet it sported only three stuffed chairs and a rather worn settee.

"Shall I show her ladyship up to her room?" the woman that Evie guessed was Ballymore's housekeeper asked with a flick of her gaze and a genuinely warm smile.

"No," snapped the irritated duke, with his very large, very firm hand wrapped around Evie's. "I'll send for you when she's ready to go up, Mrs. Wilde."

"Very good, Your Grace."

The duke's demeanor didn't surprise the older woman in the least. She nodded agreeably, spun on her heel, and left Evie alone with him.

"I can explain," Evie told him.

"Not here, you won't." Then he was off again, and Evie had no choice but to follow.

He led her through the great open hall toward a bank of stairs, up one flight, and then through an arched wooden door. The minute they crossed the threshold, he released her and closed them into the room alone.

Evie turned to find he'd stayed there—back pressed to the door, arms lashed across his chest. Those dark brows of his dipped down now, forming a displeased *V*. He scrutinized her—her mussed hair, rumpled traveling gown, and muck-encrusted boots—with an increasingly displeased glare.

"You may do your explaining now," he said quietly.

Evie bit her lip, and his gaze locked on the spot. If he hadn't received the countess's letter, hadn't truly expected her arrival, then she understood his displeasure. Even empathized with it. She wasn't a countess, but she was a lady and didn't wish to be treated otherwise.

The explanation she'd worked out in her head in the coach had been replaced with chagrin she couldn't repress.

"Did you not receive a letter from Lady Waverly, Your Grace?" Evie flicked her gaze to the chaos atop his desk. In fact, some of it had spilled to the floor.

He blinked, looked momentarily dazed, and then a flare of real anger lit his gaze.

"I'll ask the questions, if you please." He was fairly bristling, and he locked his arms tighter over his chest as if he was trying to keep his frustrations locked inside. "I know we've met before. I remember . . . that night. But we never exchanged names. Who are you?"

He flicked his gaze from the tip of her boots to her hair, which was practically unbound since so many pins had loosened or been lost as she napped in the coach. She felt another pin dislodging as he assessed her.

And suddenly she felt her embarrassment spark into ire. She'd made a long journey on her employer's behalf. This wasn't some scheme.

"Your tone isn't at all what I would expect of a nobleman when speaking to a lady."

"My tone?" Those pale eyes of his flashed with molten silver. "You came all the way from London to chastise me about my tone? And yet you do not have the decency to even explain what you've done with my—" He cut the sentence off as if someone had pressed a hand to his mouth. He flattened his lips. A relief, since his mouth vied with his eyes for being the most distracting thing about the man. "If I've been rude, it is only because you are not the lady I was expecting."

"Yes, I know." Evie waited a beat just to be ornery. "I'm sorry, but she was unable to make the journey and sent me in her stead."

He dipped his head as if he needed time to work out what, in Evie's mind, was a very simple explanation.

"My name is Evelyn Graves. I am her ladyship's secretary."

The duke stilled as if shocked, and then everything about him—his posture, the hard lines of his voice, those distracting eyes—softened. He all but sagged against the door.

"So . . ." He lifted a finger like a governess preparing to lecture. "Let me get this straight. Lady Waverly changed her mind about coming, and you came instead? And you're her secretary?" He sounded most confused about this bit, as if he couldn't imagine she was telling the truth. After a moment of silence, he added, "Unchaperoned?"

Evie considered pointing out that *he* was the one who'd all but dragged her into this room. And locked her in. Alone. With him.

"Her ladyship"—Evie wanted to get this part right for the sake of Lady Waverly's pride—"had another commitment she could not miss."

"Our event didn't merit her attendance. That part I understand."

"She sent a letter." Evie felt certain about that. Lady Waverly wouldn't forget, and her employer would wish to explain her absence in her own way.

Evie was tempted to dig through the pile on the desk behind him.

"I didn't receive any letter, but I am sorry she won't be able to attend the charity event." A frown still knotted his forehead into deep grooves. "But you, Miss Graves. Why did she send you?"

There was such exasperation in his tone that it felt like an insult, even if she could hardly have expected him to be pleased at her arrival.

"She sent me to help, Your Grace. Much has to be arranged, and she did not wish the remaining details to be a burden on you or your staff."

"You'll stand in her place. Is that the idea?"

Was the man being purposely obtuse? Had she not just said as much?

"I'm not the countess, but I have helped organize all of her social and charitable events for the past three years. She believed I could be helpful to you."

"How long, Miss Graves?"

"I'll stay until the event."

"Of course." He waved a hand at her dismissively. She imagined he wished he had a magician's power and could make her disappear entirely. "And Lady Waverly does not intend to come to Ireland at all?"

"No."

The answer struck him like a blow. He jerked back, scrubbed a hand across his jaw, and offered her a pained look. Apparently, he didn't see any purpose in her presence at all, and perhaps he was right.

"I'm sorry, Your Grace." Suddenly, all the fatigue of the journey and the realization of how much of a mistake this whole trip might have been swept over her.

He straightened his shoulders and took her in again, but this time there was an electric flicker in his gaze. A spark of what had passed between them in Lady Waverly's garden.

"None of this is your fault," he said quietly. "You must be exhausted after your journey. And"—he swept a hand up and gestured at her—"your hair."

Evie reached a hand up to push in the pin she'd

felt drooping as they conversed. But as soon as she touched the knot at her nape, the pin slid free and plinked to the carpet. Then another followed suit.

The duke approached and knelt to retrieve them.

Face flaring with the heat of embarrassment, Evie worked quickly to at least gather her thick waves into something approximating tidiness.

The duke rose and stood before her, offering the missing pins palm up, as he watched her intently. A far different perusal than when they'd entered the study together.

Evie swallowed hard as she reached for the pins. A little tremor ran through her when she touched her hand to his, and she pulled away quickly, reaching up to secure the knot at her nape. But when she pushed one in, another slid out.

Poorly timed and irrepressible laughter bubbled up. To hide it, Evie bent to pick up the fallen pin and noticed a cluster of papers that had drifted off the grand oak desk in the center of the room and onto the floor. Among the pile, she noticed Lady Waverly's neat script.

Evie collected the letter.

"You needn't, Miss Graves. I must have knocked them—"

"The countess's letter." Evie held it up for him to see.

"Ah." He looked chagrined as he stared down at the note.

"Your Grace, I assure you. I'm good at organizing. Good at helping. Lady Waverly asked me to come for a little over a week and do just that. To make sure the charity event can still go on without her."

He stared at her. Yet his gaze didn't feel assessing. It felt as if he was asking a question without any words.

"I won't be any trouble to you or your staff" was the only assurance Evie could think to offer.

OH, BUT SHE was trouble.

Alex didn't know quite what to make of Miss Evelyn Graves, but the moment she'd tumbled into his arms in the carriage circle, he'd known she would vex him.

The moment he'd recognized her, and his gaze locked with her vibrant green eyes, a strange jolt of energy had sped the beat of his pulse. He'd felt caught. Seen as he rarely felt with anyone. As he rarely allowed with anyone.

There'd been consternation, of course, since she was not the lady he needed. But what had unnerved him even as he escorted her to the door was that he did not feel as disappointed as he should have.

Something about her shockingly direct gaze drew him. And her nearness had heated his blood, at least until she'd looked as if she was about to cast up her accounts and tumbled into his arms.

Yet even now, as she watched him, he felt the

same inexplicable draw he'd felt from the first moment he'd met her months ago.

She was such a beauty. Not just the simple appeal of fine eyes and a pert nose and Cupid's-bow lips. Miss Evelyn Graves had a lush allure. Some might call her eyes too big, her nose too long, or her lips too full. Alex found all those excesses irritatingly appealing.

She was the kind of lady that he would have remembered if he'd passed her on a London street or glimpsed her for a moment across a ballroom. Let alone found himself crouching above her on a moonlit night.

But a distracting beauty was the last thing he needed.

He needed a wife.

And Katharine Waverly was out of the question now. She clearly had no interest in him, and he could hardly beg the countess to visit.

He needed a new plan.

"Your Grace?" She'd been watching him, waiting, but he was ever aware of her presence. With her about, he couldn't think.

"Forgive me, Miss Graves." He stepped away from her and toward the window because he hoped it might allow him a moment of clarity.

Staring out onto the overgrown gardens behind the castle, he spotted Bel convening with his aunt. Had they come out when Miss Graves arrived?

Good grief, his whole attention had tunneled

into singular focus on the beauty who stared out at him with sea-glass green eyes.

If Givens was right, and the man was rarely wrong, his uncle would arrive before the charitable event. And without any potential bride for Alex anywhere in sight, he'd assume the castle would soon be his.

"Are you not going to read Lady Waverly's letter?" Her voice had a husky quality that sparked something in Alex he had no business feeling.

And she was right.

He tore unceremoniously at the paper and scanned the note.

Lady Waverly gave no real specifics about her decision not to come. A conflict in her schedule, as Miss Graves had said. But she heaped praise on the young woman she'd sent in her stead.

Miss Graves is the most competent of young ladies and will manage the charity event with much the same skill and finesse as I myself would. You may trust in her intelligence, honesty, and biddable nature.

Alex couldn't help but glance at Miss Graves over the letter's top edge at that description.

Biddable? He somehow doubted that description. The lady fairly bristled with an energy that felt wholly unbridled.

"She speaks highly of you," he told her.

A watercolor wash of pink shaded her cheeks.

Alex wondered if the pink extended below the collar of her blouse. Good God, where had that come from?

He crumpled the letter in his hand and headed toward the door. She was too much—those vibrant eyes, untamable waves of mahogany hair, and lips that made one wish to—

"Mrs. Wilde will see to a room for you," he told her without looking back.

"Your Grace, there is much to discuss regarding the event you're set to host. When might we—"

"Later. Right now, I need to think." He glanced back once, and a single long curling wave of hair slipped down across her shoulder.

His fingers trembled with the urge to tuck it back behind her ear. Or better yet, to dispense with every damn pin and stroke his fingers through her hair.

"I must think," he shouted, more to himself than at her.

Then he strode from the room, closed the door behind him, and all but raced toward the stable yard.

Chapter Five

"Here you are then, my lady."

"Oh, I'm not—" Evie tried.

But the housekeeper was already halfway across the room, opening the long rose-hued velvet drapes.

"I'll have Magda come up to unpack your traveling case."

"I can manage that myself." Lady Waverly had insisted that Evie bring a few of her gowns in case the Pierponts preferred to dine in formal attire. Evie had planned innumerable dinner parties for aristocrats, but she'd rarely had occasion to dine with nobles and didn't bother with the expense of fancy gowns. Still, even with all that she'd brought, Evie could unpack without troubling a servant.

"Nonsense, my lady." The housekeeper smiled with genuine warmth.

"I'm afraid I'm not who you think I am, Mrs. Wilde."

"Oh, not at all, my lady. You're very welcome here, I assure you." She glanced around the room and then pointed to a door on the far wall. "Bathing and dressing room is through there." She turned and gestured to a door along the opposite wall that was prettier and covered partially in the same pale pink wallpaper as the room itself. "Sitting room through there."

"Goodness." Evie hadn't been led to a simple guest chamber. She'd been led to a suite—the suite intended for Lady Waverly, who Mrs. Wilde still believed she was.

After taking it all in, Evie spun to face the older woman, intending to correct her.

"Please ring if you need assistance with anything at all." With that, the housekeeper nodded, opened the chamber door, and departed.

Evie let out a long, weary sigh.

Rennick would correct everyone's misunderstanding soon enough. And maybe it was best that he be the one to do so. Egos were a delicate thing when it came to nobility.

The memory of the man she'd met in the garden and her experience with the one who'd locked her in his study with him were so incongruent that she still couldn't merge them in her mind. The two versions of the duke were like mismatched puzzle pieces. Or perhaps she was just too weary to put all the aspects of the distractingly handsome man together in her mind.

Evie made her way toward the bed. It beckoned her with plump pillows and a creamy white counterpane.

Sitting on the edge, she couldn't help but note

how good it felt compared to the coach's uphol-
stered bench and the stiff bed she'd slept in at an
inn near Dublin. She flopped back and let out a
contented moan.

Her eyelids grew heavy only a moment later.

Perhaps a nap was in order. Then she'd wash, put
on a fresh gown, and see if she and the changeable
Duke of Rennick could work together. And maybe
have a wander around the castle. Lady Waverly
had insisted that she treat this trip as a holiday, at
least in part.

Lifting her arm, she bent it over her eyes to block
out the warm afternoon light streaming in from
the window.

Then she caught a scent. Crushed juniper berries
with a hint of clove. A masculine scent. His scent.

He'd caught her, held her. Even while his tone
was a veritable growl of irritation, his touch had
been warm, his body comfortingly solid.

Evie savored the scent as she drifted . . .

The bedchamber latch twisted, and the door
swung open.

"Oh, you are in here." A light feminine voice
filled the room.

Evie sat up, blinking at the pretty blonde who
swept in like a whirlwind of plum satin and silk. A
tall dark-haired woman trailed behind her with the
same energy and excitement.

"We're so glad you've come, my dear. And
please forgive us for not greeting you out front."

The blonde approached as if she'd embrace her but stopped short. "Did the journey make you as weary as it tends to make me?" She looked around the chamber, a wistfulness suddenly coming into her gaze. "When we came here as children, the trip felt as if it took no time at all. Now I'm afraid I remember every bump and jostle along the way."

"Are these flowers all right?" The older woman stood next to a gorgeous display of blooms that Evie had barely noticed. Now that she did, she nodded eagerly.

"They're beautiful."

"Aunt Oona is very particular about gardening and choosing just the right flower for every person and every occasion." The blonde gasped and laid a hand on her chest. "Goodness, we haven't been introduced properly. We were in the garden when you arrived, you see."

"It's quite all right." Evie stood and was grateful all the wooziness of the journey had dissipated.

"This is our aunt, Oona McQuillan, and I'm Alex's sister, Belinda. I'm sure he's mentioned me in the letters you've exchanged, though I fear little of it was complimentary. I do torment him at times."

"I'm afraid there's some confusion, which is entirely understandable."

The clock on the mantel let out a resonant chime, and the duke's aunt cast a worried glance its way.

"I've an appointment with Lady Wilcox. Will you excuse me, ladies?"

Belinda swept over to give her aunt a kiss on the cheek, and Ms. McQuillan offered Evie a nod and a welcoming grin. Once she'd gone, Lady Belinda smiled expectantly.

"Is this your first visit to Ireland, Lady Waverly?"

"I'm sorry, but I'm not Lady Waverly. She was unable to come and sent me to help with the charity event. I'm her secretary, Evelyn Graves."

"Goodness, that's unexpected."

Evie thought it best not to point out that a letter explaining everything had been misplaced by the duke.

Lady Belinda studied her a moment. "Nothing serious has kept the countess away, I hope."

"Not at all. A scheduling conflict."

"I see." Lady Belinda frowned and then glanced toward the window. "How odd that he didn't say anything."

"The duke?"

"I saw him storming down the hall and asked if you'd arrived. Or rather, if Lady Waverly had arrived. He merely said she had."

"I think it was all a bit of a shock."

"Yes." Lady Belinda assessed her now, as intensely as her brother had, though with a soft smile curving her lips. "I rather think it must have been. How strange that she sent you, considering the circumstances."

"Circumstances?" Evie wasn't sure if Lady Belinda referred to what Lady Waverly suspected: the duke's intentions toward her employer. "Do you mean a potential courtship?"

"Yes." The duke's sister scoffed. "Such an odd word to think of in connection with my brother. He's fended off marriage-minded ladies in the past and avoided the very notion of matrimony for so long, but it's no longer an option since he inherited."

Considering the way the Duke of Rennick looked, she could readily believe that young ladies had noticed him and pursued him for years.

Evie swallowed hard and hoped her expression gave nothing away.

"She sent you to handle the charity event, is that it?" Lady Belinda settled on a cushioned bench beside the bed.

"Yes, my lady." Evie sat on the edge of the bed. Suddenly, she was full of nervous energy again and didn't think she could nap if she tried. "Do you think the duke will allow me to help?"

"I imagine so." The duke's sister leaned a bit closer. "Between you and me, I don't think he would have participated at all if not for Lady Waverly's interest. Not that he doesn't love horses and giving to worthy causes, but he's never terribly comfortable at social events, and there's another matter weighing on him of late."

Wonderful. She'd come to assist with an event

that the man would probably have happily declined an invitation to.

"I feel as if this journey may have been folly. Perhaps the duke will not wish to participate at all."

"But he must. The luncheon is to be hosted here, and he wouldn't wish for you to speak poorly of him when you return to London."

"I'm not here to spy on him, my lady."

"No, of course not," Lady Belinda reassured. "But if he's beastly, you'd be remiss not to tell the lady who sent you."

"Is he beastly?" The words were out before Evie could stop them.

The duke had been so confusing. That face of his had haunted her dreams for months, and she'd never imagined she'd see it again, let alone feel his warm, hard body against hers.

Lady Belinda laughed, a low, appealing sound filled with mischief. "You're not asking an objective observer, Miss Graves. As his younger sister, I'd have to say *yes*. At times, he can be beastly, though he's never cruel."

Evie wanted her to say more, but she'd already been extraordinarily forthcoming. Her openness was charming, and Evie felt comfortable with her.

"Alexander can be hard to know," Lady Belinda continued. "He has such a busy mind. He's not effusive and tries very hard not to be impulsive. He may appear exhaustingly even-tempered or cool, but all that containment comes at great effort."

Evie recalled that flash in his study. He'd given every indication of being on the verge of outrage, but he'd never let the emotion out.

"However, I'm sure he'll be agreeable to you while you're here. He'll recognize that none of this is your fault. Talk to him." She grinned. "He can be a reasonable man. Quite tediously logical at times. And since he's a bit taciturn, he makes for an excellent listener."

"Then I will speak to him and hope it goes better than our first encounter."

"Heavens, he wasn't rude, was he?"

"Surprised at my arrival, I think." In truth, Evie wasn't sure what Alexander, Duke of Rennick, thought of her at all.

"Hmm." Lady Belinda stood. "I should leave you to rest. I've just made the journey myself and still feel it in my bones."

She looked as fresh and vivacious as anyone Evie had ever met, but she appreciated the offer of understanding.

"Thank you, my lady."

Lady Belinda nodded and made her way to the door, then stopped with her hand on the latch and turned back.

"May I call you Evelyn? And will you call me Belinda? I'm scandalous when it comes to etiquette, I know, but I've never cared for it much."

"I would like that."

"I'll see you at dinner then, Evelyn."

Evie nodded, and then another thought came. "Belinda, do you know when would be a good time to speak to the duke?"

"You might catch him before dinner. I suspect he was heading for the stables earlier, and you'll want to see the ponies, of course." She nodded decisively. "I'd start there."

Lady Belinda took in her traveling gown.

Evie glanced down at her rumpled bodice and skirt self-consciously. "I'll change before dinner."

"Of course, my dear. I was just thinking that if you wish to ride while you're here, I have a riding habit you could wear. I'll have it sent to your room." She cocked her head toward the window again. "Hopefully, my dear brother will be in a better mood after his afternoon dash across the countryside."

Evie hadn't ridden a horse in years and couldn't imagine tackling it after a day of travel, but she would wash and change and try to find the duke.

For some reason, the prospect of it made her pulse thrum faster.

ALEX HAD GIVEN Sherlock his head for most of their ride, but the stallion recognized the approach toward Ballymore's stables and slowed on his own. Alex stroked the horse's neck, thanking him for a much-needed diversion. They hadn't gone as far as they did some days, but he suspected they'd both needed this impromptu run across the fields, through the copse, and up to the standing stones.

They'd stopped there, and Alex had paced the windswept grass, winding his way around the stones, wishing they'd drop some brilliant solution into his brain.

He'd rather enjoyed the couple of days when he'd thought Lady Waverly might be a solution. Not that he'd been certain a quick courtship and marriage would take place, but telling himself it might had allowed his mind to at least put that single worry aside.

And then the wrong lady had tumbled out of the coach. A lady who, he had to admit, he'd thought of often. One he'd even fancied he might see again one day on some visit to London. Now that she was here, the beauty had an urgency for an event that he couldn't give a damn about.

What was he supposed to do with Miss Graves? Should he send her packing back to London?

The fact was that *he* should return to London. Nearly every lady who'd been on the list of prospective brides—he'd assembled the latest list one evening out of drunken urgency—was in the city this time of year. But he couldn't leave Ireland if his uncle was on his way to Ballymore.

He'd shelter his family from that man's machinations in any way he could.

Lost in thought, Alex let Sherlock lead the way back to the stables without much effort from him, but up ahead, a flash of vibrant color caught his eye.

Miss Graves approached wearing a carnation-pink day dress. She'd dispensed with her hairpins and a tangle of thick reddish-brown waves hung over her shoulder, collected with a ribbon that matched her gown.

She looked lovely, summery even, in the cool autumn breeze. Like she'd just wandered away from a picnic.

Unfortunately, she was wandering straight toward his stallion, and Sherlock, like most horses, could spook if something caught him beyond his line of sight.

Alex adjusted direction so they drew alongside her.

"I wondered if we might have a word, Your Grace." She had to lift her hand to shade her eyes from the sun as she looked up at him.

Alex tried not to stare at her lips.

"If you've had sufficient time to think, of course," she said in a pert tone.

Was she daring to tease him?

"Somehow, I suspect that you'd insist on talking whether I had or not, Miss Graves."

"Possibly," she said and then had the audacity to grin.

Alex felt like a fool riding while she walked, so he pulled Sherlock to a stop and jumped down from the saddle.

"He's not one of the Connemara ponies." As soon

as she spoke of Sherlock, the wily beast nudged his head in her direction.

"He's a stallion my father purchased on his sole trip to Ireland."

She glanced over at Alex, surprise lifting her brows.

"He only came once?"

"The castle . . . wasn't to his taste." The most succinct way of describing his father's scathing opinion of Ballymore's imperfections.

"Ah, I see. He wasn't fond of a charming castle set among lush rolling green hills?"

Alex tipped his head, studying her in return. "You find it charming, do you?"

"What I've seen of it, yes. And this landscape is beautiful." She looked out over the field ahead of them, the lands beyond the castle that led toward the sea. Colors brightened and muted across the fields as windblown clouds hid and revealed the sun. In the distance, the sky churned in a kaleidoscope of hues as a line of late-afternoon light gilded dark roiling storm clouds above.

She was right. He was determined to hold on to the castle for his family, but the land was magical too. His grandfather had emigrated from Ireland during the devastation of the famine and had made a fortune in American oil. He'd purchased the crumbling castle as a wedding gift for his eldest daughter, Alex's mother, as an extravagant way to honor her Irish heritage.

Alex felt a surprising sense of pride in how much Miss Graves admired a place that had meant so much to his mother and siblings. He'd rarely seen it through the eyes of another.

When she caught him watching her, she admitted, "Lady Waverly thought I would enjoy this trip."

"Is that how she persuaded you, Miss Graves? The promise of a holiday?"

She frowned, and all the pleasure he'd just seen on her face vanished.

"The countess is my employer, Your Grace. I didn't ask to come." She pressed her lips together before continuing. "In the past, travel made me quite ill. Though I did well this journey, I assure you I didn't come thinking it would be a freewheeling getaway. The countess sent me with a check to present at the charity event and a few words that I hope you will relay to the gathering on her behalf."

He'd offended her and hadn't intended to. She'd been sent out of Lady Waverly's sense of duty and commitment, and that was something he understood.

The fact that the countess's decision had upset what he'd seen as an easy answer to his marriage dilemma wasn't Miss Graves's doing, nor was the fact that he'd yet to come up with any alternative.

"I hope you do enjoy your time here, Miss Graves. At dinner, tell my sister and aunt what you'd like to see and do. Belinda is an accomplished horse-woman, and my aunt resides at the castle much of the year. She will happily spend an hour giving you a tour of the gardens."

Miss Graves nodded, but as they entered the stable yards and one of the stable hands took Sherlock's reins, she turned to him.

"Not you?"

Alex tipped his head in question.

"You won't show me the castle yourself, Your Grace?"

The question took him by surprise. Not because it was an unusual request but because of the fierce rush of determination that he do just as she asked.

That he be the one to show her all the crumbling bits, admirable aspects, and secret nooks of the castle, and the land around it too. He wanted to hear her thoughts about all he showed her, and perhaps he'd be lucky enough to spark that delight that had broken over her face a moment ago.

The prospect of spending time with her was too appealing. Especially when he had no time to lose.

Yet, somehow, that made him want it even more.

His mind spun with possibilities. Walking with her near the standing stones, touching her again, listening to her ramble on as she had so charmingly that night in the garden. And suddenly everything he needed to do, all his duties, his need to find a bride, felt like nothing more than a nuisance in comparison to time spent with Miss Evelyn Graves.

But he couldn't afford a dalliance—neither the distraction of it nor the pleasure.

"I'm afraid not, Miss Graves. I have a pressing matter that commands my attention." He gestured for her to join him on the path back toward the castle. He didn't look at her as they walked side by side. He knew his resistance would crumble if he did.

Chapter Six

Evie managed to unpack her traveling trunk on her own, but deciding which dress to wear to dinner was another matter entirely. The dresses Lady Waverly had loaned her were excessively lavish to Evie. Finer than any gown she'd ever have need of.

Even if the Pierponts did dine formally, as Lady Waverly suspected, would her simple evening gown work, or was it a night for silk and satin?

After realizing she'd taken too much time debating, she opted for her own finest dress. It was a bit out of fashion and perhaps a bit frayed at the hem. She'd worn the gown dozens of times, but its elegant lines hugged her body, and its robin's-egg blue fabric and darker velvet accents always gave her a boost of confidence. Tonight she suspected she'd need it.

The duke unnerved her if only because she couldn't decipher him.

He was both oddly familiar but also a mercurial stranger who glowered at her one moment and shot her a heated stare the next.

She wasn't sure what had possessed her to ask him to be her guide to Ballymore.

Had he truly considered marrying Lady Waverly? She struggled to see him as the fortune-hunting sort.

Not that she assumed a handsome face meant a man couldn't have sinister motives. She knew the opposite was often true. But there was something about the duke: he might repress his emotions sometimes, but she sensed he wasn't a man of pretense. If he wore a mask, it served to conceal his emotions rather than to charm others.

Though it was early, Evie decided to head downstairs and steal a moment to explore a bit of the castle before dinner. She checked herself one last time in the cheval mirror in the suite's dressing room and then stepped into the hallway.

"Goodness, you're a sight for this weary traveler's eyes."

Evie's back stiffened at the playful masculine voice. She turned to find a young man—dark hair, dark eyes, chiseled jaw very much like the duke's—ogling her.

"Was that directed at me?" she asked, trying for an imperious tone and that single arched-brow look Lady Waverly excelled at.

"Absolutely." He smiled without a hint of shame and then approached. "Rupert Pierpont, brother to the duke, at your service." With that, he sketched an overly dramatic bow. "And you must be Miss Graves. Aunt Oona did say we had a lady visitor."

"Is this how you introduce yourself to all lady visitors?"

"Only the pretty ones." He winked, but it only served to make him appear more of a youthful scamp than a true Lothario.

"I'm heading down to dinner, my lord."

"As am I. Starving, if truth be told." He crooked his outstretched arm. "Travel makes me fiercely peckish. Allow me to escort you, Miss Graves?"

"If you promise to mind your manners, Lord Rupert."

"I could, but what fun would that be?"

Evie laughed but relented and took the young man's arm.

When they descended the long staircase toward the main hall, they found Lady Belinda and Ms. McQuillan sitting together chatting in front of the unlit fireplace.

The duke was nowhere in sight. Evie chastised herself for looking for the man first off and with ridiculous eagerness. He intrigued her, confounded her. She wasn't used to observing others and having no real sense of what they thought or felt.

"Rupert, tell me you're not pestering Miss Graves." Lady Belinda approached and took Evie's free arm.

"I *beg* your pardon. I was a perfect gentleman."

The two siblings turned expectant gazes on her—both the same dark honey-brown, so different from their brother's slate blue.

"*Perfect* may be a bit of a stretch, my lord, but I do appreciate the escort."

Lord Rupert let out a bark of laughter. "Oh no! You're one of those young ladies who won't tolerate my nonsense. I must warn you that they're my favorite sort."

"Forgive him, Evelyn. My brother is a terrible flirt. And when I say *terrible*, I do mean he's not very good at it."

Once again, Lord Rupert took the teasing in stride and plopped gracelessly into an overstuffed chair near his aunt.

"I'm not one to fuss about menus, but if Cook hasn't added her colcannon, I shall throw a rather sizable tantrum," he vowed.

At that comment, Lady Belinda began a soliloquy about her little brother's proclivity for tantrums as a child.

Evie lost track of the conversation.

The thud of footsteps on the stairwell consumed her attention. She couldn't yet see him, but she could sense the Duke of Rennick's approach. He loomed in her periphery—tall and intense and dark but for the sapphire sheen of his waistcoat.

"I thought you were detained by a social engagement in London," the duke called out, his gaze fixed on his younger brother.

Lord Rupert busied himself at a drinks cart while Rennick descended the stairs. Then the young scamp took a sip of his drink before offering a reply.

"Unfortunately, the only young lady I truly wished to dance with at that party declined to attend. She received a marriage proposal she could not refuse." He shot the duke a playful glare. "From a duke, of course."

"What lady could resist a bachelor duke?" Ms. McQuillan winked at her nephew, but he didn't take notice.

Rennick stalked toward the drinks cart, put his hand on a decanter, and then appeared to think better of it. He turned away from the cart and began pacing the perimeter of the room.

Unlike everyone else, who exuded a relaxed, cheerful ease, Rennick seemed determined to brood. He stalked the high-ceilinged room, peering out the arched, diamond-paned windows as if looking for some danger lurking among the sheep and horses and endless fields of green.

Evie resisted the urge to approach and peek over his shoulder to see what he found so interesting.

Moments later, another set of footsteps approached, clipping quickly on the stone floor.

"Dinner is served, Your Grace." The kindly butler Evie had seen when she arrived stood in the doorway to deliver the announcement.

Lord Rupert was at her side in an instant. "Shall I escort you in to dinner, Miss Graves?"

"Am I not host in this castle, brother?" Rennick's voice echoed through the room and carried a playful tone that didn't match his expression.

Lord Rupert's smile remained fixed as he offered his brother a sharp nod. "I defer to you in all things."

"You've never deferred to anyone in your life, and I like you better for it," the duke quipped as he approached and offered Evie his arm. The look he cast his brother was warm, but Evie spied a sadness that made her curious. The two verbally sparred but interacted as if it was their natural way of relating to one another. Perhaps brothers were different from sisters in that regard.

As Evie and the duke proceeded into the dining room ahead of the others, she dared a whispered query for his ears alone.

"Is something troubling you, Your Grace?" Once it was out, she realized the foolishness of her question. He'd said earlier he was preoccupied with some matter, and of course, there was the fact that the wrong woman had arrived this afternoon. "I'm sorry. That was a silly thing to ask under the circumstances. But you seem uneasy."

To her shock, that comment inspired a smile. The expression sharpened the angles of his jaw and etched creases in his cheeks. The smile transformed him from a fine-looking man to a devastatingly handsome one in a flash.

"Is that your way of telling me I'm a rotten host?"

Evie instinctively tightened her grip on his arm. She hated being rude, but she'd been raised to be honest and speak her mind and found she sometimes stumbled into impudence without truly trying.

"It's all right," he said quietly. "The news about Lady Waverly was a shock."

"As was my arrival."

"As was your arrival." He gazed at her again, and when their eyes met, Evie glimpsed something of the man behind the cool demeanor. "Though the only true surprise there was when you fell out of the carriage."

Evie laughed and then pressed her lips together. "Did I ever thank you for catching me?"

"I believe so. It's difficult to recall. I was preoccupied with keeping you on your feet."

"Heavens, if I rambled, I don't recall. Though I do admit to talking a bit more than usual when I'm nervous."

"Only a bit," he said with a grin, though he kept his gaze focused ahead as they approached the candlelit table.

The dining room was the opposite of the great hall in every way. With a low, decorative ceiling and pale blue damask covering the walls, the space had a cozy feel despite the enormous table that stretched nearly the length of the room.

Evie was pleased to see that all the place settings had been arranged at the end of the table nearest two enormous windows that looked out onto the windswept hills behind the castle.

Rennick led her to a chair just to the left of his at the head of the table. Soon Lady Belinda had settled into the chair across from Evie, and Lord Rupert beside her. The duke helped his aunt into the chair next to Evie's before sitting down himself.

As everyone began tucking into the soup course, Lord Rupert lifted his head.

"So what exactly happened to your future bride?"

The duke stilled with a spoonful of soup midair, head bent, and shot his brother a withering glare.

"I told you I'll explain everything later," Lady Belinda put in, waving at her younger brother as if to deter him.

"She had a scheduling conflict." Evie couldn't fathom any reason for secrecy.

"Good God, that's all? One would think she'd just come at a different time." Lord Rupert sipped a bit of wine and turned his attention to his brother. "So will you head to London to court her properly?"

The two brothers were seated several feet away

from each other, yet they might as well have been facing off.

Evie understood sibling rivalry. Sybil had challenged her plenty, but there was an undercurrent between the brothers that she didn't understand.

"The countess was coming for the charity event. Perhaps that's why she didn't opt to come at a different time," Evie put in after waiting a moment or two to see whether the duke would answer.

"Well, we must thank her for sending someone to take care of the event in her absence. We could send her a bouquet of flowers as a sign of gratitude," Ms. McQuillan put in. "Or perhaps you should deliver them in person, nephew."

"That's not possible." The duke spoke with a lighter, more pleasant tone to his aunt than he had to anyone yet. "But flowers are a fine idea, and I'll respond to her letter too."

"Surely you won't propose via letter," Lord Rupert bellowed in an outrage that Evie wasn't certain was sincere.

It was hard to tell. From the moment she'd met the young lord, he'd performed a role. Careless rogue. Flirtatious bon vivant. None of it truly fit him seamlessly.

She studied the duke and then his brother. Both men wore a mask: one of seriousness and the other of joviality. They made for an odd balance, and a palpable tension.

Finally, when the table had fallen quiet, the duke lifted his head and announced, "I have no intention of proposing to the countess."

"But it would have been such a good match." His aunt sounded genuinely dismayed.

"There could still be a way." Lady Belinda looked around the table as if seeking suggestions. "Might the countess come another time? Next month, perhaps?"

"She's hosting a charity event next month in anticipation of the holiday season. It's always quite elaborate," Evie told them. Then she cleared her throat and said what needed to be said, no matter how awkward. "But the more important factor is that Lady Waverly has no intention of marrying again."

Everyone turned their gaze her way.

"She said as much to you?" Rennick spoke to her quietly, as if no one else was in the room.

"She did."

"Heavens, your employer speaks to you very freely." Ms. McQuillan dropped her jaw in shock.

"I'm lucky," Evie acknowledged. It was a thought she'd had after her visit with the Duchess of Vyne too. "She allows me to speak my mind, and in turn, she trusts me enough to do the same."

Footmen standing sentry in the dining room cleared the table, and then others carried in the next course. While they filled each plate, the wind picked up outside. Gusts buffeted the broad sash windows. Storm clouds that had hung in the distance an hour ago rolled closer, darkening the autumn sky.

"That weather is foreboding," Ms. McQuillan said with a shiver that caused her to pull her shawl together at her neck.

"It is indeed," Lady Belinda murmured softly and then tipped her gaze toward the duke. "Will there be enough time to find another . . . option?"

He settled back in his chair, glanced at his sister, then at Evie, and took a sip of wine. "Let's discuss it later, shall we? Miss Graves doesn't need to be regaled with our family dilemma."

"I disagree." Lady Belinda folded her arms, just as Sybil did when she'd decided to dig in her heels and win an argument. "Obviously Miss Graves is discreet. Lady Waverly trusts her unequivocally. And she's spent the last few years in the thick of the London Season."

"Oh, I wasn't a guest at—" Evie started, but Lady Belinda didn't allow her to get the words out.

"I know you may not have attended balls and soirees, Miss Graves, but Lady Waverly hosted many, and you were involved in their planning."

The memory of the first time she'd ever seen Alexander, Duke of Rennick, flashed in Evie's mind. He was the first nobleman she'd ever spoken to informally during all her years of employment with Lady Waverly. For a moment, she was back there in the garden with him. The glowworm's flicker lit her mind's eye, and she shivered at the memory of the duke's broad-shouldered body above her.

When the images receded, Evie found the duke's sister staring her way. "Yes, my lady. I helped plan Lady Waverly's parties and balls."

"Then you must have met many eligible noble-women."

"Bel." The duke's tone indicated that he'd had enough. "Miss Graves needn't play matchmaker for me."

Evie took a sip of wine the minute she felt herself begin to blush.

The duke tapped his fingers on the table and watched her. She couldn't divine whether he was angry or embarrassed or just as uncomfortable with the conversation as she was.

"The dilemma is that it's a matter of timing," Lady Belinda explained. "Our father included a cruel dictate in his will that Alexander must marry within six months of inheriting." She shrugged. "And now Lady Waverly isn't an option."

"Good grief, Bel, must we air all the details for our guest?" Ms. McQuillan laid her silverware down with a clatter, as if the whole topic had put her off food entirely.

Echoing the mood at the table, the wind roared outside and then rain began to patter against the windowpanes. Evie had never experienced such an awkward dinner in her life. Undeniably, the duke faced a dilemma. Marriage on a time line was cruel, or at the very least unfair.

"Uncle George is the more immediate problem," the duke said before emptying his wine glass.

"What's this?" their aunt said. "Tell me that awful man has not been invited here."

"Not invited, but he's on his way nonetheless."

"Like a vulture come to pick over the castle," Rupert put in.

Lightning cracked across the darkening sky, and Lady Belinda jumped and clasped a hand against her chest. "Why don't we gather in the drawing room early? We can sit by the fire and have dessert served there."

Evie liked that. Since the group was small, everyone retired to the same room after dinner rather than splitting off—men in one room and ladies in another—as was the fashion at most of Lady Waverly's dinner parties.

The drawing room was even more inviting than the dining room. Low ceilinged and papered in gold, its dark emerald drapes were pulled closed against the storm. The scent and crackle of a freshly laid fire added to the room's appeal.

After they'd all made short work of a tasty little pudding with caramel sauce that the servants had arranged on a low table between them, the duke offered everyone whiskey, though only he, his brother, and his aunt partook.

"Time for parlor games," Ms. McQuillan said

with an eagerness that no one else appeared to feel. Apparently, she'd blissfully forgotten the uncomfortable conversation at dinner.

"Charades," Rupert declared decisively. "I'm excellent at charades."

"Forget your charades. We must talk about what to do when Uncle George descends on Ballymore." Belinda had picked up a knickknack, a polished stone that had been atop the mantel, and began turning it over in her hands.

"Just because her ladyship didn't come, that doesn't mean you can't tell George that you'll marry her." Ms. McQuillan dug behind one of the pillows on the settee as she spoke and pulled out a skein of yarn with knitting needles tucked inside.

"You're suggesting that Alex lie?" Rupert's tone was incredulous, and he emphasized it by scoffing as soon as the words were out. "Our paragon of a brother wouldn't think of it."

Evie couldn't help but flick her gaze toward the duke, curious what he'd make of that assessment. He maintained a stoic mask that gave nothing away.

"There is an obvious answer." The duke's aunt lilted the words softly, not looking at anyone, her whole attention focused on her knitting.

Everyone in the room cast their gaze her way.

"She'll explain eventually," Rupert said confidently. "Our family loves a dramatic pause."

"Miss Rowena Raymond," Ms. McQuillan said with a decisive poke of her needle into the yarn.

"No!" came the chorus from the duke and his brother.

"Who is she?" Evie decided if they were going to include her in their discussions, she wanted all the facts.

"An admirer of Rupert's." The duke's tone emerged roughly, and he rose from his chair as if agitated. After pacing a moment, he joined Belinda near the fireplace.

"She was until my brother inherited," Rupert added as if the matter didn't concern him much at all. "Now she'd far prefer a duke, and I wouldn't have married her anyway."

"A rather snappish young lady," Belinda told Evie as she settled onto the sofa beside her. "We've known the Raymonds since childhood, but I don't think she and Alex would suit. And I know for certain that she and Rupert would drive each other around the bend."

"She possesses every requirement for a duchess." Their aunt laid down her knitting and took a sip of whiskey. "And she loves horses and Ballymore. A very practical choice, Alexander."

Whatever reply the duke intended, it was cut short by a ruckus of raised voices outside the drawing-room door.

Rennick's gaze snapped toward the sound, and he immediately crossed over and opened the door.

"What's the—"

An older man burst across the threshold and into the drawing room. Then he stopped in his tracks and tugged on the rain-splattered lapels of his overcoat.

Ms. McQuillan gasped, Lord Rupert emptied his glass, and Belinda wrapped her arms around herself as if the man had brought the weather inside. No one spoke to the intruder, and he noted each reaction, tracing his gaze across one face and then the next.

"So this is the kind of familial welcome I get," he groused.

The butler stepped into the room a moment later. "Forgive me, Your Grace. He would not give his name and forced his way in." The steel-haired butler eyed the man warily. "Shall we have him removed?"

"You wouldn't bloody dare," the intruder barked.

"Leave him, Mullins. I know who he is."

The butler gave a sharp nod and departed. Evie noticed he did not pull the drawing-room door completely shut.

"Is there aught to drink? Bloody freezing out there in this torrent."

Lady Belinda reached for Evie's hand and stood, drawing her along to stand near the fire. This put them as far away from the rain-drenched visitor who'd burst in on them as possible.

Did she fear some violence from the man?

"No one invited you to make the journey, Uncle George." Lord Rupert stood too but made his way to the drinks cart as if the man's presence was more irritant than threat.

He handed his uncle a finger of whiskey.

"Drink that and go," Rennick said in a low voice so full of warning that the hairs at Evie's nape prickled.

Their uncle frowned and scraped his glance over each of them in turn once more.

"No hospitality to be found here, is there?"

"Did you truly expect any, Pierpont?" Ms. McQuillan was the only one who kept her seat. She'd laid her knitting aside and glared at the duke's uncle.

"Oona. How are you, old girl? It's been a long while. I heard my brother let you make this old crumbling pile your home."

"Since my father purchased the castle, yes, it always felt like home."

"Especially since your sister paired off with a duke, allowing you to remain unmarried, childless, free."

There was history between the two. Evie could see it in the way their gazes held wariness as if born of an old enmity, but as Pierpont flicked his gaze around the room, there was a wistfulness in his expression too. He'd visited before, Evie suspected.

"It's time for you to go, Pierpont." The duke

stepped forward and looked as if he yearned to remove the man bodily, but he did not touch him.

With his height and the breadth of his shoulders, he towered over the older man.

The uncle flinched but didn't budge. He looked the duke in the eye, emptied his glass with one final swig. "I thought perhaps we should talk, but I see this is not the moment for it."

For the first time, he noticed Evie. He stared at her, studying her, then dropping his gaze to her gown.

"Well, how do you do? I take it you're the fiancée."

"Yes," Lord Rupert affirmed.

"No," the duke said in that same low growl. "You will not speak to her, and her presence here is none of your concern."

"Isn't it?" Their uncle appeared genuinely confused, even as Rennick took a step closer, all but blocking Pierpont's view of Evie. "If the young lady changes her mind at the last minute, all of this"—he spun his finger in the air—"will apparently fall to me. So odd, since the dukedom did not."

"We'll never allow that," the duke's aunt shouted, crossing her arms over her chest.

"You won't have much choice, Oona. My brother could be cruel, as you well knew, but the law is the law." Pierpont slammed his empty glass onto the table next to her, making her jump. Then he turned his attention once more to Evie.

His perusal made her skin itch as he pointed straight at her.

"You all better make sure this pretty young lass doesn't change her mind."

"Get out." The duke pointed too, straight toward the drawing-room door.

"Now that it's done raining for a bit, I'll make my way back to the inn." Pierpont smiled at his nephew, but it held none of the anger he reserved for Ms. McQuillan. "Invite me for a meal. I'd like to meet your future duchess properly."

Before the duke could reply, the man turned on his heel and marched out of the room. He had the air of someone who'd done what he'd come to do. As far as Evie could tell, that intention was to upset everyone.

And he'd succeeded.

Lady Belinda clasped a hand over her mouth. Ms. McQuillan hung her head and made a frustrated tsking sound. Even Lord Rupert had lost his sense of joie de vivre.

"I'm sorry for that, Miss Graves. Aunt Oona. All of you." Rennick's stoic facade had faltered. He looked tired, pained, as if the older man's visit had turned all of his worries up a notch. "Perhaps it's best we all retire for the evening."

Evie stood to follow the duke's aunt, brother, and sister upstairs. But after they'd crossed the threshold, she couldn't resist glancing back at the duke.

"I'll take you on that tour tomorrow," he told her in a warmer voice than he'd used all night. "To make up for all of this."

Evie nodded and followed the others toward the stairs.

On the way up, her heartbeat sped at the prospect of time alone with the duke.

Chapter Seven

Evie lay on her back and closed her eyes again. As exhausted as she was, sleep wouldn't come.

Willing her mind to settle, she decided counting might help. But what to count? Sheep? Irish ponies? The number of times she'd caught the Duke of Rennick staring at her?

When she closed her eyes, she saw only him.

His storm-cloud gaze and inscrutable murmurs. The hard edge of his jaw set in concentration or consternation. The way his dark hair managed to be both disheveled and enticing. The way he'd looked—so dark and imposing—standing in front of Ballymore's door when she'd arrived.

That brought a memory of the moment he'd recognized her and the frustrating shield he'd slid neatly into place.

What did the duke think of her? Of anything?

It was so hard to tell. She'd never wished to be a fortune teller in her life, not until she'd met him.

People played the roles that were expected of them. And they bit their tongues for the sake of politeness. That she understood. False smiles. Feigned joviality. Mundane conversation hiding what they really felt or wished to say. Those skills were the backbone of high society.

But the duke was the most confounding man she'd ever met, because it felt as if he had something to say *to her*, or at least he found it necessary to study her. Yet whenever they spoke, he revealed next to nothing. And not out of nervousness or a lack of anything to say. He'd not been that way when they'd met as strangers in a lantern-lit garden.

Unease in her company was an insufficient explanation for Rennick's stoic brooding.

And nothing explained all the times she'd caught his gaze on her tonight.

He'd watched her openly, from under his dark brows, surreptitiously when he thought no one would notice. By rights, she should have called him out for rudeness or at least asked him why. Perhaps she could coax it out of him with straightforward questioning.

And then there was the very inconvenient fact that it matched none of what she imagined about the man she'd met in Lady Waverly's garden.

That night, that moment, still blazed in her memory. He'd been so expressive. Even lost his temper for a moment when he'd first stumbled over her.

And then he'd smiled. His whole face had lit with wonder and interest when he'd spotted the glowworm, and then he'd noticed her with an interest she wasn't used to. He'd studied her, as if she was as fascinating and incandescent as that creature. That part wasn't some fancy she'd spun after revisiting the memory time and time again. Nor had she fabricated the warmth of his skin when she'd collected her pendant from his palm.

Oh, she'd called herself a fool and pushed that moment from her mind so many times that she believed, eventually, she'd forget.

But she never had. Not a single moment.

Evie let out a little growl of frustration.

The wind howled as if in sympathy. A moment later, a gust sparked the embers in the fireplace into flame.

Between the whistling wind, the creaks and groans of the castle, and flashes of firelight, her body and mind were restless. Reading always helped, but she'd finished the book she'd brought along on the journey from England.

On the way to the drawing room, she'd spied bookshelves through an open doorway. The temptation to explore what she guessed was the library had been irresistible. Now even more so.

She glanced at the mantel clock. It was just past midnight. Surely everyone would be abed and asleep.

Making quick work of her plan before she could think better of it, Evie buttoned her thick, quilted

robe all the way to her neck in case she encountered a servant and took up a candle from the desk
in her room.

Halfway across her bedchamber, she stopped at
the sound of footsteps in the hall outside her door.

Her heart thrashed against her ribs, and she held
her breath, straining to hear, wondering if the
footsteps were approaching her door or another.

But no one knocked, and after a moment, she
couldn't hear any movement in the hall. That was
when she spotted it. Someone had slid a piece of
paper under her door. Evie rushed over, snatched it
up, and her pulse thudded like a drum in her ears
as she read the duke's note.

*If you're still awake, meet me in the library
downstairs*

—R

Evie closed her hand around the scrap of paper
and pulled the door open, but the duke was gone.

She stood staring out into the dark hall, debating
what she should do.

The infuriating man had read her mind. How
could he have known she was on her way down
to explore the library? And why hadn't he simply
knocked on her door if he wished to speak to her?
Or, more appropriately, waited until morning?

Even as she debated, she found herself pulling the

door shut behind her and making her way to the stairwell.

This was an opportunity to speak to him privately. He couldn't very well be silent and brooding when it was just the two of them. And what if he had something to convey about the charity event?

Of course she had to go.

As she made her way downstairs, the night in July flashed in her mind. The wild thrashing of her heart had less to do with nerves and more with her eagerness to encounter once more that man she'd met in the garden.

ALEX POKED AT the kindling until the flickering sparks lengthened into flames.

He'd chastised himself from the moment he'd slipped the note under Miss Graves's door. For a long moment after doing it, he'd simply stared at the sliver of light under her doorframe and considered whether he could somehow reach in and retrieve the note.

What the hell's teeth had possessed him?

Inviting a pretty, unwed lady to a midnight assignation would have been the quickest path to scandal under any other circumstances.

Perhaps it was that they'd already had a midnight meeting once.

No, if he was honest with himself, it was his own need to make things right.

He wished to apologize. Every time he thought

of his uncle bursting into the room and mistaking Miss Graves for his fiancée, he winced. She'd already been sent to Ireland with another's responsibilities on her shoulders. His dilemma was not her burden, and he had no wish to make her journey a miserable one.

In fact, he was eager for her to enjoy as much of the experience as she could.

He'd seen her eye the library when he'd escorted her to dinner. Unable to sleep, he'd come down half-expecting to find her tucked up on a settee with a book. That night in Lady Waverly's garden, she'd said that was where she would have preferred to go to read.

But of course, he hadn't found her in the darkened, book-lined room.

She had to be exhausted after such a long day.

He laid the fire iron aside and held his hands out toward the flames, letting the warmth soothe a bit of the tension knotting his muscles.

The staff didn't usually lay a fire in the library anymore. Aunt Oona thought the room too dour and preferred her suite upstairs or the soaring conservatory that had been added to the castle a few years ago.

His siblings didn't have much use for it either. Rupert and Belinda had never been inclined to escape into books as he had.

Alex had been the one who'd loved the library. And his mother too, though she'd also complained about how dim and cold the room could be during winter months. There were no windows, which he'd liked as a boy. It made him feel safe somehow.

He stood before the fire and checked the clock on the mantel. Enough time had passed. Miss Graves was asleep, and he would simply have to deal with the embarrassment of the note when she found it in the morning.

Though he still felt unsettled and doubted sleep would come even if he climbed the stairs and lay in his bed.

He approached a shelf where the latest bookstore acquisitions had been placed and pulled out *A Study in Scarlet*. The book was one he'd read before, but he kept forgetting to read Conan Doyle's follow-up, *The Sign of the Four*.

Settling onto the worn leather settee near the fire, he opened to the first page of the book at the precise moment the library door slid open.

His breath snagged in his throat, and he couldn't force out the greeting or the apology he knew he should offer.

Miss Graves looked lovely, even in the bulky robe she'd buttoned to her neck. Caught in a loose ribbon, her auburn hair hung over her shoulder just as it had when they'd met, but now her cheeks were flushed, and her green eyes flared with irritation.

"Why did you ask me to meet you?"

Alex put his book aside and stood, fighting the smile that threatened. Another lady might offer him a lecture on the impropriety of them meeting alone. But that wasn't Miss Graves at all.

She asked straightforward questions. No one else in his life did. It unnerved him, and yet he admired her for it.

"Because I owe you an apology." He swallowed and added the more loathsome part. "And I have something to ask of you."

"Why?" If possible, she looked even more fetching when her brows arched in confusion. "The apology, I mean."

"The business with my uncle. I know it must have been awkward for you. And Rupert—"

"Your brother was trying to protect you," she allowed.

"I don't think his concern was for me. It's the castle, you see. None of us want to let it go."

She crossed her arms. "I don't understand."

"My father's will. The requirement that I marry soon. The penalty is the transfer of Ballymore to my uncle."

"Oh." She sounded genuinely bereft. "Your family would take that hard, I think."

"As would I."

"Which is why you wished to marry my employer." Tipping her head, she looked at him as if attempting to read his thoughts.

"Shall we sit?" He gestured toward a wingback, but she sat on the settee by the fire.

Alex settled next to her, leaving a bit of distance,

though he realized all of this was miles beyond the bounds of propriety.

"What must you think of me, Miss Graves?" he said quietly.

"I confess I do not know what to think of you." She stared at the fire, not looking at him.

"Am I such a mystery?" Alex found he wanted her gaze on him, even if those searching eyes of hers saw right through him.

"You are." She uncrossed her arms and turned toward him.

"Ask me what you wish, and I'll do my best to solve the mystery." He settled back, stretching out one arm along the back of the settee. Some wild impulse made him want to open up to Miss Graves. For some reason, he cared what she thought of him.

"Anything at all, Your Grace?"

"Yes." His pulse began to race, realizing that he was doing something for Evelyn Graves that he rarely did for anyone. Laying himself bare. Being vulnerable. "But"—he lifted one finger, wanting something else too—"I get to ask a few questions of my own. And one favor, which you may certainly decline."

"Very well," she agreed with a nod. "I have nothing to hide."

"Nor do I."

She laughed, and the sound resonated warm and low, melting any shred of doubt about his choice to invite her to meet him.

"You find me funny, Miss Graves?"

"I find you inscrutable. But let's begin this game of questions. Me first."

"Ladies first, of course."

"Do you love her?"

Alex choked. It took him a moment to realize she meant her employer, and he cleared his throat, swallowing the lump of guilt that he richly deserved.

"I suspect you already know the answer to that question. But no. I hardly know her. In truth, she was my aunt's choice more than my own. A practical choice." He winced at that, though just a few days ago he'd found some logic and potential convenience in the match.

"She's wealthy," Miss Graves put in quietly as if it provided the explanation she sought.

"Indeed, but I'd only ever met her once. That night."

Her green gaze fixed on his, and her nearness made his mouth water. The wild thought came that he should have kissed her that night. He'd considered it and then imagined it often since.

"You have things in common with her," she said.

"I suppose," Alex admitted. "Horses. Charitable endeavors."

"But not the most important thing." She cast her gaze at the fire a moment and then back at him. "A desire to marry."

Alex couldn't help but chuckle at his own hubris

to even consider a match with the countess. In his selfish single-mindedness, he'd presumed Lady Waverly would wish to be a duchess.

"I assumed too much."

Miss Graves dipped her head in agreement. She looked contemplative, as if she'd gotten lost in her own musings.

"What are you thinking?" he asked softly.

"That I understand."

He wasn't expecting that. "Do you?"

"Making a practical choice? Yes, of course. Especially to protect one's family." She looked around the library, and her gaze came to rest on a landscape that had been painted of the castle in the past century. "Or, in this case, to protect a place that matters to your family."

"Yes, that's it exactly. Do you have family to protect?"

"I have a younger sister. Sybil. She's going to become a doctor."

"And your parents?"

"Both of them are gone, which is what led me to the practical choice of becoming Lady Waverly's secretary."

"And you're quite good at it. That much Lady Waverly made clear in her letter." Alex realized now that all the organizational wizardry the countess was often lauded for was likely down to the woman sitting just a few inches from him.

For a moment, her gaze turned serious and

searching. "Did you ever ask her about that night-—"

"No," he cut in. "I considered asking but couldn't imagine how to broach the topic."

"'Who was that strange girl in your garden?'" she said in a low imitation of his voice, then smiled.

"And did *you* ever ask?" Alex was shocked by how much he wanted to hear that she had.

"No. Why would I?" She shrugged. "I knew it was unlikely we'd ever meet again."

"And yet we have." This time when their gazes met, something in the center of his chest burned, like one of the fireplace embers had planted itself there and sparked to life.

"And yet we have," she repeated and then swallowed hard.

Alex wondered if she felt that same spark kindling between them.

"What is the favor, Your Grace?" she asked, the words almost a whisper.

Alex stood and ran a hand through his hair, gripping the back of his neck. He wished he'd never mentioned the favor at all. He wasn't certain asking her was the right thing to do. It was expedient and might stave off his uncle, but he hated putting an honorable young woman in such a position.

"You won't shock me. I'm not easily shocked," she told him confidently.

He turned back to her and decided to get it out and let her deny him if she wished.

"My uncle is here to cause trouble and will cause a great deal more if he knows I have no real prospect of a bride and only a few months left to fulfill the requirement of my father's will."

She cocked her head. "Earlier, he mistook me for your fiancée."

"He did."

"But you denied it." She stood too, coming to stand near him by the fire. "Now you regret that? His incorrect assumption would help you."

"I know what I'm asking is not honorable or even fair to you. But if you could allow him to believe that you're Lady Waverly and have agreed to be my bride, it might be enough to send him on his way."

"Will he come back again?"

"I think it's likely." He could see her weighing what he was asking of her, and he had the impulse to rub his finger across the spot where furrows appeared on her forehead as she contemplated.

"If he comes again, I'll do it."

"You must feel free to say no. I would understand. Dealing with my uncle and the provisions of the will is my burden. Not yours."

She smiled. "I already said I would, and now you're trying to talk me out of it."

"I'm trying to be less of a cad while also absolutely being a cad."

"Your uncle makes everyone uncomfortable. If he comes and makes the assumption again, I won't correct him."

"Thank you. I'm in your debt."

She looked down and twisted her finger around the ribbon at the front of her robe. Then she tipped her head up, looking amused. Alex found himself leaning closer, eager to bask in the warmth she exuded.

"You pointed out the only glowworm I've ever seen in my life. I feel as if I owe you something for that."

Never in his life had he felt so immediately drawn to and yet at ease with a lady, especially one who aroused him as she did. And it had all been there from that first moment. He'd been holding her hand when he spotted the glowworm. And yes, the little luminescent creature had caught his notice, but she had intrigued him more.

He reached for her, unable to stop himself. Then he hesitated, his fingers hovering near the flushed slope of her cheek.

She tipped her head to close the distance, and he stroked his fingers across her skin. Sliding a silken strand of hair behind her ear, he leaned closer, breathing in her scent—something rich and floral, like the flowers in the garden where he'd first met her.

Her lips parted, and he expected one of them would surely come to their senses.

But she said nothing.

And he wanted nothing so much as to kiss her.

"I told myself I'd never see you again," she whispered. "But I hoped."

Alex swallowed hard, his mind whirring with thoughts, images, memories of that night in Lady Waverly's garden that had become etched and gilded in his mind. A strange encounter but something special and set apart, having nothing to do with the day-to-day duties of his ordinary life.

Over the months, he'd kept it as a treasure, revisiting every detail when a day weighed him down.

"I recall that night fondly," he finally admitted. Immediately, he felt it was too little, a half-arsed confession that didn't fully express any of his true feelings.

"As do I." She appeared suddenly sheepish, perhaps embarrassed.

Alex felt like a fool. Any eloquence he'd ever possessed had evaporated, and when she started to pull away, desperation clawed inside him. To give her reason to stay. To express even a small measure of how she aroused and excited him.

"I was thrilled," he blurted.

Her brow pinched in puzzlement. "When?"

"Today. When I looked into that carriage, and it was you."

"Even when I fell out?"

"Especially then." He'd gotten to hold her, and touching her was just as good as he remembered.

"I thought perhaps my journey was folly. I knew as soon as I saw the runner that you didn't know—"

"It doesn't matter." Alex reached for her again, cupping her cheek in his palm. "You're here now, and I'm glad you are."

She nibbled her lower lip, and he ached to draw that full, rose-tinted flesh between his own teeth.

"I should go," she whispered.

Alex released her but found himself yearning to touch her again. Touching her, spending time with her, eased something inside of him. But he understood that he'd taken liberties.

"Forgive me—"

"There's nothing to forgive." She looked as stunned as he felt but not offended. Not regretful.

He was grateful for that.

"It's late," she breathed.

"Yes, of course." He nodded but didn't agree at all. To hell with the hour. Given the choice, he would have bidden her stay, even if it was only to talk.

But those were selfish thoughts. The lady needed sleep.

"Thank you for coming down." The words were awkward and yet another incomplete expression of what he was feeling. "For allowing me to apologize."

"Once again"—her mouth curved in a soft smile—"there's nothing to apologize for."

He hoped she meant the way he couldn't stop himself from touching her more than the business with his uncle.

"Good night." She nodded and then headed for the door.

Alex stepped forward, unwilling to let her go. "If you'd still like a tour of the castle—"

"I would."

"Tomorrow?"

She grinned, and he felt as if he'd won some prize. "Tomorrow."

Chapter Eight

Sitting in the drawing room after breakfast the next morning, Evie tried to keep her attention on the book of sketches Lady Belinda was determined to show her rather than on the doorway. Ms. Mc-Quillan knitted contentedly in a chair by a lovely diamond-paned window.

"This one is my favorite," Lady Belinda said as she ran her hand along the edge of the page. "The artist's idea of what Ballymore might have looked like during the years when it was all but abandoned, before my grandfather purchased it."

Evie glanced down to find a colorful pastel sketch that captured the facade of the castle in loose, lively strokes. The field around the castle was depicted as wild, craggy, and overrun with vines and an abandoned garden. Nothing like the current garden that appeared lush but well-maintained.

Evie longed to be out in the greenery rather than stuck on a settee. After two days of travel, her body ached for movement.

When Lady Belinda turned the page, she couldn't

resist lifting her gaze to the threshold and then the clock on the mantel.

"This time of the morning," Lady Belinda said quietly, "he's usually in his study."

"And does he mind being interrupted in his study?"

She lifted her gaze to Evie's and offered a mischievous, knowing smile.

"Not by you, I suspect." Lady Belinda flicked her gaze toward her aunt, who didn't acknowledge their conversation, whether she was eavesdropping or not.

"There's something between you," Lady Belinda whispered. "I noticed it last night."

Evie let out a quiet scoff, but no words came to deny it. In fact, her cheeks betrayed her. She felt the heat rising up her neck. Lady Belinda couldn't know about last night.

The way he'd touched her by the firelight. She'd come so close to kissing him. When she'd awoken this morning, she'd debated with herself whether it had been anything more than a fanciful dream. But then she'd spotted the note he'd slid under her door that she'd left lying on her bedside table.

There *was* something between them, but even she couldn't name it yet.

"He said he'd show me the castle and the countryside."

Lady Belinda's eyes widened. "Then the time has

come. The riding habit I mentioned? I had a servant deliver it to your room this morning."

"Thank you." Evie still wasn't certain the riding skills she'd mastered while being raised in the country would come back to her, but she appreciated Belinda's thoughtfulness.

"Go." Lady Belinda made a little shooing motion with her hand. "I'll distract Aunt Oona."

Evie stifled a chuckle and made her way across the room.

After climbing the stairs to her room, she stood in shock for a moment as she found the clothes Lady Belinda had directed a maid to lay out on her bed.

The shirt was simple, roomy, and soft to the touch. The blue coat beside it was more tailored but looked as if it would fit, but the next garment shocked her. Beside the shirt and coat lay a pair of trousers.

Evie lifted them and nibbled her lower lip. She hadn't worn trousers in years and had missed them. They were practical and comfortable, or at least they had been when she and her sister had sewn themselves pairs that they could wear when riding astride. Apparently, Lady Belinda preferred riding astride too.

Within minutes, Evie had removed her skirt and petticoat and slid the trousers up over her hips. She felt a bit scandalous but vastly more comfortable than she would have wearing a skirt and riding sidesaddle.

Walking out of her room in search of the duke, she expected some reaction from the servants she passed. But they hardly showed her any notice, except for a single nod from a young maid.

"Can you tell me where to find the duke's study?" Evie guessed it was the room he'd led her to after she'd arrived, but she wasn't certain.

"Just that way and up the stairs, my lady."

Evie's guess was right, and she climbed the stairs that led to what looked to be an older part of the castle. Before she reached the top, she heard footsteps approaching from above.

The duke appeared at the top of the stairs. "I was coming to find you."

"Likewise," Evie told him.

The duke descended until he was on the step above her.

"Are you having second thoughts?" The concern in his gaze lit something in her chest, and warmth bloomed there.

"About a tour? No."

"What we talked about last night."

"No." She meant it. "Once I've decided on something, I'm committed."

"Thank you." He descended until they stood on the same step, but he still towered over her.

In that *thank you*, he acknowledged what she

couldn't admit the night before, hadn't even fully spelled out for herself. That she was doing this for him. That in doing it, she was acknowledging what Lady Belinda had said too—that there was something between them.

"We should head out while the weather holds." He glanced down, taking in her trousers.

Evie bit her lip.

Then his gaze lifted to hers and held there. "We should find you an overcoat too. It's set to rain, and if I take you toward the coast, we'll be gone awhile."

Evie nodded and let him descend first.

A servant waited for them in the great hall and offered the duke an overcoat and gloves. When he asked for the same for Evie, a maid brought them within moments.

"They're Bel's," he told her, "but she won't mind."

Once they were outdoors, she followed him to the stables.

"I haven't ridden in a while," she admitted.

"But you used to?"

"Yes, all the time. Before I moved to London three years ago."

"Then you'll do fine." He glanced back with the hint of a smile. "The stretch to the coast can be precarious, but the horses are much more sure-footed than we'd be."

As they entered the stable, a young man doffed his hat in Evie's direction.

"My lady," the young man said, "we're preparing Jane Eyre for you now. She's sweet and strong. Won't give you a bit trouble."

"That sounds perfect." Evie turned a glance toward the duke once the young man had gone.

"My mother." Rennick shrugged. "She took a fancy to naming horses after her favorite characters from novels."

Another young man led an enormous dark reddish-brown horse with a shiny black mane into the stable yard. The same one the duke had been riding the day before. Something about the horse felt wild, as if his power was barely contained and he longed to run.

"He's full of fire." Nervousness made Evie fuss with her gloves. In London, there was no reason to ride. Lady Waverly did so most days, as did many nobles. Being seen on the Rotten Row stretch of Hyde Park still mattered to many. But, of course, Evie had never been invited.

"Did you enjoy it when you rode in the past?"

"Yes," Evie said earnestly. Memories of the days when she and Sybil and her father lived at their modest home in Hampstead brought a rush of wistfulness.

"I think it will come back to you. And, by the way, this is Sherlock." He led the lithe creature toward her, his fist wrapped around his reins, the other hand on his neck in a soothing gesture.

"He's the horse that made me decide that I could make a go of this."

"Make a go of . . . ?"

For a moment, the duke assessed her, then he dipped his head in an almost abashed sort of gesture.

"Prepare yourself. I tend to go on about this, or so my family's told me."

Evie chuckled, and the nervousness that had seized her ebbed away. "You mean you have the capacity to talk too much too? I never would have guessed, but I might be able to sympathize."

"I never said you talked too much, Miss Graves."

"You did acknowledge I rambled *a bit* when we met." Evie couldn't help but smile ruefully. "But out with it, Your Grace. Ramble all you like." Good grief, if she could get him to be more open, she'd happily ride the tallest horse in the stable.

"Says the verbose and well-spoken lady," he said with a wicked grin. Was he teasing her?

Any response on the tip of Evie's tongue evaporated as another horse walked into the yard with the stable hand.

"Miss Jane for you, my lady."

The horse was a jaw-dropping beauty. White with splashes of gray, and eyelashes that any woman would envy. She was smaller than the duke's stallion, walked with grace, and exuded calm.

Meanwhile, his mount stomped his hoof as if eager to be moving on past their chitchat.

"She's gorgeous." Evie took the mare's reins from the young man.

"Less worried about riding now?" Rennick approached, so close that Evie's heart began hammering. His nearness tended to do that to her.

"Yes." Riding had become secondary to how his proximity unsettled her, though not in an unappealing way. When his coat sleeve brushed hers, it was as if a tiny electrical charge danced along her skin.

"If you don't mind, I'll make sure you get in the saddle all right," he quietly assured her.

The mare wasn't nearly as tall as the duke's horse, but Evie was grateful for his offer to help. It made her less worried she'd fumble the whole thing and end up on her backside.

He reached out and steadied the stirrup. She clutched Jane's reins and a handful of her mane, and then heaved herself into the saddle. Her momentum threatened to tip her over the other side, but she felt the heat of the duke's steadying hands on her arm and thigh.

But only for a moment.

"Feel steady?" he asked, no longer touching her, though he stood close enough for his chest to brush her leg.

"I do." Evie reached out to pat the mare's neck

as he'd done to his stallion. "She has a reassuring demeanor."

That brought a smile to his lips. "That's why she was my mother's favorite."

He was up into his saddle in one graceful motion. Clearly, the man took riding seriously. Of course he did. The Equestrian Society of Ireland was hosting their event at his castle.

Sherlock instantly began to edge forward, but Rennick held him in check, waiting for Evie to bring Jane up alongside them.

"We'll head west. There are some landmarks I can show you along the way, but it's a clear day for a good view from the coast. Then, when we return, I can show you around the castle on foot."

Evie nodded, and they were off. Once they were beyond the immediate castle grounds, the terrain became craggier, but the horses knew their way.

"You never told me."

He glanced over, and the wind caught his dark hair, sifting it in wild waves. It made him look dangerous, but his eyes weren't as stormy as they'd been yesterday. He looked almost at ease.

"The thing your family says you go on about too much."

ALEX STUDIED MISS Evelyn Graves, wondering if she'd react the way Belinda did, the way his aunt and brother did. Perhaps his aspirations *were* too fanciful, too improbable. Then he got caught up in noticing the way the wind reddened her cheeks and how the sunlight found the fiery strands of red in her chestnut hair.

"I want to support the development of uniquely Irish horse breeds and improve treatment of horses in general," he confessed, though he wasn't sure why he was divulging so much. Something about Miss Graves made him wish to. That ease between them that he'd felt even that night in Lady Waverly's garden. Ease combined with being thoroughly enticed by her. He could admit to himself now that in the months since they'd met, he craved that feeling.

He'd rarely spoken about his hopes and plans in full detail to anyone but Aurelius Byrne, another Irish horseman who'd once chaired a local horse association and the Equestrian Society.

"Jane is a Connemara pony. But a new breed could combine the Irish pony's robust features and the sleekness and speed of a thoroughbred. Such a breed would be valuable and sought-after."

"For racing?"

"Not just racing. Equestrian events, pleasure riding, or even to lead tours across the countryside. The local economy has struggled in recent years, but if we expanded Ballymore's stables, we could help grow that economy. Even now, there's talk of devising a horse show here like the ones in Dublin and London. Working together, the various horse associations in the country and the

Equestrian Society have rather ambitious plans to establish a farrier school, a horse sanctuary, and a veterinary hospital."

It did sound like a formidable challenge, even to his own ears. And there was always the matter of funding.

"That sounds like something Lady Waverly would support," she said as if reading his thoughts. "Is that where her donation will go?"

"In a sense, yes." Alex nodded. "It will go toward the Equestrian Society's efforts."

"She's a member of the Ladies' Committee of the Royal Society for the Prevention of Cruelty to Animals. I suspect she'd support the hospital and sanctuary. They sound like wonderful ideas."

Her approval came in an animated tone that made him believe she meant it. But he noticed her watching him, her brow furrowed.

"Your family doesn't encourage these goals?"

"I think they see them as a distraction from what my focus should be. The dukedom, the requirement in my father's will."

Their eyes met, and he wished he could see the thoughts whirring in her clever mind.

She turned toward the landscape ahead. "Marrying a wealthy debutante would certainly help with all your aspirations."

"You're sounding suspiciously like my sister and Aunt Oona."

"They're being practical. In the last few years, I've learned about the things we must do out of necessity." The sadness in her tone made him curious, and he suspected she thought his goals, however wonderful they sounded, were impractical.

"My goodness." She pointed to the row of mountains in the distance. "They look utterly magical."

"The Twelve Bens."

Miss Graves slowed her horse and stared wonderstruck, just as he did every time he ascended the rise near the castle and saw the mountains stretched out in the distance.

"This countryside is like something in a dream," she breathed, then looked back at him, her eyes aglow. "I never imagined I'd see mountains and the ocean all in the same day."

"We're not to the coast yet."

"How much farther?" she asked eagerly.

"Far enough for you to tell me what's made you practical in the last few years."

"My father." Once the two words were out, she swallowed hard and tried for a look he knew well. The attempt to feign ease when you felt anything but. "The loss of him. My sister and I were quite on our own."

"I'm sorry, but what of your family?"

She stared out toward the mountains again,

her expression hidden from his view. Finally, she turned back, straightened her shoulders, and looked at him squarely.

"I don't have any, other than my sister. My father's family did not approve of his marriage to my mother, and my mother had lost both of her parents by the time she married my father."

"Why didn't they approve?"

"She wasn't titled. Not noble born." There was a bit of bitterness in her tone, and he empathized and understood.

"Neither was my mother."

Her green eyes widened, and the sun lightened them to a pale jade. "Was she not?"

"No, but she was quite wealthy. Or at least my grandfather was. Not always, mind you. He left Ireland in the direst state of poverty, made a fortune in the United States, and by the time he brought his daughters to London to hunt for husbands, he came as one of America's wealthiest oil barons."

"There's the difference, then." Her voice had brightened. "My mother was not wealthy."

"But were they happy?" Alex had no idea where that question came from. It was very much something Bel would ask.

"Yes, very. I suppose that has value, doesn't it?"

Since they'd started their trek, Alex had sensed Sherlock's desire to stretch his legs. The horse was unsettled, and suddenly the animal's unease matched his own. Miss Graves's question didn't have an easy answer. At least not for him.

Bel had eloped with her newspaperman, and she did seem to be happy with him. He imagined Rupert would fall under the spell of some society diamond. And yet Alex's father had urged him to think of marriage as being as simple and uncomplicated as a transaction. The role of duchess came with duties and expectations. Perhaps fewer, now that Estings was no longer a working estate but a beautiful shell for an American millionaire to fill with his baubles. But the role was not one he'd ask any woman to take on lightly.

So was happiness truly his aim? The prospect of repairing Ballymore and expanding the stable, of funding a hospital or school—those things sparked hope in him. But happiness?

At his side, Miss Graves let out a breath of laughter. "You're taking an awfully long time to consider the value of happiness, Your Grace. I would have thought it an easy question."

"Just considering my answer thoroughly, Miss Graves."

She grinned with a mischievousness that made him long to touch his fingers to her lips. To finally kiss her as he'd wished to do last night.

"This path ahead looks less uneven," she noted. "Shall we go a little faster?"

As if he'd understood every word, Sherlock lifted his head, tugging at his reins.

"Let's," Alex said, then tapped the stallion's belly with his heel.

Without a second's hesitation, the horse took flight. A quick canter at first, and Alex looked back to check that Miss Graves was all right with the speed.

She sat her horse well and looked as confident as any lady equestrian.

"You're better at this than you let on," he called against the wind.

"I remember everything all of a sudden. Shall we race?"

Alex chuckled. "See that stone outcropping ahead? Race you there."

It was far enough to let the horses gain speed but also to allow them to slow down safely.

Without a word, Miss Graves leaned over the saddle, gave Jane Eyre her head, and the accommodating mare knew just what to do. Sherlock did too. The stallion flew past the pony, as Alex knew he would. He was an animal built for speed, yet when they reached the widest part of the path, Sherlock fell into a steady gait as if he'd decided to allow Jane to catch up. They nearly paced each other for a bit, and Miss Graves turned her head to offer Alex a beaming smile.

The sweetness of it made his heart stutter in his

chest, and he could swear he felt something in him give way.

She flicked her gaze at him again, and he offered her a smile in return.

"Watch out!"

Alex turned and saw that Sherlock was headed for the stones. He'd been trained to jump, but not on stony ground. Alex pulled on the stallion's reins, and Sherlock tugged his head, not wanting to relent. In his nimbleness, the animal cut hard left, and Alex's body heaved right. Straight out of the saddle.

He hit the ground on his side and let go of the reins, rather than tug on the stallion's head.

A moment later, Miss Graves was kneeling on the grass beside him.

"Are you all right?" She pressed a hand to his arm and jostled him as if she wasn't sure he was conscious.

Alex rolled onto his back, and the sky wobbled a bit before Miss Graves's lovely face appeared above him.

"I'll be sore, but I'm uninjured." Alex lifted his head. "Where's Sherlock?"

Miss Graves gestured behind them. "He and Jane are in the tall grass. Neither are keen to approach the stones now."

She reached up and swept her fingers across the hair that had fallen onto his brow.

"You're sure you're well?"

He hesitated to reassure her, if only to keep her hands on him.

Finally he nodded. But when she pulled back, he reached for her, his hand against her smooth, wind-reddened cheek.

"This reminds me of the night we met."

She smiled and rested a hand on his chest. "Our circumstances were reversed. Shall I help you up this time?"

"Would you?"

Never lowering her gaze, she used his chest for leverage, stood, and then held out her hand.

Alex took it and watched her, wishing their hands were bare as they'd been that night. Then he braced himself to rise, and Miss Graves pulled to help with his momentum. An unexpected twinge in his hip made him groan, and she immediately moved to stand beside him, her arm around his waist as if she feared he'd topple over.

He didn't mind at all and wrapped his arm around her shoulders, savoring the warmth of her body against his.

"Do you want to get a better look at the stones?" he asked her when he'd caught his breath.

"Will it bother you to walk for a bit?"

"Not if I can keep you close by," he told her.

She smiled at that but wouldn't look at him.

"For stability, of course."

"Of course," she said with a chuckle.

The stones were weathered, some with patches

of lichen. As they approached, he sensed tension in his companion.

"They've seen ages of time pass. They feel sacred."

"They likely were to those who put them here."

"And still standing."

"They have an excellent view." Alex guided her around the subtle mound that delineated the perimeter of the circle of ancient stones, and they walked on as the land sloped downward.

Beside him, Miss Graves let out a gasp.

"Is that it?" she asked breathily. "Is that the ocean?"

Alex nodded, and she slipped from under his arm and rushed forward. They were perhaps two miles from a stony beach that lapped the western coastal waters, but from this spot, one could see a vast, unending line of water strung out along the horizon.

"If only I could see all the way to America."

"You'd likely see the Aran Islands first," Alex said, delighted at her excitement.

"It's so vast." She glanced back at him. "Thank you for showing me."

"Thank you for riding out with me."

She returned to where he stood. "I understand why you want to make your home here. Why all your goals and plans are for the life you can make in Ireland. I've been here but a day, and I've already seen wonders."

Alex reached out and tucked a few windswept strands of hair behind her ear.

He liked the way she viewed the world, the way she listened and observed. And he realized in that moment that what she thought of this land and his ideas mattered to him.

"Will you take me back and show me the rest?"

Chapter Nine

By the time the castle came into view, Evie felt newly invigorated by all she'd seen and at ease with the duke in a way she'd never been with any man in her life.

He sensed it too, if the easy smiles he offered her as the horses made their way back to the stable yard were any indication. But for a scuff on his boot and grass stains on the elbow of his riding coat, he looked no worse for wear after his fall.

Once they were near enough to the stable for a groom to approach, the duke was the first to jump down from his horse. He immediately approached her and Jane, stripping off his gloves as he did.

"May I help you down?"

Evie reversed everything she'd done to mount the horse and felt the duke's hands at her waist as she lowered herself to the ground.

She'd forgotten the part where her legs would feel wobbly after riding and was grateful for the heated support of his hands and body at her back.

When she turned to him, he kept his hold on her. So long that one of the stablemen let out a chuckle.

Then Rennick finally stepped back and together they started up the path back to the castle.

"I still owe you a castle tour," the duke said quietly.

"You do," Evie agreed.

"After lunch?"

"That sounds perfect. Unless . . ." Looking ahead, Evie spotted a maid making her way toward them, her gait quick.

"Pardon me, Your Grace. Your aunt wishes you to know a visitor has come and asked that you join them in the dining room for luncheon."

"I've invited no one. What visitor?" The duke suddenly sounded as cool and reserved as he had the day she'd arrived.

The maid shot Evie a glance and then returned her attention to the duke.

"Lady Rowena Raymond, Your Grace."

"Bloody—"

"Thank you," Evie told the maid, who already looked frightened and surely didn't deserve cursing, as she was merely the messenger.

The girl looked pleased to be dismissed, bobbed a curtsy, and departed quickly.

"I'm sorry," the duke said immediately. "I didn't know my aunt had invited her."

"I know. She's matchmaking." Evie understood even if it caused a little of her joy of the last couple hours to ebb away. "She's being practical," Evie added because that was what she understood most of all.

"Like hell she is." He strode ahead as if he intended to march inside and send the visiting lady on her way. Then he stopped, drew in a deep breath, and turned back to Evie. "I'm still going to take you on that tour. You have my word."

"Of course. We can do it tomorrow if need be." Evie tried for a reassuring smile and reminded herself that what she'd come for was a charity event. Anything else—whatever she felt for the duke—was wholly impractical. "You should perhaps change." Evie pointed to his dirtied cuff, though in truth he looked magnificent. Windblown hair, skin brightened by the sun, and still with a bit of that ease they'd found as they'd ridden across the countryside. Though the two furrowed lines between his brows undercut a bit of that.

He nodded his head and stared at the ground. "I'll change and then go and make an appearance in the dining room. Perhaps we can reconvene in an hour or so."

Evie hadn't expected him to invite her to join the luncheon. She understood why he couldn't. And if he did, who would she come as? Lady Waverly, or her secretary? Feigning her identity for someone else held no appeal at all.

"I like that plan," Evie told him.

"Good." The duke lifted his arm, offering it

to her, as if they were heading into a park for a promenade rather than into his castle where he was about to take lunch with a lady he might very well wed.

Evie took it, ignoring the hint of warning in her heart that told her that at some point she needed to stop touching him and letting him touch her.

Later, she'd put distance between them. Now she wanted him to know how much she'd enjoyed and appreciated their ride to the ocean coast.

They entered through a door that led into the conservatory and then into the great hall. He nodded and released her as they parted ways.

"Until later, Miss Graves."

Before Evie could offer a reply, a voice rang out in the great hall as two ladies, the duke's aunt and a pretty blonde, stepped into the room.

"There you are, Alexander." The blonde lady swept forward, all elegance and silk, but though she held a smile on her face, her eyes were filled with thunder.

Her gaze scoured over Evie from head to toe, and one tawny brow inched up as she took in her riding trousers.

"And you must be the secretary who everyone thought was a wealthy countess. I'd heard the great Lady Waverly had arrived, and yet here you are instead." The scrape of her gaze down to Evie's trousers and muddy boots and up again to her windblown hair fairly shouted that she couldn't imagine how anyone would make that mistake. "It's so amusing that she sent you."

Evie shot the duke's aunt a look that she deflected by focusing on the duke.

"We didn't know quite when you'd return, so we decided to take tea near the fire. Will you join us, Alexander?"

Before offering any reply, the duke turned his gaze on Evie. She felt his perusal like the warm touch of his fingers, and when she glanced back, he seemed to read something in her expression.

"We've just been riding, and both of us could do with a bit of refreshing. But I'll join you two afterward."

With that he gestured toward the stairwell, indicating Evie should precede him.

"Don't leave us waiting, Alexander," Rowena said in a singsong tone. "It's been too long, and there's a great deal of catching up to do."

He made no reply and simply nodded.

Evie preceded him up the stairs, but as soon as they were clear of the great hall, he drew up beside her.

"I'm sorry for her rudeness. I'll speak to her."

Evie kept on until she reached the door of her guest room because her heartbeat had begun racing, and everything she wanted to say to him couldn't truly be laid at his feet. Lady Rowena's sharp tongue and snide perusal wasn't his fault. But it stung, and all Evie wanted was to get away from all of them.

At her door, she stopped with her hand on the latch.

"I don't know if I can maintain the subterfuge with your uncle. I know I agreed to do so, but even he will realize I'm not a noblewoman."

The duke shocked her by resting his hand over hers and pushing down so that they turned the latch on her bedroom door as one.

Evie entered her room, and he followed behind, closing the door.

"Your Grace, you shouldn't be in here."

"Agreed, but we also can't talk in the hallway. There are always servants about, and our servants are acquainted with Rowena's staff."

Evie tried to hold her temper in check. She could ascribe it to offense or propriety, but what she truly felt was a possessiveness she had no right to.

"Is she acquainted with Lady Waverly?" Evie wasn't certain why Lady Rowena would rush over upon hearing of the countess's arrival.

"Not that I'm aware of, though it makes sense that they would have met at some point. They're both accomplished equestrians, but the Raymonds mostly spend their time here in Galway or in Dublin."

"Then she's been invited to the charity luncheon?"

"No," the duke said evenly, "I did not include her on that list."

"Why? If she's wealthy and an equestrian, she'll likely donate. And her donation could help with all of the goals you talked about. In fact, if she resides chiefly in Ireland, isn't she a member of your equestrian society?" Evie realized she was rambling, her words slipping out before her brain had a chance to sift them.

"She's not a member." The duke drew closer. "I'm sorry I asked you to lie about being Lady Waverly if my uncle returns, and I certainly don't expect you to accept Rowena's rudeness. She was out of order, and I will insist that she offer you an apology."

Evie shook her head. "That's not necessary."

Her main wish was to never see the young lady again, though she felt certain she would. She'd meant what she'd said to the duke: if Lady Rowena Raymond might donate to his causes, she should be invited to the event.

"I disagree. I won't tolerate mistreatment of a guest in my home."

Evie would allow him to speak to the young woman. Indeed, she doubted she could stop him, but another worry took shape in her mind. "Is she acquainted with your uncle? If she is—"

"No." He took another step closer and lifted a hand as if he'd reach for her but didn't. "My uncle has only ever been to Ballymore once before. Many years ago. And it went about as well as his visit last evening."

For a moment, they simply watched each other. She had a sense that he wanted to say something. Or ask something. There was a question in his gaze, but she wasn't certain of the answer he was seeking.

What she truly wanted to know wasn't her business to ask. Did he care for Lady Rowena? His aunt seemed to believe she was the next best prospect to be his bride.

Instead, she blurted, "She calls you Alexander." Evie regretted the words the moment they were out.

Rennick tensed and then finally reached for her. He ran his fingertips along her jaw, tipping her chin up gently.

Evie's breath caught as he bent his head until their lips were but a breath apart.

"I'd rather hear you say my name," he whispered.

Evie swallowed hard and closed her eyes, struggling to find a reason not to give in to what he was offering. She couldn't, not with the towering heat of him so near, so enticing.

When she opened her eyes, he looked curious. As if wondering what she wanted, what she felt.

The connection between them was undeniable. Irresistible.

When she pressed a hand to his chest, she understood. Even through the fabric of his shirt, she felt the galloping beat of his heart.

She wasn't alone in this desire.

"Alexander," she whispered.

And he took her lips.

ALEX TOUCHED HIS mouth to hers.

He told himself to tame his hunger, but when she curled her fingers around the placket of his shirt, he lost the fight.

She responded eagerly, opening to him, and a jolt of pleasure raced down his spine. One hand came up, and she laid it on his chest, the heat of her palm warming him, soothing him, melting every bit of tension in his body.

When the longcase clock in the corner of her room chimed, the sound broke the delicious spell they'd both been under.

She pulled back and reached up to run her fingers over her bee-stung lips.

"Goodness," she breathed and then gifted him with a beaming smile.

"Goodness, indeed." Alex bent to trace his lips against her cheek, inhaling her floral scent. "Shall I shock you further?"

"Yes." The word came instantly, and her eagerness made him grin.

"I've wanted to do that since the night we met."

Alex eased back, assessing her reaction.

She'd drawn her lower lip between her teeth. "It crossed my mind too."

"Crossed your mind," he teased, pulling her closer, flush against his body.

She let out a throaty chuckle and eased a finger between the buttons of his shirt.

"I should have."

She shook her head. "No, we would have caused a scandal."

"Hmm." He resisted saying what he felt—that he wouldn't have minded creating a scandal with her—because it made no sense to the man he'd been before he kissed her.

Something in him, something he'd kept locked away, felt as if it had been released from its bonds. He felt reckless. A bit wild.

"Come downstairs with me."

"No, it will be too awkward. And Lady Rowena won't—"

"Attending the luncheon will be awkward regardless. But it might be bearable with you there."

"Alexander—"

"Alex," he corrected and bent to kiss her forehead.

"Then it's Evie."

They both chuckled, and he pulled her in for one more kiss.

"Besides," he told her as he forced himself to stop kissing her, "you were right. She should be invited to the luncheon, but that invitation should come from you."

"Why must it come from me?"

"Because I have no wish to encourage her." With that, he released Evie and made his way to the door.

But he couldn't make himself leave without one more look. He already wanted more.

"Let's go down together. Meet me in the hall in a quarter of an hour."

Alex rushed back to his room and shucked his boots and clothes, then dressed in a clean suit. By the time he entered the hallway again, Evie was stepping out of her room.

"You're certain you want me to accompany you?" She looked hopeful he'd decline, but not inviting her felt too much like allowing Rowena's rudeness to stand. He would demand the apology Evie deserved.

"Of course I'm certain."

She still looked wary, but they descended the stairs together and found the great hall empty.

"They've gone to the dining room, Your Grace." The housekeeper emerged from a hallway as if she'd been watching for the duke's arrival. "Your aunt asked me to send you that way."

"Thank you, Mrs. Wilde."

The ladies were laughing when Alex entered the room with Evie, and Belinda had joined the party.

"I told you they'd join us," Bel said as she rose

from her chair and came over to take Evie by the arm. "Come sit by me, my dear."

Alex took his seat at the head of the table, and two servants sprang into movement to begin serving.

"I should be quite peeved with you, Alexander." Rowena sat to Alex's left and gestured at him, though he moved his hand before she could touch him. "Lady Belinda says you have a fete planned next week for the Equestrian Society, and I was not invited."

"You are invited, Lady Rowena," Evie said in a soothing tone. "And I certainly hope you'll attend."

"Miss Graves, forgive me for the misunderstanding earlier. Lady Belinda was kind enough to set me right as to the situation with Lady Waverly." Rowena tipped her head, assessing Evie.

Her perusal set Alex on edge. One more snide remark and he'd be tempted to send her on her way.

"She says that your employer has great faith in you and your abilities."

"Yes, my lady. She sent me to help organize the event next week."

Rowena nodded thoughtfully, then lifted her gaze toward Alex before saying, "And yet you still found time for a ride across the countryside."

Alex cut in. "I insisted on taking Miss Graves out. Whatever else her purpose here may be, she's a guest and has never visited Ireland before."

"Ah yes, the Pierpont hospitality," Rowena said

with a sarcastic bite. "And yet I had to come without an invitation."

"But we're so pleased you did," Bel put in with one of her sunny smiles. "And you will come to the luncheon next week, won't you?"

Rowena shot Alex an assessing look. He held still, his face a congenial mask. He knew she'd agree. They'd known each other since childhood, and Rowena liked being included in any social occasion.

Still, it was clear she viewed Evie's presence as a challenge.

"Of course I will. Anything for the Pierponts. Our families have been acquainted for so long that it's almost as if we're all family."

"Who knows," Aunt Oona said from her side of the table. "Perhaps one day we will be."

Alex tensed his jaw before the rest of his muscles followed suit. He tried to catch his aunt's gaze, but she simply smiled at Rowena and carried on tucking into her lunch.

He'd need to have a word with his aunt.

Even before Evie's arrival, he'd been certain that he and Rowena would never suit. She had a history with Rupert that would make a match awkward, even if Rupert insisted he did not care.

Now the prospect of marrying Rowena, or any woman his aunt pushed his way, was impossible. Unthinkable.

He couldn't marry his neighbor or any other

noblewoman when his every thought was of the mahogany-haired beauty who'd taken up residence in a guest room.

He cast his gaze her way, past everyone else at the table. After a moment, she noticed his regard and looked back at him.

She gifted him with one of the soft smiles like the ones they'd shared on their ride, and he felt tension seep from his muscles. Everyone else, the cluttered table, the din of conversation, all of it fell away.

Alex swallowed hard but couldn't tear his gaze from hers.

He could get lost in those green eyes, and it terrified him how much he wanted to.

Chapter Ten

The next morning, Evie woke early, spread out all of the notes she'd taken before departing London, and decided on a strategy to begin planning for the charity event. That was why she was in Ireland, after all.

Not to watch a gorgeous duke tumble head over feet off a horse, and certainly not to tumble herself into some impossible—

What was it? For a lady who fancied herself a writer, not a single word sufficed to define what had happened between her and the Duke of Rennick.

They'd touched each other far too much, and they'd kissed each other far too long, and . . . Heaven help her, she'd adored every minute of it.

But that wasn't what she'd come for.

Gathering up her lists and her trusty notebook and pen, she headed downstairs, knowing that the staff, at least, would be up and busy at this hour.

A maid helpfully directed her to the kitchen, and Evie stood in awe for a moment, taking in the soaring ceiling and enormous hearth dominating the room. Her own family's kitchen had been modest.

Sometimes far too small if she and Sybil and Papa had all occupied it at the same time. And Lady Waverly's London kitchen was tiled in spotless white and had been outfitted with every modern convenience.

A tall woman with rich red hair approached, wiping her hands on an apron. "What can I do for you, my lady?"

The warm lilt of her Irish accent combined with a welcoming, if curious, smile made Evie feel as though her day was off to a good start.

"I am Miss Graves, secretary to Lady Waverly." Evie had only agreed to pretend to be the countess for one man, and she wished to set Ballymore's staff right regarding her identity. "I was hoping to speak with the cook at Ballymore about the charity luncheon next week."

"Well, you've found the cook. I'm Mrs. Frain. What is it about the luncheon you'd like to know, miss?"

"Is the menu set?"

The lady tipped her head, assessing Evie. "I've heard nothing from His Grace or Ms. McQuillan, though if there's anything special to be ordered, I suspect they'll inform me soon." The statuesque woman shrugged. "Thought I'd prepare the usual menu we serve for the family, especially considering I was told by Lady Belinda that only five guests would be coming."

"Five guests?" Evie said in astonishment.

Lady Waverly would consider that a small, intimate luncheon. For anything related to her charitable causes, her strategy and Evie's was to invite as many as they could think of who might enjoy the camaraderie of like-minded people and be willing to donate even the smallest gift to a worthy cause.

"Are there to be more, Miss Graves?"

"I certainly hope so. This event is meant to be special and, as I understand it, serve as inducement for guests to donate to worthy endeavors."

"I see." She turned away from Evie and reached for what appeared to be a very old book, its binding weathered. Bits of paper had been stuffed in around the edges. "My inherited book of receipts. I can find something special in here, unless you've suggestions."

"I do have a few." Evie drew out a document with a list of the dishes that were universally popular at Lady Waverly's events while also being easy on the kitchen staff. "Everything about the luncheon should be pleasant and memorable, but these are some dishes that have been a success in the past."

Mrs. Frain took the document and gave it due consideration. "We'll need to order in much of the fruit, but the rest looks quite doable."

"Excellent." Evie smiled, and the older woman nodded agreeably. Then she frowned and raised her gaze to Evie.

"Must the menu be exactly this?"

"No, not at all. In fact, if there's something the

family favors or that uses local produce in season, I would welcome any suggestions."

"Let me see what I can do, miss. There's a wee strawberry tart the late duchess adored. Always went over a treat when guests came to Ballymore."

"Thank you, Mrs. Frain. That sounds perfect. And let me get you an accurate count of attendees."

"As soon as you do, I'll assemble an order for the master's approval."

"I'll have it to you as soon as I can. Now, can you direct me to the castle's gardener?"

Mrs. Frain looked surprised by the question. "I've some herbs, vegetables, and fruit growing in the greenhouse outside the kitchen, but if you mean flowers, the only one who tends the formal garden at Ballymore is Ms. McQuillan."

"And I take it she's not up at this hour?"

"Oh, she might be, miss," Mrs. Frain said with a wink. "You never know with that one."

Evie decided to head straight to the garden rather than seeking out Alexander's aunt.

The *duke's* aunt. She needed to get back to thinking of him as someone she'd work with for a short while and likely never see again in her life.

Out in the garden, she immediately appreciated how the flowers and shrubs were laid out in neat rows but that there was still a bit of wildness to the whole. This late in the season, the flowers that remained stood so tall and thick that they reached to her knees or required wood frames for support.

And beyond the garden, a copse of trees rustled in the morning breeze. A scent came with that breeze, one she'd adored since childhood.

Weaving past trellises of climbing vines, Evie found rows of lush buttercups and pink asters. A tall Tudor rosebush still held some blooms. Evie dipped her head and closed her eyes, drinking in their sweet scent that brought even sweeter memories. Of Papa and home and even flashes of her mother's smiling face.

They were going on her list to include in the decorations for the event. She noticed hollyhocks and a few still-blooming dahlias that would make for beautiful bouquets too. Flowers tended to make people hopeful, and since every initiative the duke had mentioned was cause for hope, plentiful bouquets would be a perfect decoration.

As she continued through the garden, she noticed one section farther in the grove surrounded by a low wrought iron gate. Not enough to keep anyone out. Just a means of delineating one part of the garden from another. Venturing in, Evie froze after a few steps.

Almost hidden by one of the trees, she saw a man standing stock-still in the garden. A man she recognized.

The duke's uncle stood looking down at a thicket of tall grass. Then he shifted, lifting his head and staring straight at Evie as if he'd noted her presence long before she'd noticed his.

"My lady, you're a garden fancier, are you?"

"I am fond of them, yes." The man made her wary, uncertain, but she'd agreed to uphold the misunderstanding with him that she was her employer. The prospect of lying made her queasy.

For reasons she didn't fully understand, every one of the Pierponts and Ms. McQuillan gave every indication they loathed the man, and he'd exhibited no great love for them in return. But one thing she knew for certain. The duke and his family would not welcome his presence at Ballymore.

"Are you going to tell them?" The silver-haired man somehow read her very thoughts.

"Is there a reason I shouldn't? If you ought not to be here, perhaps you should go."

He smiled, and she couldn't detect any malice in it. If anything, he looked sad, defeated.

"Oh, I should not be here for certain, Lady Waverly. But I could not return to England without visiting her one last time." He gestured toward the ground, and Evie suddenly understood why this section of the garden was set apart. "I loved her, you see. And she once vowed that she loved me, but why marry a spare when you can have a duke?"

Evie dared a few steps closer, and her suspicions were confirmed. George Pierpont stood at the grave of Alexander's mother, Maeve, Duchess of Rennick.

"I did wonder if I should warn you," he said softly now that she stood closer.

"Warn me about what?"

He studied her a moment, as if weighing his reply or deciding whether to speak at all.

"Rennick is like his father. He can play the convivial gent well enough, but his heart is hard. Cold."

Evie knew that wasn't true. She'd seen proof that Alexander was a man of passion and kindness, even tenderness, but she didn't think it was her place to confide anything about the duke to this man.

"Marcus made Maeve miserable and destroyed any chance I ever had at happiness." Pierpont's voice rose, and his cheeks began to darken. "He was a wastrel, a gambling fool, and never appreciated what he had." He gestured toward the castle. "They think of me as the villain, but it was him. The only time I ever visited Ireland, I was crueler than I intended. A bitter fool. They are the product of a marriage that made Maeve and me miserable."

"That's hardly their fault. Children are not responsible for their parents' choices."

"Oh, I never blamed them, but it was hard seeing them. They mistook my misery for loathing, and they loathe me in return. Perhaps they should."

"Have you tried letting the bitterness go?" Evie spoke the words softly. She understood being angry at one's circumstances. After her mother's death, her father had been in turmoil for months. Much like Pierpont described, he'd believed happiness had been stolen from him. But he'd come back to himself when he began counting his blessings again, realizing how loved he was by Evie and her sister.

"I have tried," he finally admitted.

"It didn't seem that way a couple evenings ago."

Pierpont considered her comment with a clenched jaw, then his shoulders visibly sagged. "No, I suppose it did not. I only said I've tried to let the old resentments go, not that I've succeeded in vanquishing them."

"But you'll keep trying?"

"Of course. It's what she would want." He kept his gaze fixed on the duchess's headstone as he spoke. "Believe it or not, I came this time with the thought of making amends with all of them." He waved toward the castle again. "But while Belinda and Rupert have Maeve's kind heart, Rennick is apparently as unbending as his father. A heart of stone."

"That's unfair and unkind."

Pierpont scoffed. "Good heavens, do you love the joyless drudge?" He took a step closer. "Do you know what he did to Lord Drake? Has no one told you what he's capable of?"

She'd never heard anything about a Lord Drake,

but she knew Pierpont was baiting her and held her ground. A bit of empathy for the duke's uncle had welled up inside her. Despite his behavior when he burst into the drawing room, he now struck her as more wrongheaded than menacing. A man struggling with his past.

"He's marrying you for your money, my lady. Just as Marcus married Maeve for her father's fortune." He reached for Evie's wrist, holding her loosely.

She didn't pull away immediately, innately sensing that he did not intend her harm.

"Escape while you can."

"If you'll forgive me for saying so, sir, I believe you're the one who's trapped. By past pain and regrets."

He nodded and loosened his hold. "You see a great deal, Lady Waverly. Perhaps you are wiser than I gave you credit for."

Just as he released her, a deep, angry male voice rang out through the garden.

"You're not welcome here."

They both turned to see Alexander striding toward them. Even from a distance, Evie noted the tightness in his jaw, his fisted hands at his sides.

Within moments, he'd planted himself in front of Evie, blocking her from his uncle's view. Then he glanced back at her.

"Did he harm you?"

"Not at all." Evie moved to stand beside the duke. She didn't feel as if she needed protection from Lord George Pierpont. "We merely talked."

"About what?" Alexander demanded.

"Nothing that would concern you, Rennick."

"Leave and do not return. Ballymore will not be yours."

Pierpont nodded again, his head turned down, his stature slumped. He looked suddenly exhausted. "Then you should marry this lady, nephew." He lifted his gaze to Evie. "And appreciate her beyond her fortune."

"How dare you?" Alexander stepped toward his uncle, and Evie moved to face him, one hand against his chest.

"Just let him go," she pleaded softly. "He means no harm."

Alexander looked at her as if she'd gone mad. He was breathing hard. She could feel his heart beating fiercely beneath her palm.

He didn't even look up when Evie sensed Pierpont making his way out of the garden.

"What were you doing out here with him?"

"I wasn't with him. I'd come out to see what flowers we might use to decorate for the luncheon. He was here." Evie lowered her gaze. "At your mother's grave."

At that, he looked as if something in him had eased. He lifted his hand and laid it over hers, still pressed to his waistcoat.

"I'm sorry I barked at you. He's always been a thorn in our family's side."

"Did you know he cared for your mother?"

Alexander's frown told her the answer. "No. Did he tell you that?"

"Yes," Evie admitted. "He said he loved her and that she cared for him, but she chose your father instead."

Alex turned his head, staring off in the direction his uncle had gone. "She didn't choose my father. Her father did. He wanted a duke for his daughter. I had no idea she and my uncle . . ." His voice ebbed. "It makes a great deal of sense."

"He still thinks I'm Lady Waverly," Evie assured him. "But he never mentioned inheriting the castle at all. Perhaps it's not what he truly wants."

"Or he's convinced I'll marry you." He wrapped an arm around her waist and gazed down at her as if he meant *her*, not the subterfuge his uncle was meant to believe.

For a moment, Evie forgot to breathe. Then she shook her head, dragging herself out of the spell he cast over her so easily.

"We should discuss the luncheon," she told him, irritated that her voice emerged with a husky tremor.

"Of course." He released her.

Evie lowered her hand and crossed her arms around her notebook, clasping it to her chest like a shield against his masculine appeal.

"Shall we combine it with the castle tour I promised you?"

Evie had known from the moment she awoke that the logical strategy was to avoid him as much as possible, but now that they were together again, she realized part of her had hoped for just this.

"Yes, I'd like that."

He eyed her armful of documents. "You look extremely prepared."

"I was sent to help you plan," she reminded him. "And based on what I learned this morning, we have quite a bit to do."

That piqued his interest. One dark brow angled in question. "Do we?"

"How many people did you invite?"

"Ah," he said. "You've discovered that the local equestrian society is rather small."

"Rather?"

"All right, very."

"We have to invite more than five people, Alexander. This is a charity event, so we should cast the net as wide as we're able."

He leaned toward her as they walked. "Not to quibble, but it's seven if you include yourself and Belinda. Two more if Aunt Oona and Rupert join in."

Evie chuckled. "We need *donors*. People who care about the causes you and the society do. They need not be members, only horse lovers. Or anyone who could be persuaded to care about their welfare."

He said nothing, but Evie couldn't miss his smile out of the corner of her eye.

As they approached the door they'd used yesterday to enter the castle, he reached for the latch and held it open for her. But at the last moment, he turned, blocking her way.

"I'm glad you're here, Evelyn Graves."

Evie didn't know what to say in reply. The lump in her throat made it doubtful she could speak if she'd tried.

He was confusing her. Perhaps confusing himself.

Without waiting for a reply, he replaced the warmth in his gaze with that very proper mien she'd encountered the day she'd arrived.

"Shall we?" He stepped aside.

Evie entered the conservatory and did her best to narrow her thoughts to one single purpose: the upcoming luncheon.

"I'm assuming you planned to host the event in the great hall."

He pursed his lips. "I'd assumed we'd serve in the dining room and then gather in the drawing room."

"Lady Waverly sometimes conducts her speeches and calls for benevolence *during* a meal so that guests don't feel rushed to eat and yet also don't lose sight of the event's real purpose."

"You're suggesting we move tables into the great hall?"

"Yes. And maybe drinks before or after here." Evie stared up at the soaring glass and ironwork conservatory walls. The sunlight warmed her face, and there was something terribly appealing about being surrounded by greenery while the autumn wind chilled the air outdoors.

"It's worth considering." He gestured toward a door off the great hall that Evie hadn't noticed before. "We can start the tour here."

Beyond the door, a stone staircase wound upward, curving so that she couldn't see where it led.

"This is the oldest part of the castle, and much of it is in need of repair. But there are some parts I can show you."

Evie followed him up, and he looked back now and then as if to ensure she was still behind him.

They emerged onto a polished inlaid floor in a narrow corridor papered in faded red damask. Lining both walls were rows of gilt-framed art.

"It's a portrait gallery, though they're not all portraits," the duke explained.

He was suddenly nervous, watchful. Then he stopped in front of a portrait of a man with hair as black as his and the same chiseled jaw, though his eyes were dark, his mouth thin and mirthless.

"Speak to a dozen noblemen who knew him, and they'll tell you he was convivial. But I think the portraitist captured the truth of it." He glanced down at Evie, and the bleakness in his gaze reminded her of the pain she'd seen in his uncle's eyes. "He was a ruthless man. I have no desire to follow in his footsteps."

"Then you won't." He wasn't what his uncle had called him. There was nothing truly cold or heartless about him, though he could hide his emotions, his thoughts, well.

A hint of smile curved his lips. "You sound very certain of that."

"I tend to trust my intuition."

"I thought you were a lady in favor of practicality."

"Why not both? I can trust my intuition and still make practical choices."

He stepped closer, and Evie was aware of him as she'd been in her room. Aware that if she reached for him, he'd respond in kind. If she kissed him, she'd forget everything else.

She glanced at the paintings to keep herself from falling into the stormy sea-blue of his eyes.

"Are those your horses?" she asked, pointing to a lushly painted landscape with white- and bay-colored horses in the foreground.

"My mother's. And that one's Sherlock as a colt."

Evie approached the painting. "It's beautiful. Can we move it to the great hall for the luncheon? Remind the guests why they've come."

"If you like."

"Do you have any ideas about who else we could ask?"

"I can think of a few others who raise or breed horses, but I know of a man who'd know of even more. Aurelius Byrne, a famed horse trainer. Retired.

He and my mother were friends, and he cares about horses as much as she did. As much as I do."

"We should speak to him."

"He lives a ways outside the village. We could call on him tomorrow."

"Good." Evie continued perusing the paintings, and Alexander accompanied her, watching her as if intrigued by her reaction to each. Midway down the hall, they encountered two carved doors with gilded handles. "What's in there?"

"That is, or was, Ballymore's main ballroom."

When Evie started toward the double doors, he reached for her, one large, warm hand wrapped around her upper arm that sent a shiver from the spot all the way to her toes.

"We should proceed carefully," he warned, his voice a low rumble.

"Is it dangerous?" Evie wasn't sure if they were talking about the ballroom or the spark between them.

"There's some damage to the floor on the far side," he said as he pushed the doors open. "But it's a beauty worth seeing." He walked to the far wall and peeled back one pair of long dusty velvet drapes.

The chandeliers caught her eye immediately, their crystals glinting in the sudden burst of sunlight. She could imagine how grand it would be with candles lit, a band warming their instruments, ladies and gentlemen mingling in their finery.

"You look as if you've gone off someplace far away," he said quietly.

"Just imagining what it must have been."

"Once upon a time, it was quite resplendent, though not as long as I've lived at Ballymore." He crossed his arms and kept his attention on her, seemingly determined to ignore the grandeur of the room. "Mother rarely hosted here on a grand scale. Just family. A few close friends."

"And none of you ever came up here and considered dancing?"

His mouth tightened, and he finally cast his gaze up to take in the room, then looked at her apologetically. "I'm not very good at dancing, I'm afraid."

"Were you not dancing the night we met?"

"In all honesty, I was escaping from a dance."

"Escaping?"

"Are you going to make me recount the whole debacle? All the painful details?"

Evie laughed. "Goodness, I had no idea you were in such distress that evening."

"Well, I was. I came to the ball out of a sense of duty to my father and felt the discomfort I always do in large gatherings the moment I stepped through the door. My attempt at dancing . . ." He winced as if recalling it in vivid detail. "I was awkward. Out of practice. Nearly toppled my partner onto the floor, but thank God I didn't."

"It does sound miserable."

"It was. I was." He fixed his gaze on her, the way he had a habit of doing, as if he wished to memorize her features, see inside her mind. "Until I met a beauty in the garden."

"That night, I wondered if you'd ask me to dance." Evie grinned. "Now I know you wouldn't have under any circumstances."

"I'd be willing to try again. With you." He unclasped his hands and stepped toward her, then he held out his hand.

Evie had never met a man who could turn her insides molten, make her knees quiver with just a look or the deep rumble of his voice. She couldn't *not* react to him. Even when she willed her mind to do so, her body responded of its own accord.

"I . . . didn't mean now."

"Why not now?"

Evie laid her hand in his, and he immediately drew her closer, a hand at her back. That gentle pressure was all the urging she needed to get lost in the scent and nearness of him.

"Remember, I'm not good at this. Keep close."

"I won't let you fall," she whispered.

"You can't keep me from it, Evelyn." He nuzzled her cheek, and they moved through the steps slowly.

When Evie lifted her head, the intensity in his

gaze made her toes curl in her boots. She felt suddenly dizzy, breathless.

She was the one who was falling. No logic or practicality could keep her from it.

Like the characters in her stories, she couldn't help but follow her heart.

Chapter Eleven

Alex had ridden, washed again, and found himself out in the stables once more. His chief stableman, Skerret, advised him about the imminent birth of a colt and the potential purchase of a young stallion from a neighboring farm. In mentioning that he planned to visit Aurelius Byrne, Skerret expressed interest in any foal that might come off Devilly, one of Byrne's famous draft horses. Alex promised to inquire.

Afterward, he busied himself in the tack room, anything to keep his hands working, his mind occupied, and avoid any possibility of running into Aunt Oona. She had a wild energy to her now to match him with any eligible lady who might be nearby or even as far as Dublin or London. He'd forbidden her from doing any more meddling until after the charity luncheon.

But that wasn't far off, and the prospect of meeting the requirements of his father's will pressed on him like an ever-tightening vise. Anger burned in his chest anytime he thought of Marcus Pierpont's machinations. Had his father ever truly cared for anyone?

Recalling that look in his uncle's eyes in the garden, Alex had come to suspect Evelyn was right. The man didn't want Ballymore. But Alex did. His family did. He couldn't bear to lose it.

Yet there was something else he'd begun to dread more—the day when Evelyn Graves would pack her bags and walk out of his life.

Her arrival had been a shock, but her presence had proved a balm. And a torment.

Sleep had eluded him since her arrival. Not that worry hadn't caused plenty of sleepless nights before. But now he lay awake thinking of her, consumed with fantasies of touching her, tasting her. The notion of laying her out across his bed and losing himself in her had become more vivid night by night. So compelling that he'd found himself out of bed, pulling trousers on, and contemplating going to her—but he wouldn't.

He'd noted the times she retreated. The times when she tried to put the distance between them that she believed their relationship required. Or perhaps the professionalism that Lady Waverly would expect of her.

But he wanted her, and she wanted him. Beyond doubt, there was a magnetic connection between them. And he didn't want to lose it.

"There you are." Aunt Oona rounded the corner

and stood at the threshold of the tack room. "I might almost think you're hiding from me, my boy."

"Keeping busy. That's all." Alex removed his gloves and faced her, already wary because there was a suspicious tone in her voice. A sprightliness that was only present when she was meddling. "Is anything amiss?"

"Not at all. But I did want to ensure that you'll be available and amenable to dine with Lady Rowena and her family tomorrow."

"Aunt Oona." Alex squared his shoulders and fixed his gaze on hers. "Hear me because I do not care to repeat this. I am not going to marry Lady Rowena. She knows that. We are not well-matched, and Rowena's feelings are engaged elsewhere."

His aunt tsked and entered the room, approaching until they were close enough to speak quietly.

"As are yours," she said on an irritated whisper. "You're besotted with that girl, and it can only lead to folly."

Besotted. That was the word he'd used when Bel had gone off to elope with her newspaperman.

Was he besotted with Evelyn?

"You can't even deny it." Aunt Oona leaned closer. "That girl hasn't a penny to her name. On top of everything, this is a complication you do not need. She's a *secretary*." She pronounced the word as if it were the most scandalous thing a woman could be.

"She's intelligent, kind, curious, and here to help us. I love you, Aunt Oona, but you will speak of her respectfully or not at all."

For a long, silent moment they stared at each other, and he knew she was willing him to concede that she was right: his feelings for Evelyn were a complication. But they didn't feel that way. They felt as natural as the next breath he took, as inevitable as the sun setting this evening.

Behind him, someone cleared their throat. Aunt Oona's gaze shifted and then widened.

Alex had known a second before that Evelyn was near. His senses had ignited, and he'd caught her scent on the air. What he hadn't expected was that she'd make her way down the whole row of stable stalls and enter the tack room from the opposite side.

"Miss Graves," his aunt said evenly.

"Sorry to interrupt, Ms. McQuillan, but the duke and I are traveling today, and I feared I might be late."

"Traveling?" Aunt Oona's voice rose so high, it emerged as a squeal. "I had no news of your departure. What of our guests tomorrow, Alexander?"

"Oh, it's just a short day trip," Evelyn quickly explained. "To visit a Mr. Byrne, isn't it?"

There was a glint of mischief in Evelyn's gaze, and he wondered exactly how much she'd heard.

"You're visiting Aurelius Byrne?" Aunt Oona's tone had turned incredulous. "Whatever are you thinking?"

Evelyn took a breath as if to answer, but Alex stayed her with a look. His aunt would harangue them all morning. And Evelyn was right. They needed to get on their way.

"Byrne knows more about horse training and breeding than perhaps anyone in Ireland. And he knows plenty of nobles who'd support our causes."

"Our causes?"

Of course, they weren't *her* causes. All she cared about was keeping Ballymore. But Alex wanted more. He'd always wanted more, and the last five years he'd convinced himself those goals should be secondary. Not anymore.

If he could make a go of breeding horses, attracting buyers interested in uniquely Irish breeds, and expanding Ballymore's facilities to include equine medical care, the income wouldn't be as quickly achieved as pocketing a wealthy bride's fortune, but it would matter more and feel worthwhile.

"We'll be back soon," Alex told his aunt, then dismissed her with a nod.

She huffed for a moment, glared at him, and didn't spare Evelyn a glance before departing.

"She's not pleased." Evelyn's tone was matter-of-fact.

"Aunt Oona is entitled to her opinions, but so am I. And all we need to worry about is getting on the road. I've had a pony cart prepared, and I think the weather should hold through the morning."

"Excellent." She smiled as if pleased, and he

was grateful for it after the confrontation with his aunt.

He noted the notebook clutched to her chest. The lady was never without a pen and something to write on.

"You look prepared, as always." They walked side by side, the sleeve of his coat brushing hers. That simple contact made him feel lighter. All the irritation of a moment ago melted into the pleasure of having her near again.

"One should always be prepared," she said, her tone teasing. "We're hoping Mr. Byrne will help us with the guest list, so I need to be prepared to make one."

"We'll have to get invitations out quickly."

"I can help with that. I've created more invitations for Lady Waverly than I can count."

He offered his hand and helped her up into the cart, then settled onto the bench beside her.

As on their ride together, she was attentive to the countryside, eager to take everything in.

"Why doesn't your aunt like Mr. Byrne?"

"His reputation isn't spotless," Alex shared, "though that hardly detracts from his experience and knowledge. He turned his noble patrons against him when he confronted one of them quite publicly."

"Oh?"

"My aunt would tell you he was drunk and attacked a viscount in his home."

She turned her face toward his. "And what do you say?"

"I heard the story from Byrne himself. As he tells it, he discovered a certain viscount was running a dog-fighting ring. Byrne knew the man well. Trained his horses, taught his family to ride, helped the viscount fill his stable with thoroughbreds. But he noticed that the nobleman had a cruel streak."

"And what did he do about it?"

"Made a scene at one of the viscount's country-house parties. Showed the guests evidence of their host's cruelty. Some probably didn't care and may have bet on dogs themselves, but enough were outraged. Byrne was fired but apparently rescued a few of the dogs and reported it all to the authorities first."

"I already like him."

Alex laughed and tipped his face toward hers. "I thought you might." He hesitated a moment and then admitted, "We became friends after I had a bit of a scandal of my own."

"Well, you must tell me about that one too." She wasn't appalled or taken aback that he'd just admitted to being embroiled in a scandal. All he could detect was her usual curiosity.

"It happened in London," he started. The memories came in a rush. "I came upon a nobleman beating a horse. The gelding hadn't gotten his hansom to some meeting on time, apparently."

"That's terrible. What did you do?"

Alex turned toward her. He suspected this would be when he'd see the disgust he'd come to expect when people heard what he'd done.

"I took the viscount's cane from his hands and hit him, much as he'd struck the poor animal still attached to the cab. Then I used my fists."

"I see." She didn't look horrified, only contemplative. "Do you know what happened to the horse?"

Alex smiled at her query, both surprised and charmed that her main concern was for the most innocent party of all.

"I bought the horse from the cabbie. I suppose I'm a bit of a soft touch and have purchased a few horses that are too broken down to work. Byrne does the same. In fact, he's taken in the handful I've purchased. He gives them food and pasture and lets them retire, so to speak."

"That's wonderful. I'm so glad someone does." She swallowed hard as if some deep emotion had welled up inside of her, then turned to him with a gentle smile. "When one is down on one's luck, every bit of assistance, especially if it's offered respectfully, is such a gift. Animals deserve that too."

"Agreed." Alex felt close to her in that moment, not just in a physical sense but as if their hearts and minds were in accord, at least on this topic.

They talked for the rest of the trip. Evelyn excelled at asking questions that caused him to expose parts of himself he didn't normally offer up in polite conversation. She was good at putting him at ease and keeping him talking, and she listened with genuine interest.

Yet after a while, he noticed that she'd revealed little of herself, despite him offering up questions in between hers.

"So now you know I once had thoughts of being a doctor—"

"Like my grandfather and soon my sister."

"Precisely." Alex waited a beat, glanced down at her, and said softly, "But you haven't told me what you longed to be when you were younger."

She knew his aspirations, and he found he desperately wanted to know hers.

"Oh, I still want to be what I longed to be when I was younger."

"Which is . . . ?" He leaned against her gently, savoring the warmth of her body and the little hitch in her breathing as she looked up at him. "Are you going to make me drag it out of you, Miss Graves?"

She let out a little growl of frustration. "It's just that I know what you'll say. The questions you'll ask."

"Well, now I'm offended," he said with mock anger.

"No, no," she said, turning to lay a hand on his arm. "It's what everyone asks when I tell them."

"Perhaps I'm singular." He glanced at her, at where her bare hand lay on his arm. He had the wildest urge to kiss every single finger. "Maybe I'll surprise you."

"Very well." She shook her head, closed her eyes, took a deep breath, and said, "I'm a writer. In addition to the writing that I do for the countess, I also pen stories. Have since I was a girl."

"Stories." He tried to imagine what sort of stories a lady like Evelyn Graves might write. "About what?"

Evelyn clapped a hand over her mouth, and her eyes danced with mirth. "That's the first question."

"Oh, very well," Alex grumbled. "It's the logical one."

"Romantic stories," she admitted quietly. "Love. Adventure." She eyed him warily, then crossed her arms. "You may find that silly."

"I don't." He was wholeheartedly offended now. "Love is a more than worthy subject for any writer's pen."

"Agreed."

They rode in silence as Byrne's property came into view over a rise in the road.

When he adjusted the reins to direct the horse into the drive, Alex risked a glance at Evelyn. She wore an inscrutable expression, but she was at ease. No longer crossing her arms, but no longer touching his either.

"Would you ever consider letting me read one of your stories?"

She chuckled and beamed at him. "That's the other question."

Alex gritted his teeth but couldn't hold onto his irritation when she continued to smile as he turned the cart into the front drive of Byrne's country house.

"Very well," he conceded with a tone more peevish than he'd ever used in his life. "I am as unsurprising as everyone else."

"You've surprised me many times," she said as he climbed down from the cart, and he held out his hands to help her descend. "And I'm sure you will again."

"I shall make it my chief endeavor." Rather than merely offer her his hand, he wrapped his hands around her waist, and she stepped down in his arms.

When she tipped her head up, the sunlight kissed her skin, lightened her eyes. He noticed gold sparkling amidst the green.

"Chief endeavor after charity-luncheon planning, of course," she told him with a cheeky grin.

"Of course."

He released her, and she turned to gather her notebook. Then they both froze at the distinct and harrowing sound of someone cocking a shotgun.

"Who goes there?" Aurelius Byrne ambled forward, shotgun pointed at Alex. "Alexander?"

"It is I, Mr. Byrne. And this is Miss Graves."

For the first time, the barrel-chested, bearded

man noticed Evelyn, and he immediately lowered his rifle.

"Forgive me, lass." The man's narrowed eyes widened as he took Evelyn in. "Can I offer you tea and a fire to warm yourself by in recompense?"

Alex didn't miss that this offer was entirely offered to the beauty beside him.

"I would like that very much, Mr. Byrne."

The old man kept his shotgun pointed down, hidden under one arm, and offered her his other as if he'd just asked her to join him for a whirl around a ballroom.

She took his arm and smiled back at Alex.

Good grief, he'd suspected she would be able to soothe Byrne's gruffness over the course of their visit, but the very sight of her had dulled the man's usual wariness.

Byrne's home gave every evidence of bachelor status. Dark hues dominated in every piece of furniture and fabric and wallpaper. Books lined bookshelves but also sat in haphazard piles. Teacups were scattered atop them. Or whiskey tumblers.

The old man led Evelyn to a worn leather chair by a low-burning fire. Then he gestured to Alex to join him in the kitchen. While he took a cast-iron pot off a neatly polished hob and poured steaming water into a teapot, he glanced back at Alex.

"What brings you here, Rennick?"

"That lady in your front room."

"Lovely as she is, she could convince a man of anything. Even visiting an old criminal like me."

"We're having a charity luncheon next week."

Byrne eyed him skeptically. "My purse isn't flush, man."

"We're more interested in your mind. Your connections."

He let out a chuckle that turned into a cough. "By God, Duke, have you not heard how my days went arseways after that business with the viscount?"

"You can't have lost all your clients. The prince regent called on your expertise."

"Once upon a time, lad. Once upon a time."

Alex took the tray that Byrne filled with teacups, a teapot, and a small decanter that he suspected contained whiskey.

Evelyn was examining the framed paintings and photographs covering his drawing room walls when they joined her. Most included horses. A few featured gatherings of equestrians at horse shows or hunts.

"Is that . . . the queen, Mr. Byrne?" Evie asked, pointing to a photograph above the mantel. Byrne stood with reins in his hands, while one of the royal princesses sat atop a sleek pony. The queen stood stoically at the princess's side.

"It is, miss. Long time past." Apparently, Byrne wasn't interested in recounting that memory. He pointed instead to a portrait of a noble bay-colored horse. "The greatest thoroughbred I ever trained."

"Who are these people?" Evelyn asked of one of the group photos that included perhaps fifty individuals, all kitted out in equestrian garb. The date at the bottom indicated it was taken five years previously.

"Do you expect an old man to remember every name?" Byrne teased as he splashed tea into everyone's cup.

"If you could remember a few, it would help us." Evelyn glanced at Alex, and he nodded, content for her to take the lead. "His Grace is a local head of the Equestrian Society, and my employer holds a similar role in the London chapter."

"Who's that?" Byrne settled into an enormous wingback near the fire and added a generous pour of whiskey to his tea.

"Lady Katharine Waverly."

"Ah, of course. The lady of causes. Never saw a needy thing she didn't wish to save or throw her wealth at."

"Yes, that's her." Evelyn cast her gaze down and took a sip of tea.

Alex wondered if she was seeing herself in that description. How desperate had she been when she'd sought employment with the countess?

"We're holding a charity luncheon at Ballymore, Byrne." Alex decided to cut to the chase. "Any suggestions you can give us would be helpful. Any owners, riders, or even horse-show organizers who might be interested in donating."

"Still looking to establish your schools and hospital?"

"The society is considering a sanctuary too. You were mentioned in that discussion."

Byrne let out a low, rumbling chuckle. "In whispered tones, I'm sure. Not many of your ilk will even speak my name."

"My mother did."

The older man turned his whole attention toward Alex, his clear blue eyes wary and curious. "A fine woman. I still miss her." For a moment, the old man appeared to be lost in memories, and when he raised his head, he offered them a sad smile. "I'll give you names, Miss Graves. Get yourself a writing implement, and I'll offer those I can recall."

Evelyn pulled out the notebook she'd tucked beside her. Her pen was poised over the paper a moment later.

"No," Byrne said, his hand slicing through the air. He pointed to a battered wooden bureau with half a dozen drawers. "Second drawer down, you'll find a list of everyone who attended that particular event. And guest lists of a few others over the years. Will that help you at all?"

Evelyn choked on a gasp that was half laughter, half relieved exhale. "That will help us very much indeed, Mr. Byrne." She was up and tugging out the drawer before the retired horseman could reply.

While she busied herself sifting documents and

pulling a few from the drawer, Byrne turned his attention Alex's way.

"A lovely lass you've found yourself, Rennick."

Alex nodded, unwilling to quibble with the assessment. Yes, he'd been the one to first stumble over Evelyn in that lantern-lit garden, but now it felt much more as if she had found him. The most honest, fundamental parts of himself that few ever got to see.

"Keep her."

The mumbled words came so softly that Alex wasn't sure if Byrne had spoken them or they'd welled up from someplace deep inside himself.

But then Evelyn, who'd given every appearance of being too engaged with the documents she'd found to pay any mind to their exchange, shot him a look over her shoulder.

There was a question hidden in the depths of her green gaze. Alex wished they were alone so she could ask it.

Chapter Twelve

Rain slid down the neck of Evie's coat, and she turned up her collar, trying to stave off the icy drops. Precipitation had come on lightly at first, a delicate patter so intermittent they didn't feel like a shower at all. But ten minutes in, the sky unleashed a torrent, and gusts kicked up to whip the rain into her face and Alex's.

He'd immediately risen from his seat, lifted the bench, and produced a dusty blanket from inside. She'd stretched it atop both of them as he drove the horse and cart as fast as he dared.

Then suddenly, Alexander turned off the road onto a path sheltered by high thickets on each side. Rain had pooled into puddles, and the sky had grown so dark that it felt like night. But their cart horse gave every indication she knew where she was going.

But Evie was curious too. "Where are we going?"

"There's a public house not far down this way," he told her. "Or at least there used to be. We can wait out the storm there."

Oh, to be dry and warm and get a bite to eat.

Evie nodded eagerly, though Alexander was too busy keeping his eyes on the lane ahead. In the dim light, with the greenery leaning in on both sides, they'd be in trouble if they encountered another vehicle coming the opposite way.

Evie let out a relieved breath when the well-lit pub came into view. It was as hidden by the thickets and lush tree cover as the lane itself, but clearly locals knew it. Several light carriages and carts were tucked in under a thatched overhang.

Alex somehow managed to fit their cart in too. Then he swiftly jumped down and secured their horse to a post. Evie clambered out after him.

"Let's go get warm." He lifted his arm, sheltering her inside his long overcoat with him, and they both bent their heads against the rain and headed for the door.

The warmth they sought found them the moment they pulled open the pub's door. A wall of peat-scented heat, along with the aromas of roasted meat and fresh-baked bread, welcomed them. Despite the weather, Evie was surprised to see only a few people gathered around the tables.

"Welcome," the publican called from behind the bar.

Alexander approached and spoke to the man while Evie made her way to the fire, removing the damp blanket from her shoulders, and then holding her hands out so that at least some part of her felt dry.

"He doesn't think the storm means to stop for a while," Alex said as he drew up beside her and held his hands out too.

Evie couldn't help but notice how much larger they were than hers and remember how they felt against her skin. They'd only touched in the most practical of ways today, and she knew she was foolish to yearn for more. Yet she did.

"What does he suggest?"

Alex glanced down at her, then behind them as if to ensure no one overheard their exchange.

"He's offered us a room for the night."

"Just one?" Evie heard her voice lilt over those two words. The prospect of it thrilled her in a way she knew it shouldn't. Desire rose in her each time they were within a few feet of each other: a seed planted that first night had bloomed into something richer. She'd never wanted any man as she wanted him. Never had her body reacted before her mind could make sense of what she was feeling.

She'd already been alone with Alexander, touched him, kissed him—good heavens, that kiss.

Alexander didn't appear quite so intrigued by the prospect. Or, if he was, he was hiding it well.

"I realize it would be gravely inappropriate." He turned to her then, his face set in grim lines. "I've already been careless with your virtue—"

"No," Evie stopped him before he went on blaming himself for encounters that she participated in, wanted. "I have no regrets, Alexander. I don't wish you to have any either."

She was quite sure of what she felt, but perhaps *he* regretted how close they'd become in such a short stretch of days.

"Do you have regrets?" she dared to ask.

"Where you're concerned? Absolutely not."

That brought a smile to her face. "Good." She took a step closer and laid a hand on his chest. His shirt was damp but no longer soaked, but it was his heartbeat she sought. For a moment, she stood silently, reveling in the heat in his gaze and the strong, reassuring thud against her palm. "I think we should take that room."

He smiled, a dazzling flash that made her pulse race. "I was hoping you'd say that."

"Should we eat first? Have something to drink?" Out of the corner of her eye, she felt the assessing gaze of the publican and a few others in a corner booth.

"If you like." He cupped her cheek and tipped her head, almost as if he meant to kiss her right then and there. "Or we could have food sent up."

"Maybe that's best." Evie had already made the decision in her mind. She wanted this moment, these few hours with Alexander, in a way that was private and theirs alone.

But though most in the pub gave them a glance and continued eating or drinking, a few gazes followed their movements.

She realized they were opening themselves to gossip the longer they lingered.

"I'll return in a moment."

The fire had begun to warm Evie's hands and dry her dress, but there was a different sort of warmth kindling inside her too. Anticipation. Eagerness. And strangely, though logic dictated she should feel fear—for her reputation, for her future—she didn't. At least not yet.

"We can go up," Alex said quietly as he approached. "The publican will have food and drink brought to us."

Evie followed him upstairs, and he led her into a cozy room with a freshly laid fire. Though not spacious, the room featured both a sizable bed and a round table with two chairs. Simple cotton curtains were pulled at a mullioned window. Rain whipped against the panes as the sky darkened.

"Second thoughts?" he asked her quietly.

"Not at all. Just looking." Evie turned her gaze to his. While she'd taken in the room, he'd been watching her, almost warily. "Are *you* having second thoughts?"

He shook his head in answer. "Will it shock you if I admit that since the day you arrived, I've thought often of how we might spend time on our own?"

Evie smiled. His admission made her feel almost giddy, a reminder she needed. That what she felt for him, the desire and attraction, wasn't one-sided. They were in this together. They felt the same.

"Come and get warm." He spoke the words in a low, husky tone that charged the air between them.

Evie approached, and he gave her space to stand closest to the fire. Without speaking a word, he moved behind her, then reached around to remove her coat. Evie glanced over her shoulder and watched as he laid the garment aside and shed his own.

Then he came back to her, the heated wall of his body sheltering her from behind. He wrapped an arm around her, and Evie reached up to press her hand against his in the spot where he held her.

That simple connection—her hand joined with his—was still as powerful as the night they'd met. It felt natural and right, and yet it also filled her with a fizzing sort of energy. As if when they were together like this, every sensation, every experience was more vivid.

He bent his head and nuzzled her cheek. Evie turned her head, and he touched his mouth to hers.

"I want this more than you can imagine," he whispered and then kissed her. A languid, melting kiss, his tongue teasing at the seam of her lips until she opened to him.

At a knock on the door, he groaned and released her.

Evie touched a finger to her lips and caught

her breath. Suddenly, the last thing she wanted was food, despite the savory smell that filled the room.

He poured wine for both of them and brought a glass to her.

"Still hungry?"

She was, but it was for him, for his kiss, his nearness. Still, she nodded and took a sip of wine. He cut a few pieces of bread, spread butter on one piece, and held it out, offering it to her. Rather than take it from him with her hand, she bent to take a bite.

Alex smiled and then took a bite himself. He lifted the last morsel to her lips.

She took the bite, pulling it into her mouth along with the tip of his finger.

"Such a seductress," he murmured.

Evie had never been called such a thing in her life, never thought of herself that way either. But, then again, she'd never met a man she wished to seduce. Never met a man who made her determined to wield her feminine wiles. The loveliest part was that Alexander required no seduction—she felt how much he wanted her in every touch, saw it in every glance—and yet she knew he enjoyed her flirtation too.

"I suppose we should get out of this wet clothing," she told him and then reached for the buttons on his shirt.

"We really should." He watched her as if fascinated, allowing her to undress him.

Evie reveled in every new inch of skin she exposed. Even as she unbuttoned the fastenings of his shirt, she swept a finger up through the dusting of hair on his chest, then bit her lip when she pushed the garment from his shoulders.

"Heavens," she breathed. She'd known his shoulders were wide. That had been clear even in that moment when he'd bent over her in the darkness of Lady Waverly's garden. But now she realized that much of that width was muscle. Beautiful arcs and curves were highlighted in the fire glow.

He let her explore, standing patiently, studying her face, as her hands roved over his shoulders, the sinew at his neck, the line down the center of his chest. Then, looking up to lock her gaze with his, Evie lowered her hands to the band of his trousers.

"Don't stop now," he whispered.

"Oh, I don't intend to," she told him as she unfastened buttons and edged the fabric down over his hips.

"Slowly," he told her.

She eased his trousers off slowly, but once they were past his hips, they slipped down on their own.

"I can help with the rest." He bent to remove his boots.

Evie stepped back and watched as he pushed his

trousers away and then slid off his drawers. He stood before her bare, the firelight licking at his skin.

She approached to touch him, unable to resist. First his chest, trailing her fingers through the line of hair that ran to his belly. Then she wrapped her fingers around the hard length of him, curious and thrilled that she excited him. That he wanted her.

"That's for you," he whispered huskily.

Evie swallowed hard when he reached out and began undoing her bodice. She still held him, didn't want to let him go. Though when she moved her hand, letting her fingers rove, he let out a low sound. She wasn't sure if it was a moan of pleasure or a groan of discomfort.

"Did I do something wrong?"

He bent his head and whispered in her ear, "You couldn't, but if you keep touching me that way, I may lose control."

Evie rather liked the idea. How would Alexander, Duke of Rennick, be without a shred of control?

She helped with the fastenings of her bodice, and Alex slid his hands down to her skirt, finding the hooks, slipping them apart easily. Then she stepped out of her petticoat.

Alex bent to kiss her neck, tugging gently at the light fabric of her chemise to reveal more and more skin. Evie tried to focus on her corset, but each kiss, each stroke of his fingers made her body hum with need. When she was finally free of it, he reached for the hem of her chemise, and she lifted her arms as he slipped the garment over her head.

Alex bent to kiss her neck again, stroked his tongue along her collarbone, and then trailed kisses down between her breasts.

Her pins began to loosen, and she reached up to pull them out.

"I've wanted to remove those so many times."

Evie let out a husky laugh. "Have you?"

"Mmm," he said as he stroked his fingers through the strands as she freed them. When he drew his fingers down, there was a clink of metal against metal as the ring he always wore brushed against the pendant at her neck. He lifted the pendant and smiled. She knew they both were remembering the night they met.

She'd wanted him even then. There was no denying that to herself anymore.

He pushed her hair aside and bent to take her nipple into the heated haven of his mouth. The warm, teasing insistence of his tongue against the sensitive peak turned her insides molten. Made her thighs quiver, her core pulse with need.

When he stood again, he cupped her cheek. "No doubts?"

"No. Please." The *please* came out unbidden. She wanted him desperately in that moment, wanted to be close to him in ways she'd never yearned for with any man.

He took her lips, wrapped his arms around her, and drew her toward the bed.

She reached between them to work the ribbon free on her drawers, the last stitch of clothing she wore, but the knot she'd tied resisted.

"Let me," he whispered. "Lie back, sweet."

Evie did, and Alex knelt over her, just as he had that night they'd met. The delicious difference now was that she could touch him. And she did, stroking her hands over his shoulders, the corded muscles of his arms. He turned to catch her fingers, kissing her hand, her arm, all while his fingers worked at the knotted ribbon at her waist.

"You could cut it," she whispered, glancing at the knife that had been sent up with the food.

Alex chuckled and bent, kissing her stomach, his fingers still working the knot. "My impatient beauty."

His patience was driving her mad. She reached down, ready to tear the fabric herself, but he'd freed the ribbon and gripped the fabric, sliding it with maddening slowness over her hips and then off altogether.

Evie reached for him, expecting him to settle between her thighs, but he lowered himself beside her, his head near her breast, and drew his fingers lightly along her leg. He traced a path to her curls, and then slid a finger along her wet hot center.

"Mercy," she breathed and wrapped her hand around his neck. The single stroke made her body shudder; the next parting her, seeking her heat, made her buck her hips off the bed.

Alex bent and pressed a kiss to her belly, a soft, almost soothing kiss. Then he dipped his head, using his tongue as he had his finger, seeking, exploring. She reached down to sink her fingers into his hair, another hand braced on the hot, shifting muscles of his shoulder.

When he slid a finger inside her, she gasped at the pleasure of it, and then his tongue flicked at a spot that seemed the center of her. Evie's every breath, every sensation became fixed on that spot. On Alex's heated tongue against her core, his hand braced against her thigh. With each stroke, pleasure built and pushed her further, higher.

She held her breath, her body tensed, she closed her eyes and clutched at Alex, digging her fingers into his warmth. Pleasure burst through her, and a bone-melting sense of satisfaction chased after.

"Alex," she breathed, feeling him but needing to see him, kiss him.

And he knew. He understood without her saying the words.

Arching over her, he braced himself above her. But Evie wanted him closer. She wrapped a hand around his neck, another at his shoulder. Then she noticed the redness of his skin. Marks where her fingers had gripped him.

"I'm sorry, I was—"

"Perfect," he told her with a finger at her lips. "Exquisite. Delicious."

Evie smiled. "All right. You needn't overdo it."

He ran his fingertip along the seam of her lips, then he bent to kiss her. A deep, hungry kiss, his tongue stroking in to taste her.

"I mean," he said huskily against her lips, "every word I say to you. You are beautiful." He stroked his fingers through her hair splayed out on the bed. "I adore you."

He meant it. She could see it in his awestruck gaze, feel it in every tender touch. And the loveliest feeling filled her heart. A feeling that every moment with him was exactly where she belonged.

With the most gorgeous man she'd ever met, a duke of the realm stroking her body to the heights of pleasure she'd never known, and she felt at home. Safe, secure, adored. Even if only for these precious moments, within the four bounding walls of this tiny room.

Without another word, Alex bent and kissed her again, and finally settled between her thighs.

Evie let out a moan of pleasure as he rocked against her. She wanted him, needed him, and bucked up to get him closer.

"You know I'm not patient," she whispered as she nuzzled his cheek.

He arched up to look into her eyes as he filled her.

When she gasped at the feel of him, adjusting to the sensation, Evie lifted her hand to cup his face.

Alex turned to press a kiss against her palm as he stroked inside her, creating a rhythm that built that feeling again. The sense that she was climbing, but this time they were together. She could see that he'd lost himself in it too.

The controlled duke was someplace else. In Alex's eyes, she saw only hunger for her. He bent his head to kiss her neck, then took a nipple into his mouth. Not tenderly like the first time. He nipped with his teeth.

Evie rushed toward the edge then, pulling Alex up so she could see his face again.

"Come with me," he urged on a gravelly rasp as he thrust deeper, harder. No controlled rhythm now, just the need for her. For them to be like this. Together.

Evie followed him, heard his guttural groan as she flew over that edge once more. A moment later, her body boneless and sated, she called his name as if he wasn't still beside her.

"I'm here, love," he said, drawing her into the heat of his body, the warm embrace of his arms. "I'm not going anywhere."

"Within this little room, in your arms, everything feels safe. Feels perfect."

"I agree. Let's stay forever."

Evie chuckled at that and nipped at the skin of his neck. "Let's stay a little longer."

The rain had stopped. They could return to Ballymore.

But Alex pulled the covers up over them, and Evie found that they fit together in a way that felt right, and she didn't want the moment to end too soon. It might be the only time they'd ever be together in this way. She knew that. Accepted it. And that made her more determined to hold onto it as long as she could.

Chapter Thirteen

Sunlight warmed Alex's skin, and Evie heated the length of his body. With her face tucked against his neck, her soft breath tickled his skin. Then she sensed that he was awake and shifted away from him.

He stroked across her shoulder, threading his fingers through her thick waves of hair, urging her to stay. Alex wanted to savor the moment, stamp it on his memory, draw it out as long as they were able. She seemed willing to do the same and snugged herself against him with a contented sigh.

As they lay in the early morning quiet, he knew peace as he couldn't ever remember feeling before in his life. No thought of what he should do next, and no guilt for lingering in the sweetness of the sensation.

"We should return," she whispered against his skin.

"Mmm," he murmured.

Such a practical beauty.

Alex looked down at Evie, at her auburn hair splayed on his chest, her arm draped across his stomach. She still had her eyes closed, but he could feel that her body had begun to tense.

He had the urge to roll her onto her back and make love to her again. Or better yet, let her climb atop him and set the pace to find her own pleasure.

"Your family will be worried." She lifted her head to gaze at him.

She looked absolutely delicious with her mussed hair, bee-stung lips, and green eyes luminescent in the sunglow.

"I know you're right, but I'm struggling to muster a single urge to leave this bed."

"Are you that fond of the bed?" she teased, her voice warm and early-morning raspy.

"I'm fond of having your bare skin against me from head to toe."

She smiled, and he traced the shape of her lips with his fingertips, feeling a wave of tenderness.

"Thank you," he told her.

"For keeping you warm?"

"For the peace I woke with, for every moment of last night. For that smile to let me know you have no regrets."

"I don't. I wanted this. But . . ." She eased away from him and sat up in bed, taking the edge of the coverlet with her. "We should return."

Alex groaned and ran a hand over his stubbled face. "I suppose we should."

"There will be questions."

Alex sat up too, settling against the bedframe, and reached down to take her hand.

"Please don't worry. I'll tell them whatever I must, and you needn't worry about Bel and Rupert."

"Your aunt—"

"Is my concern. Not yours. I'll speak to her."

Evie nodded but worry lingered in her gaze, and he understood. Bel and Rupert wouldn't offer a single word of judgment, even if they noticed that something had changed between him and Evie. If they did, Bel wouldn't be at all surprised, and Rupert had already noted his attraction to Evie.

But his aunt would be vocal. Alex suspected she would become even more insufferable in her insistence that he marry Rowena.

If that had been unlikely before, it was impossible now. He wanted . . .

Evie bent to kiss him, one sweet taste of her lips before she climbed out of bed. He watched in tantalized arousal as she brushed her fingers through her hair and gathered it at her nape. Then she looked around for pins. He spotted one next to the bed and leaned out to collect it, and then another nearby.

"Thank you," she said, glancing at him over her shoulder.

"You look like a siren," he murmured, reaching out to stroke his curled fingers down the soft slope of her back.

She smiled almost proudly but then said in a

teasing tone, "Well, I promise not to lure you to your demise."

"Much appreciated, beauty."

Once she'd stood and slipped on her chemise, Alex realized she was in earnest about them being on their way.

With a sigh of regret, he flicked the covers back and collected his own discarded clothing. While buttoning his trousers, he caught Evie watching him out of the corner of her eye as she fastened the buttons on her bodice.

"If you change your mind and wish to stay longer, I'm open to being convinced."

She laughed, a delicious, full-throated sound.

Too soon, they were both finished dressing. Evie faced him, putting one last pin in her hair.

"Do I look at all presentable?"

"You look wonderful."

She approached and pushed playfully at his chest. "You must be honest."

"I told you not to worry. Trust me to deal with Aunt Oona." He took her hand and didn't let go until they were out of the room and at the top of the stairs.

Another couple was up early and taking food at one of the tables, and the publican's wife offered a nod, but no one else noticed them as they made their way toward the door. Though Evie cast her gaze around, even looking over her shoulder as if she expected a London scandal-sheet writer to jump out of the shadows.

Once outside, Alex prepared the horse and cart while Evie examined a cluster of flowers at the edge of the public house.

"Your Grace."

At the call, Alex snapped his head toward his hired man, Givens, who emerged around the side of the pub leading a horse by its reins. "I was just on my way to Ballymore, Your Grace."

Alex turned toward Evie. She looked more curious than concerned about Givens noticing her presence, but she didn't approach.

"Givens, of course you're here at the inn." Alex had been so consumed with escaping the rain and spending time alone with Evie, he'd somehow forgotten that Givens, and possibly his uncle, were among the guests staying at the Hart and Crow.

Alex examined the two windows facing the front of the public house and wondered if his uncle was watching them from behind one of curtained panes.

"Oh, he's not here anymore, Your Grace."

"Well, that's a bloody relief. I want no more uninvited visits from him, Givens."

The older man cast his gaze at the ground and clutched the hat he'd removed with a white-knuckle grip. "Then I may have bad news for you.

Each morning, I inquire of the proprietor or his wife whether Pierpont has shown his face. Man's an early riser."

"And?"

"This morning, he rose early as usual but told the couple that he would no longer be staying at the inn." Givens offered him a stark look. "No word on whether he was returning to England, which is most likely, or heading back to Ballymore. But I was just coming out to ride over and inform you either way."

Alex clenched his jaw and tried not to turn his attention toward Evie. She remained in what looked to be a little garden at the edge of the pub, though Alex suspected Givens had noticed her presence. The man didn't miss much.

"Thank you, Givens. I'm on my way there, and I'll deal with what I find when I arrive."

"I'll head that way too." He gestured to the horse waiting patiently at his side. "I've secured a mount and can be there before you."

"Very well. Then I shall see you again soon enough."

Givens mounted the mare and was off.

Alex checked their cart and horse and then lifted a hand, inviting Evie over. "All's well, and we can set off."

"You're worried." She reached for the lapels of his coat and drew closer. "I know you don't want to hear this, but I don't think your uncle means you any ill. He seems a very brokenhearted man to me."

Alex stroked a hand along the silken line of her jaw. "You have a kind heart. And your instincts may be correct. I believe he is brokenhearted, but my father's will makes us adversaries over the inheritance of Ballymore."

"Maybe he's gone back to the castle to make amends."

Alex bent and kissed her. It was too brief, but even a taste of her steadied him somehow. "I'd much prefer that he's gone home to England. But let us go and see what we find at Ballymore."

DESPITE HOW SHE'D reassured Alex, throughout the ride back Evie's intuition told her that trouble would be waiting for them when they returned. Not from his uncle but from the rest of the family and from the circumstances themselves. They'd been gone overnight. Alone. Together.

They could manufacture some lie that might satisfy the duke's aunt, but Evie had found fibbing didn't suit her. She didn't want any further subterfuge. And yet telling the truth would cause a scandal that neither of them needed.

"It will be all right." Alex gathered the reins in one hand and clasped hers with his free one. He'd noticed that she was ruminating.

Evie relished his warmth and the comfort of his certainty.

But she wasn't certain. She didn't regret the choice she'd made, the time they'd spent. Indeed she treasured it and always would. It was as if they'd stepped out of their roles and responsibilities for a moment in time. That room in the Hart and Crow had been an intimate haven, and she'd felt free to share all of herself with the man who made her heart feel full.

Yet now, in the light of morning and on the way back to the place where their roles and responsibilities were clear, one question rang in her relentlessly practical mind. *What now?*

One practical answer came first.

"I'll have to get the invitations prepared and posted today," she told Alex, if only to get her own mind clear on what came next. "There's not much time."

"If there's a need, we can also deliver invites via telegram. A footman can take whatever messages you'd like to send to the station."

She placed her free hand atop the notebook on the bench beside her. "I'll take a closer look at Mr. Byrne's list when we get back."

And with that, the thought came that perhaps nothing had changed. Between them, yes. Inside, Evie felt different. But the circumstances around them would be much the same. She was in Ireland to see to the success of a charity event, and he was still in need of a wealthy bride.

There had been no offers or promises made except those played out between them in those perfect hours in the darkness. If that was all she'd have of moments like those, she could live with that. For those hours with Alex, she'd felt adored in a way she never had in all the years of her life before.

"Are you fretting or having regrets?" Alex lifted their clasped hands and kissed the backs of her fingers.

"Neither. Don't fret about me fretting," she said lightly, trying to reassure him.

For the remainder of the journey, they talked of everything but what they'd find when they returned. Evie pointed out stunning features of the passing landscape, including a ring of stones that she imagined having some great significance in the past. Which led to a discussion of fairies and ended with Alex asking once more if he could read any of her stories.

"A short one," he suggested in compromise.

"Maybe." She didn't want to agree to any promise she couldn't keep. Most of her writing was back in her room at Lady Waverly's town house, and even after last night, Evie couldn't imagine any way that they'd remain in contact after she returned to London.

"Well, someone has come to greet us," Alex said as they approached Ballymore.

Lady Belinda stood at the edge of the estate's stables, which had just come into view.

"How did she know when we'd arrive?" Evie waved at her.

"The rooms on that side of the castle have a view of the entire lane that approaches Ballymore." Alex pointed to windows in the tower portion of the castle, where his study was located. "Perhaps she was keeping watch."

For the first time, Evie detected a thread of worry in his tone.

"It will be all right," she told him quietly, echoing his reassurance.

He squeezed her hand and shot her a lopsided smile, and what felt like only a moment later they were pulling into the stable yard and descending from the carriage.

"Thank goodness you're all right." Lady Belinda embraced Evie the moment her feet touched the ground. "I was worried. The storm last night was fierce." She released Evie and went into her brother's arms next.

"We're fine, as you see," he told her, then pulled back and looked down at her. "But why are you trembling? What's happened?"

Lady Belinda pressed a hand to her mouth and stared wide-eyed at both of them. "Where would you like me to start?"

"Anywhere," Alex insisted. "Tell us what's happened."

She began ticking off on her fingers. "We've had a telegram from the steward at Estings. The American has decamped. And not an hour ago, Uncle George appeared again, but he refuses to speak to anyone but you." With a glance toward the castle, she added, "I think Aunt Oona is on the verge of doing the man violence."

"I'll go and talk to him," Alex said, then lifted his gaze to Evie before offering her his arm.

Lady Belinda noted the gesture and smiled. "I have to tell you the rest."

"There's more?" Alex's voice had returned to the terse tone Evie hadn't heard since the day she arrived.

"The Raymonds have been invited for lunch." Lady Belinda winced. "I'm sorry. I know you have no intentions toward Rowena, but Lady Raymond and Aunt Oona are determined that a wedding join our two families."

Evie could feel the tension rise in Alex as Lady Belinda added complications to bad news. Holding her arm in his, he looked down at her and a bit of the worry had ebbed. He even offered her the flash of a smile.

"Shall we, ladies?" he said, his gaze fixed on Evie's. "I'll start with Uncle George."

Inside the castle, they didn't have to wonder where to find Pierpont. The duke's aunt was shrieking his name in the great hall, causing it to echo into the conservatory where they'd entered.

"Leave, Pierpont, or I shall have you thrown out. We have *invited* guests who will be arriving at any moment, and your darkening presence is not welcome here."

"He's not to be thrown out until I speak to him," Alex called, his deep voice filling the room.

Ms. McQuillan's gaze locked on the spot where Evie's arm was entwined with Alex's, and her already pink cheeks flamed into scarlet.

"Where have you been, Alexander? And Miss Graves?"

"Caught out in the storm, Aunt Oona. We took shelter overnight."

"Did you indeed?" She stomped forward, shooting her nephew a gaze full of what Evie could only interpret as disappointment. "I urge you not to speak to Pierpont. The man has merely come to cause trouble, as he always does."

"Nephew, may we have a word alone?" Pierpont looked shockingly calm for the berating he'd likely endured from Ms. McQuillan before they arrived.

"This way," Alex told him, then weaved past his aunt and sister, taking Evie with him.

Pierpont joined them as Alex headed for the drawing room. Since it was to be a private meeting, Evie slipped her arm from Alex's and turned to head upstairs.

"I'll go up and change," Evie whispered to Alex.

"I'd like you to join us," he told her quietly, stopping before the open drawing-room door.

His uncle had already stepped inside.

"Please." Alex glanced at his uncle and then back at Evie. "I know it's a great deal to ask, but you have a rapport with him that I don't."

Pierpont had already taken a seat and gave no indication that he intended the meeting to be confrontational. Evie suspected the two men would do well on their own and wondered if her presence would do any good at all.

"We're a bit early, but hopefully not dreadfully so," a woman's voice rang out in the great hall. Evie turned to a see a grand older woman in a sumptuous plum day dress and an enormous feathered hat sail into the center of the hall.

"Bloody hell," Alex muttered under his breath.

The mystery of the lady's identity lasted only until Lady Rowena sailed in behind her, and another, dark-haired young lady followed in her wake.

"The Raymonds have arrived," Aunt Oona called out as if the ladies themselves weren't proof enough.

The regal one, who Evie assumed was the matriarch of the family, took in the hall in a sweeping glance that landed with curious intensity on Evie.

She approached, and only then did Evie notice a cane at her side. First, she dipped her head in Alex's direction. "Your Grace, so good of you to invite us."

Then all of her focus pivoted to Evie. "Why, you

must be Miss Graves. On loan from Lady Waverly to see to the Equestrian Society luncheon."

"I am, my lady." Evie nodded but didn't think it necessary to curtsy.

"I understand Rowena was overlooked and is now invited." She pointed to the notebook clutched under Evie's arm. "Add me to your list too, if you will. And Miss Isobel Barnes as well, if you please." She offered the dark-haired young lady a tight smile. "My niece."

"Of course you're all very welcome." Evie could utter those words with genuine enthusiasm. Even after all that had happened with Alex, she truly wanted the event to be a success.

"Excellent." The older woman turned as if searching for something she lost. "Ah, Oona. A chat and tea in the drawing room before lunch, as usual?"

"No," Alex replied before his aunt could. "The second drawing room is at your service, Aunt Oona."

From across the room, she shot him an arctic look. "Very well."

"Shall we?" Alex still stood just outside the drawing-room threshold, and he extended a hand, urging Evie to join him.

After she stepped in with him, Alex closed the door.

His uncle still sat, but he'd crossed his arms and had a bemused smile on his face. "Seems you have a bit of explaining to do, *Miss Graves*."

"No, she does not. The fault is mine, and I regret it." Alex stepped forward, as if he felt the need to defend her.

Evie understood but didn't agree. "Forgive me for the deception," she told his uncle.

"All is forgiven, Miss Graves." The older man appeared more amused than offended. "But it still leaves you with a dilemma, nephew." Pierpont studied each of them in turn. "Or perhaps not," he said cryptically.

"Why have you come, uncle?"

At that, Pierpont hung his head a moment, and then lifted his gaze to a portrait on the wall that featured a beautiful black-haired woman who Evie guessed was Alex's mother. The woman Pierpont had loved.

"I came to apologize and vow that I will not trouble you further."

Rather than soften, Alex's jaw tightened, and he crossed his arms to match his uncle's gesture. "What does that mean exactly? You forfeit any claim to Ballymore?"

"Neither of us can change what's in your father's will." George Pierpont edged forward on the settee, his elbows on his knees. "Will you marry in time?"

Evie's breath caught in her throat as she waited for Alex's answer.

He closed his eyes and then glanced her way.

"I do not know."

Evie wanted to reach for him in that moment. Not to reassure herself but to offer some comfort to him. They'd found a few hours of bliss with each other, but the reality of what must be done was always waiting on the other side.

"Well," Pierpont said as he stood and approached his nephew, "if you cannot, you may purchase the castle back from me."

Alex scoffed at that. "I have no idea what the valuation would be, but I cannot afford it."

Pierpont shrugged. "I did not name a price. That could be decided between us. I'm not a wealthy man and never expected to be. We second sons cannot rely on such things." The bitterness in his voice caused it to break. The man's eyes turned glassy, but he turned away rather than show Alex such emotion.

Going to stand before the duchess's portrait, he placed a hand on the mantel as if gathering his strength.

"I could never live here." He offered a haunted glance over his shoulder. "To always be reminded would be too much. My brother's final twist of the knife."

"And here I thought the knife was for me," Alex told him. "One final bit of coercion."

Pierpont faced them again with a bitter smile. "Either way he would win, I suppose. But we can thwart him." He approached and offered his hand for Alex to shake. "Can you agree to that, nephew?"

Evie watched emotions flicker over Alex's face: wariness, sadness, uncertainty, and then finally resolve. He reached to shake his uncle's hand.

"I'm not sure what we're agreeing to," he said as he clasped the older man's hand.

Pierpont chuckled and looked suddenly ten years younger. "That whether you marry in time or not, whether the castle comes to me or not, you will have it back. A hundred pounds, or a couple of your fine ponies. We'll find a price that satisfies us both." Leaning in, he added, "Tell your meddlesome aunt that she won't lose the roof over her head regardless, and perhaps she'll stop her matchmaking."

"That would be a miracle. But I'd welcome it." Alex clasped his uncle by the shoulder with his free hand. "Thank you, uncle."

When Alex released him, Pierpont turned his attention to Evie.

"Thank you for your honesty that day in the garden, Miss Graves."

"Of course." Evie reached out and shook his hand too.

"Stay for luncheon, uncle," Alex insisted.

"Oona won't like that."

"But we will." Alex placed a hand at Evie's back,

including her in a *we* that felt shockingly right, at least in that moment.

"Very well."

Evie led the way as they exited the drawing room and heard Pierpont whisper to Alex.

"You're going to marry that girl, aren't you?"

If Alex offered a reply, Evie didn't hear it.

Chapter Fourteen

The lunch had taken far too long, and the conversation veered into topics in which Evie took no real interest. The ladies spoke of social engagements, planned excursions to Dublin or London, a wished-for shopping trip to Paris. It reminded her why she was grateful not to be invited to Lady Waverly's many luncheons.

Only when the topic turned to horses was her interest piqued.

She'd inquired of Lady Raymond about any others she might know who'd like to attend the charity event and was promptly given three names. After that, she'd excused herself as the group entered the drawing room. Later, with the help of Ballymore's housekeeper, she was able to obtain addresses for each name Lady Raymond had mentioned.

Now Evie sat at the desk in her guest room and shook out her aching right hand. She'd been writing for hours and was on her last invitation and her fourth cup of tea. According to a maid she'd asked, she still had time to get all of them into the day's post, and two others had already been sent as telegrams to invitees who resided in London. Evie doubted they'd make the journey on such short notice, but she hoped they might still send a donation.

Focusing on neatness and ignoring the cramp in her palm, she finished the last invitation and collected all of them into a pile. The housekeeper had provided her with stamps, and soon she had the whole pile ready to go in the post.

She stood, stretching her arms over her head, and then crossed the room to tug the bellpull. When a servant didn't appear after a quarter of an hour, she scooped up the pile into her arms to take them downstairs herself.

But at the threshold, she paused. If she could, she'd planned to steer clear of the Raymonds for the remainder of their visit. And if she was honest with herself, she was avoiding Alex's aunt too. Throughout lunch, Evie had caught Ms. McQuillan watching her, almost studying her, as if she was a mystery to be deciphered.

Evie understood the worry she'd seen puckering the lady's brow. Alex had had no chance to convey what he and his uncle had agreed upon before lunch was served, and in Ms. McQuillan's view, her home was at stake.

Most of all, Evie was determined not to be a source of worry to Alex or his family.

Dinner would be served soon, and she debated taking a tray in her room.

Standing undecided with a pile of invitations in her arms, she considered whether avoiding Alex and his family was too like cowardice.

A knock on the door startled her, and a few invitations slipped to the carpet.

"Forgive me, miss." The maid, Anna, who'd helped her since she'd arrived, entered the room. She immediately bent to retrieve the fallen invitations. "How can I help?"

"These are all stamped and ready to go in the post."

Anna examined one of the envelopes in her hand. "Does it need the duke's insignia, miss?"

Evie had asked for and been given fine vellum for the invitations, and the envelopes were in a similar cream shade and much the same quality she used for Lady Waverly's correspondence. But there was no ducal insignia or imprint on any of it.

"Is it necessary?"

The young woman scrunched her lips in contemplation. "Not required, miss, but won't it help? A sort of stamp of approval from the host?"

"Yes, of course, you're right." Evie felt foolish for not thinking of it. When in London, Lady Waverly had special paper delivered from a printer with her Belgravia address engraved and gilded at the top. A duke's mark would carry even more meaning.

"Very good, miss. Should I see to retrieving it, or will you?"

"Which is quicker?"

"The duke is still entertaining the Raymonds, so

it might be quicker for me to ask Mrs. Wilde to retrieve it."

"The Raymonds are still here?"

Anna grimaced. "They're staying over for dinner as well."

A tray in her room it was, Evie decided.

"Very well. Retrieve the insignia, and I'll stamp these and bring them down to you." Evie felt the persistent click of the mantel clock at her back. "Will it be too late for the last post?"

"Not if we're quick about it, miss." Anna nodded and departed, closing the door behind her.

Not a minute later, someone rapped on her door.

Evie swung it open. "What did we forget, Anna?"

Lord Rupert stood on the threshold, dressed in elegant white tails for dinner. None of them had dressed so formally for any meal since Evie's arrival. Impressing the Raymonds mattered, at least to Rupert.

"I was going to offer to escort you down for drinks before dinner, but you don't look at all ready."

"Still working on invitations." Evie lifted the bundle in her arms as proof.

"Invitations?" Lord Rupert crossed his arms and leaned one shoulder against the doorframe. "The event is two days away. Who will agree to come on such notice?"

"Have you never gone to a party on short notice?" Judging by his bon-vivant manner, Evie thought the answer rather obvious.

"Well, you've got me there." He gestured lazily. "But surely you can set all this aside and come down for dinner." With all the drama of a Drury Lane actor, he let out an enormous sigh. "What I should say is that you will be the only bright spot. So please, dear Miss Graves, don't abandon us to the Raymonds."

Evie detected signs of nervousness and wondered if the young man still had feelings for Rowena.

"I'm exhausted, my lord. And have work yet to do. These have to get out today. As you so helpfully pointed out, the later they get into potential guests' hands the less likely they'll attend."

"My dear brother won't like this one bit." He studied her eyes as if they'd give something away even if she wouldn't admit it. "He's spent more time with you in the last few days than I think he has with anyone in years. He usually values his solitude—and the company of his horses, of course."

"On the contrary, my lord, he understands that these invitations must go out. He wants the event to be a success as much as I do."

"Hmm." His murmur of assent didn't match the dubious set of his brows. "We'll see about that, Miss Graves."

At the patter of footsteps, he turned, then stepped back to allow Anna to approach the threshold.

On a small tray she held out to Evie sat the thick gold ring that Alex wore and a black inking pad. "Thought you'd prefer this to wax, miss. It's quicker."

Seeing the ring without the man who'd been on her mind all day brought memories of the night before. The feel of that ring against her skin as he'd touched her, stroked her, until she'd forgotten everything but pleasure.

Evie swallowed hard and realized two gazes were locked on her, waiting for her response.

"This will do perfectly. Thank you, Anna. And could I trouble you for a dinner tray when the time comes?" Evie glanced at Rupert out of the corner of her eye.

He shook his head as if terribly disappointed with the request.

"Of course, miss. I'll bring it up straightaway."

When Anna had gone, Rupert drew closer, his gaze locked on the ring. "Pulled it right off his hand but won't go down to dinner. Bold as brass, you are, Miss Graves, and I admire you for it." At that, he flung his arm out and bent his head in an overdone bow and then ambled off to dinner.

Evie picked up the heavy gold ring, the metal still warm from Alex's hand. She curled her fingers around it, closed her eyes, and savored the feel of it and the memories of him, of their time together learning every inch of each other's bodies.

Then she forced herself to push the thoughts

away. Her body was already reacting as if he was near, and she couldn't deny that she longed for him still.

But she had work to do, and her memories would keep.

SOMEHOW, ALEX HAD endured the too-long lunch. All of it had irked him. The inane conversation, his aunt's inquisitive stares, and Evie seated too far away. Afterward, he'd escaped for half an hour to read the telegram from the steward in Wiltshire and craft a response for the footman to send a telegram back. The American could hie off back to New York if he pleased, but he'd signed a lease and paying for the next three months as recompense for breaking the yearlong agreement was spelled out in the contract he'd signed.

By the time he'd rejoined the Raymonds and his aunt, expecting to see them off back to their home a few miles away, Aunt Oona had herded everyone into the drawing room.

After a couple of parlor games and with the excuse of a few storm clouds rolling in, she'd invited them to stay for dinner.

Alex didn't know if his aunt was trying to drive him to madness or just forestall the discussion they would inevitably have about his overnight absence with Evie.

Evie. He'd expected her to appear for dinner and had been nearly breathless for it.

From the time she'd left the drawing room after lunch, half his thoughts had been of her. Sudden, heated memories of the night before shot through him and tightened his groin at the most inappropriate moments. But he also simply missed her presence. She brought a vibrancy with her that he felt every time she entered a room, and he felt the lack of it now whenever she was absent.

So when she hadn't appeared for dinner, it had taken every ounce of self-control he possessed to remain at the head of the table. He'd had little to contribute to the discussion during lunch and now had even less during dinner. But both Lady Raymond and Aunt Oona had forfeited any attempt at subtlety after a couple of glasses of wine.

They'd recounted Rowena's merits to him while the poor young lady looked as if she'd prefer to sink into the carpet. All of her bravado fled when Rupert was at the table, and though they took care to speak to each other in only the most civil of terms, the glances snuck between the two when they thought no one was watching told Alex that little had changed.

Alex would have a word with his brother and encourage him to offer for Rowena if that was what his heart still desired. With Alex's blessing, perhaps Lady Raymond would see sense and stop pushing her daughter his way and ignoring the lady's feelings.

Now he stood in the drawing room as the Raymonds finally took their leave, and he swigged back the last bit of whiskey in his glass.

On the matter of following one's heart, he now had his own conundrum to resolve.

In a matter of days, he'd come to a few shocking realizations. One, the organ in the center of his chest was working. Two, happiness was real and worth pursuing. Three, one woman had thoroughly and completely slipped past his defenses.

He could no longer imagine a future that didn't include Evelyn Graves. And he knew with equal certainty that she might not agree. She was, above all, a practical lady. In practical terms, he could offer her a title, a crumbling castle, a bankrupt estate, and a man with a head full of dreams that he might never be able to bring to fruition. Some ladies might yearn to be a duchess, but he was quite certain Evelyn did not.

They both lived their lives and made their choices based on necessity.

He knew only one thing for certain: what he felt for her was returned. Evie was not one for artifice or pretense, which made his request that she maintain a false identity ridiculous. It was a wonder she didn't loathe him for it.

"Alexander, we must talk." Aunt Oona had returned to the drawing room after seeing the Raymonds out.

He'd sensed her approach, but he knew suddenly and with a clarity he hadn't had until that moment that he could offer her nothing, no real answers, until he'd spoken to Evie.

"It's late, Aunt Oona," he said as he set his glass down and turned to face her. "Shall we talk tomorrow?"

"We must speak now, nephew. Whatever has"— she looked momentarily flustered—"transpired between you and Miss Graves, it is the surest sign yet that we must settle the match between you and Rowena Raymond."

"I won't be marrying Rowena, and I don't want any more visits for that purpose or scheming between you and Lady Raymond."

She opened her mouth to speak, but Alex stilled her with a raised hand.

"I would, however, support a match between Rowena and Rupert. They care for each other and have for years. Can none of you see that?"

Aunt Oona marched toward him, stepped past him, and poured herself a generous finger of whiskey from the drinks cart. Alex considered urging caution since she'd taken a good deal of wine with dinner, but he doubted she'd listen.

"Rowena's dowry will be significant," she said tightly. "If it goes to Rupert, he will use it to set up his own household, wherever that may be. Whereas if you marry Rowena"—she lifted the hand holding her glass of whiskey and a bit sloshed over the side—"all of that will come to Ballymore."

"Aunt Oona—"

"And fulfill the terms of Marcus's will."

"I am no longer confined by my father's dictates."

Her eyes bulged wildly. "You do not care if I lose my home?"

Alex couldn't help but note that she did not refer to it as *his* home, but he let it pass.

"Uncle George—"

"That man is a scoundrel of the first order. I hope you told him never to return to these shores."

"He has agreed to sell Ballymore back to me if I fail to marry in time." Alex didn't think it the right moment to mention that he had met the only woman he could ever truly consider marrying, since he hadn't had a chance to speak to the lady in question for hours.

"And you'll buy it with what, Alexander?" She was all but vibrating.

"You'll have to trust me. Uncle George will deal fairly."

She shook her head but said nothing, just sipped a bit of the whiskey in her glass.

"I suggest we both get a good night's sleep," he told her in a soothing voice that he hoped might break past her resistance and ire. "We have but a short time to prepare before guests arrive at Ballymore for the charity luncheon."

"I thought it was to be five guests. Very little preparation will be needed."

"Miss Graves has invited more to join us, and I hope they'll come." He realized he was as anxious for Evie's efforts to succeed as for the increased donations to the Equestrian Society.

"What gives her the right to decide who comes to an event you host?" She pointed one accusing finger his way, the others keeping a precarious hold on the cut-crystal tumbler. "You've let that girl turn your head."

Alex tried not to smile. His aunt was in no state of mind to understand or sympathize with his feelings.

Yet his lips curved of their own volition.

"I have," he admitted with an ease that shocked him. "And I fear there is no cure for it."

He tugged at his necktie that had felt like a constricting reminder of the man he was supposed to be all day. More and more, he'd come to realize that he was not and never would be that man. He'd given up aspects of himself after Edmund's death, knowing they would not fit the life he was supposed to have.

Now, for the first time in a long while, he knew of one thing he wanted.

"Good night, Aunt Oona. Sleep well." With that, he left her and headed upstairs.

He mused about which door he'd stop at as he mounted the steps, but there was no real debate.

He had to see her, if even for a moment.

After two raps, the door opened a sliver.

"I don't know whether you've been avoiding me or you were just busy with invitations."

Evie opened the door wider. "A bit of both," she whispered. The hint of a smile gave him hope.

"You can send me away, but I'd rather come in and talk."

Her ink-stained fingers tapped on the door latch, then she shocked him by reaching out for a handful of his shirt and pulling him inside.

Once she closed the door behind him, she came into his arms and kissed him. He took the sweetness of her mouth the way a thirsty man takes a saving drop of water.

"How could I be this hungry for you after only a few hours?" he said quietly, afraid she might come to her senses and throw him out of her room.

She stroked her fingers through the hair at his nape where her hands were entwined about his neck.

"Are you doubting my appeal, Your Grace?" she teased.

"Never. I'm quite aware of your powers, Miss Graves." He kissed her again, happily drowning in the taste of her and the warmth of her curves against him. She wore only a thin night rail, but it was still a barrier he did not want between them.

"You did say you'd come to talk," she said when they were both breathless and she had two fingers tucked between the buttons of his shirt, just so the heat of her skin against his could drive him mad.

"Yes, I think we should. Don't you?"

"About?"

One simple word begging an obvious answer had

his mind spinning. He hadn't gotten this wrong. Even now, he could feel her desire for him in the way she touched him. Yet he could also sense resistance. Back at the pub, she'd spoken of that night as set apart, a unique moment in time that had nothing to do with who they were in the world beyond those walls.

And it had been an extraordinary gift.

But he wasn't content with relegating what was between them to a moment, a memory.

"You're set to leave Ireland in less than a week, and . . ." Alex wanted to settle his mind long enough to get the words right. *I don't want you to.*

"Yes, but most important is the event in two days."

"Of course. It will be a success, no matter how many guests turn up." Alex did care about the donations that would come in and making connections, but of course it wasn't what he'd come to talk about.

"I cannot marry Rowena Raymond," he blurted. "I cannot imagine marrying anyone but you."

Evie let out a gasp, blinked several times, and released him. Then she made her way over to the chairs situated before the fire and settled on the edge of one. Alex followed and sat on the chair opposite her. He felt suddenly breathless, as if all the air had drained from his lungs.

"That is not at all what I expected you to say," she finally admitted. "I never allowed myself to think—"

"Nor I, but I am rather tired of not allowing myself to embrace what I want."

She smiled at that, and he crouched down in front of her, holding her hands.

"If it's what we both want, I have a notion that we're each willful enough to make it happen."

Evie stroked her fingers over his hand, contemplating. He understood needing time to think, and he'd always be willing to give her that.

"What if we discuss it again after the charity event?"

Alex sensed her uncertainty, imagined her fears, and knew that she did not wish to be distracted from what she'd come to do.

"Do I get to kiss you between now and then?"

She laughed as he'd hoped she would, and the sweetness of it was just what he needed.

Though she gave no answer in words, she stood, still holding his hand in hers, and led him to her bed. Then she turned to him, releasing his hands and sliding hers up his chest to twine about his neck once more.

"You can kiss me between now and then."

Alex didn't wait a single second to take that offer. He slid a hand up her back, cupped her nape with another, and took her lush mouth. He poured all he had not said into the kiss, all the yearning, all the certainty, all the hope for what their future together could hold.

She'd learned what he liked and swept her

tongue against his, a dance that set his blood on fire. He slid his hand down the soft fabric of her nightdress and stroked her breast, finding the taut bud of her nipple and rolling it between his fingers through the fabric. Then he bent and replaced his fingers with his tongue. The fabric was gauzy and thin, but still a maddening barrier between them.

Evie seemed to understand and began unfastening the ribbons that held her nightgown closed.

Alex had another idea and began lifting the hem, gathering the fabric until it was above her waist. Evie gathered the cotton into her hands from there and lifted the garment over her head. For a moment, he merely appreciated the beauty of her curves, the swell of her hips and belly, the delicious valley between her breasts. He bent to kiss that spot, running his tongue along her skin, and then taking one nipple between his lips.

"Alex." She tangled her fingers in his hair, bucked her hips as if in offering.

"Lie back, beauty. Let me taste you."

Evie sank back against the mattress, but balanced on her elbows, watching him, her gaze as heated and hungry as his.

He trailed his fingers up from her ankles, circling her knees, sweeping up slowly across her thighs. Those mahogany curls between her legs glistened with how wet and ready she was for him.

And Evie, seeming to understand what he wanted, let her lush thighs fall open. He reached for her, stroking a finger inside her, too eager to go slowly.

She arched back and let out a moan that made his cock harden painfully. God, he wanted to be inside her, but he needed the taste of her first.

He bent and stroked his tongue along her slick, pink folds. She immediately reached for him, her fingers in his hair. He loved the insistent scrape of her fingertips. She tugged gently at first, but once he'd found her sensitive bud and laved it with his tongue, her touch became fiercer. Her fingers dug deeper into his scalp, against his shoulder.

And he knew, felt, the moment when her body tensed and then every muscle ebbed into pleasure. She cried out but clasped a hand over her mouth to stifle the sound.

Alex kissed each of her thighs, her belly, the warm path of skin between her perfect breasts, and then she pulled him the rest of the way. Her hand hooked around his nape, she urged him up for a kiss.

"You'll stay," she murmured against his lips. Not a question. More of a needful command, and he loved it.

"Do you really imagine," he asked between kisses, "there is anyplace else I want to be?"

Evie immediately began working the buttons of

his shirt. Her eagerness made him chuckle, even as it stoked his own need. He toed off his boots and unbuttoned his trousers.

When she laid herself back against the bedclothes and reached her hand out to him, he felt like the luckiest man who'd ever lived. He'd never expected to feel this—this rightness, this fierce protectiveness, this love—for anyone.

"You're everything I desire," he told her as he took her hand and lowered his head to kiss the warm curve of her palm.

"I want you," she said in a low, husky murmur. "Need to feel you close."

He shed his pants and drawers and climbed onto the bed, lowering his body to hers, until there wasn't an inch of space between them.

Evie bent her knees and bucked her hips up so that he filled her. She let out a sigh of satisfaction at the first slow stroke of his cock.

"Is this close enough?" he asked as he nipped at the tender skin of her neck.

"Closer." She whispered the command softly but moved against him, one leg hitched over his hips.

Alex let her set her own pace and then reached between them, stroking her with his fingers too, until she broke against him. Shuddering, breathless, her bottom lip between her teeth to keep from crying out—though he heard her moans, felt the tremors rushing through her, and lost himself in her only moments later.

"Stay. Hold me for a bit?" she asked when he'd pulled her beside him, her leg over his, her arm draped across his chest.

"Sweetheart, I have no intention of ever letting you go."

Chapter Fifteen

After a day of prepping for the event and seeing to dozens of little details, all under the watchful eye of Alex's aunt, Evie returned to her room ready to make her excuses for dinner and sleep.

In fact, her belly was already full. Mrs. Frain had asked her to sample the strawberry tart and a few other delicacies she'd prepared for guests, and everything had been scrumptious.

As she reached back and massaged the nape of her neck, Evie went over the mental list she'd constructed. Yes, everything had been done. Flower bouquets had been arranged, even if Alex's aunt had hovered like a protective mother while the staff cut flowers and greenery from the garden.

Ballymore's staff members had been wonderfully helpful at finding extra chairs, carrying a long table into the great hall, and temporarily relocating the horse paintings from the portrait gallery. The table for the luncheon had already been prepared, and Evie did her best with place cards, though she didn't know most of the guests nearly as well as she would a gathering of London nobles for one of Lady Waverly's soirees.

Alex had been the only thing missing from today's preparations. He'd left her sometime in the early-morning hours before Anna arrived to a lay a fire in the grate. And she'd spied him through the conservatory windows once. It appeared that several horses were being added to the stables. They'd arrived in a large, enclosed carriage, apparently designed for the purpose of transporting them.

Evie decided that he was giving her the time and space she'd asked for in preparation for the luncheon, and she was grateful that he respected her wishes in such a way. Yet she couldn't deny the impulse to find some excuse to go out and see him, if only to speak for a few minutes.

She curled up in a chair by the fire, glanced at her writing lap desk, and decided she didn't have the energy to revisit her story tonight either. Perhaps she would go down to dinner. She'd commandeered most of the castle's staff for one task or another over the course of the day, and she didn't wish to be ungrateful to any of them.

Perhaps if she closed her eyes for a few minutes, she'd wake refreshed and ready to head down.

What felt like a moment later, a knock on the door roused her. According to the mantel clock, she'd drowsed for nearly an hour.

"Come in," she called, guessing it might be Anna, who checked in with her once every evening.

The latch turned, and Alex stepped inside, a covered silver tray in one hand.

"You had me worried," he said with a warming smile. "But I guessed you were tired and brought you some dinner, if you're hungry."

Evie stood and approached, hungry not for the food but the nearness of the man bearing it.

"The duke of the castle serving me personally. What have I done to deserve such service?"

"You deserve this and more." Alex set the tray on the table and kicked the door closed behind him. "I missed you today."

The urge to reach for him overwhelmed her, but he seemed to feel the same and offered the soothing stroke of his hand down her arm.

"You worked hard all day, and it shows. The great hall is transformed."

"The staff went above and beyond and should get all the praise."

"Mr. Mullins and Mrs. Wilde said much the same about you."

Evie chuckled. "If only I could win over your aunt so easily."

Alex tipped her chin up, then drew his fingers along her jaw in a way that made a delicious ribbon of warmth rush through her.

"You needn't let her worry you, Evie. She will not decide my future, and she no longer has cause for her matchmaking schemes."

"Doesn't she?" Evie bit her lip.

"You must know my feelings." He bent until his lips hovered over hers. "If you've forgotten, I'd be most happy to remind you."

Evie lifted onto her toes and kissed him. The single taste she'd wished for turned heated, hungry. The strength of his arms came around her, holding her fast. Alex's touch made her feel steady, made her forget to worry or doubt.

She reached up to stroke the thicket of black waves at his nape, felt the shift of his muscles beneath her fingertips, and the enticement to return to that protective haven that she found in his arms overwhelmed her.

"Stay with me tonight."

He laughed, and with their bodies locked together, the rumble of it echoed in her own chest.

"Darling Evie, if I had my way, I'd never spend another night without you."

In his eyes were promises she didn't know if he could keep. In her mind, she could not foresee any scenario in which a countess's secretary responsible for her sister's schooling and a duke in need of a wealthy bride could find a way to spend all their future nights together.

But she wanted to enjoy this night and each moment she had with him as if it could be their last.

Her departure was days away, and she wouldn't let it steal the bliss of this moment.

"Come," he whispered, then clasped her hand and led her to bed.

Evie sat first, her hand still in his, and with her other, she grabbed for a handful of his shirt and pulled him toward her.

"I love it when you're impatient," he told her before brushing his lips against hers. "But we have all night."

He kneeled before her then, never lowering his gaze from hers, and reached for the hem of her gown.

Evie's body pulsed with an aching need for him, for the heat of his fingers, his tongue, against her skin. But he was determined to take it slowly and reached down for the laces of her boot, tugging gently until he could slip the shoe from her foot. He repeated the ministration with the other and then shocked her by taking her one stockinged foot in his hands, kneading with his fingers.

"Good heavens." The pleasure of it made her moan.

"You've been on your feet all day. Does this feel good?" he asked in a husky rumble.

"Better than good," she said on a breath and was rewarded with a wolfish grin.

After massaging the other foot and turning her brain to blissful mush, he reached under her skirt, found the top of her stocking, and slid it down slowly. By the time both legs were bare, her bones felt like melted butter.

"I need you in my arms," she told him. Her body vibrated with need, for his heat, his body against hers.

He stood and removed his coat. He'd already

dispensed with his tie before coming to her room. Then he held out his hand, pulling Evie up off the bed and into his arms.

She felt safe in his embrace, warmed from the inside out.

"You can have me," he whispered against her hair. "For as long as you want me."

EVIE WOKE WITH a panicked clutch of worry in her chest, the way she often did before one of Lady Waverly's grand events. Then she noticed the canopy above her head and registered the warm, muscled body next to her.

Alex was awake, sitting up with his back resting against the pillows, one arm around her. He was still dressed in his trousers and shirt.

Evie still wore her nightgown.

When she looked up at him questioningly, he smiled. "You fell asleep in my arms, and I couldn't bear to leave you." He caressed her cheek and swept a fingertip over her lips. "Indeed, you asked me not to."

Evie sat up and faced him. "Thank you."

"You needn't thank me. It was exactly where I wished to be."

One glance at the clock told her they were cutting it dangerously close to Anna's arrival.

"I know," he said resignedly. "I should go." He slid off the bed and turned back to her. "It's the big day."

"It is." Despite that moment of panic when she awoke, she felt satisfied that she'd done the best she could in terms of preparations. The only real variable was whether any guests would come in response to the invitation without sending word ahead. But Mrs. Frain had been accommodating and assured her that there would be enough to feed them if they did.

Alex bent to kiss her.

"Good luck," Evie told him and then kissed him again for good measure.

When he straightened, Alex drew a hand across his stubbled jaw and frowned.

"What is it?"

"Perhaps I'm a fool for not realizing this earlier, but after all of this preparation, you're not going to attend, are you?"

"I didn't plan to, no."

He looked so bereft at that news that she reconsidered, yet it made no logical sense for her to be there. She'd come to help organize it, and she'd done that.

"I never attend Lady Waverly's events."

He nodded, but nothing in his expression indicated the answer satisfied him. "But, of course, you're not my secretary."

"That is true." Evie tried for a smile, but Alex's gaze turned questioning.

What were they? That's the question she read in those gray-blue eyes. Or perhaps it was simply the query that kept running through her head. He'd all but offered her marriage, and yet it was a notion that felt more fictional than practical. In her stories, characters overcame all odds for love.

She'd always believed in such a notion. Hadn't her parents eschewed the expectations of her father's family for love? In Alex's family, apparently Belinda had done the same. And yet neither her parents nor Belinda had a sibling who relied on their wages, or a bankrupt dukedom, or a crumbling castle to care for.

"I shall come and find you after, yes?"

"Of course. I'll be here," Evie promised. The colors of dawn through the window promised a sunny day, and that made her want to go outside and take advantage of the break in the rain. "Perhaps I'll take Jane Eyre for a walk."

That, finally, made him smile. "She'd be glad of it, and Bel might even wish to go with you. I don't think she's terribly keen on the luncheon either."

"I'll ask her."

"Good." He bent, brushed a warm kiss across her forehead, and departed.

Evie washed and dressed quickly, spoke briefly to Anna who came in a few minutes after Alex's departure, and read some of her story pages by the fire before deciding it was late enough to go down and look for Belinda in the morning room.

As she descended the stairs, the scent of the bouquets made her smile, and the sight of them gave her that sense of pride she sometimes felt when seeing everything set and ready for one of Lady Waverly's balls.

In the morning room, she found only Alex's aunt and would have spun on her heel and departed, hoping she'd gone unseen, except that the lady seemed to miss absolutely nothing and called to her immediately.

"Miss Graves, up early for one last look at your preparations?" She put her knitting aside and turned toward Evie. "You've done marvelous work, and the staff speaks highly of you."

"They've been exemplary in every way."

"Join me." She gestured toward the settee across from her. "I've tea here, and Bel should be down shortly."

Evie couldn't devise a way to decline, so she took a spot on the indicated settee. Alex's aunt didn't offer to pour her a cup from the tea service on the table between them, so Evie poured her own.

"I know you care for each other a great deal."

Evie hadn't quite gotten the rim of the cup to her lips, and she held it midair.

"You and Alexander," Ms. McQuillan clarified helpfully. "One can hardly fail to notice that you've quite . . . transformed him."

"He seems very much the man I met—" Evie clenched her teeth, realizing his aunt likely didn't know they'd met months prior to her arrival at Ballymore.

"Yes? Well, he seems quite changed to me. After Edmund's death, he altered the most drastically, and, of course, there was the scandal."

"He told me about that." Evie needed his aunt to know that the incident wasn't some currency she could use to change her opinion of Alex.

The older woman smiled. "You two have had a good deal of time to talk. Day and night."

Evie swallowed hard, but she refused to be shamed for the choices she'd made. Unless, of course, Ms. McQuillan intended to use them as some form of threat.

"Do not worry, Miss Graves. I understand discretion. Your Lady Waverly will hear nothing from me. Indeed, I'm sure she'll be happy to have you back after hearing of the work you did here."

Somewhere, in possible consequences she imagined after their night at the pub, she had considered how Lady Waverly would react if word got back to her of what had bloomed between Evie and Alex. She'd hoped it wouldn't come to that. The truth was that she didn't know how her employer would react. Lady Waverly wasn't one to shun others simply because they'd gone against society's strictures. One of her dearest friends had been part of a very public divorce scandal, and the countess had stood by her steadfastly.

But Evie suspected Lady Waverly might see things differently if the scandal emerged from within her own household. She demanded a great deal of her staff, and honesty and propriety were both high on the list.

"Let me speak plainly, Miss Graves." Alex's aunt turned on the settee to face Evie squarely. "Under other circumstances, I acknowledge that you would make a fine duchess."

Evie sipped at her tea because she had nothing to offer in response to that astounding statement.

"You're quite good at managing staff, and you seem intelligent, kind, and accomplished."

"Thank you, Ms. McQuillan." Evie spoke the words slowly. The whole conversation had begun to feel surreal.

"However, circumstances are such that it's simply not a practical match."

Practical. It was as if Ms. McQuillan knew the one word that might bring Evie closest to agreeing with her.

"My father earned great wealth in a short space of time, so my sister and I never knew poverty. But he told us of how he and his family struggled." She tipped her head thoughtfully. "I understand you've known struggle too, Miss Graves."

From the moment she'd walked into the morning room, Evie had felt caught. As if Alex's aunt had spun a web and was simply waiting for Evie to wade into it.

"I know of your father and of how you and your sister were left on your own and with very little to make your way in the world."

"How could you know that?" Even if she'd written to Lady Waverly, Evie couldn't imagine the countess divulging such details.

"You are acquainted with a friend of mine who knew your father. The Duchess of Vyne. She speaks highly of you too." She let out an exasperated chuckle. "I vow it's not a wonder that Alexander is taken with you."

"Did you know who I was before I came?"

"No, not at all. I write to Georgina weekly. Have done for years. I tell her the latest news, and, well, your arrival was certainly most unexpected."

The coincidence felt somehow in keeping with how quickly she'd taken to Ireland, how her feelings for Alex had grown so quickly. Evie mused on that night they'd met and the brief, whimsical sense she'd had that it had been fated.

But there was no doubt of Ms. McQuillan agreeing. In surprisingly kind terms, she seemed determined to persuade her to abandon any thought of her relationship with Alexander continuing past her time in Ireland.

"You depart soon, and I hope you will enjoy your remaining time here—"

"And then go on my way."

She nodded thoughtfully. "It frees Alexander to make the choices he must."

"The choices that you wish him to make."

"That duty dictates, my dear. Look what happened to your father when he did not—"

"Evelyn." Belinda swept into the room clad in her riding costume and balanced herself on the edge of the settee next to Evie. "I went to your room, but I should have known you'd be up early." She reached for Evie, clasping her hand and giving her a reassuring squeeze. "Since your work is done, shall we go out for a ride? We must take advantage of the sunshine."

"I'd like that," Evie told her, giving Belinda's hand a squeeze to express her gratitude.

"Miss Graves and I were conversing before you burst in, Belinda."

Belinda looked at her aunt with a sweet, unaffected smile. "Well, I'm stealing her now. See you in a bit, Aunt Oona."

With that, Belinda pulled Evie to her feet and led her from the morning room. Once they were in the great hall and past her aunt's gaze, Belinda turned back to Evie.

"I know you need to change into your riding gear. Meet me in the stables after you do?"

When Evie joined her ten minutes later, she found Belinda waiting with Jane and another black horse Evie hadn't seen before, both saddled and ready for their ride.

"I don't know what Aunt Oona said to you, but I suspect I should apologize on her behalf."

Evie had been going over the odd encounter in her mind, and the worst part of it was that much of what Alex's aunt had said made sense. Good, logical sense.

"Goodness, was it that bad?" Belinda laid a hand on Evie's shoulder.

"She made some very practical points. Nothing she said was inaccurate."

Belinda narrowed her eyes. "But she was attempting to dissuade you from setting your cap at Alexander."

Evie chuckled. "Set my cap at? I'm a noblewoman's secretary—"

"Nonsense. You're a clever, lovely young woman, and my brother lights up when you walk into a room."

"Does he?"

Belinda pushed her gently, teasingly, as Sybil did when she'd exasperated her. "You know he does."

A cloud reached out across the sky, blocking the sun for a moment before a breath of wind blew it past.

"Let's ride out before the weather changes its mind." Belinda offered to help Evie mount Jane, but she was able to lift her foot into the stirrup and pull herself up on her own. Jane wasn't tiny, but she wasn't nearly as tall as Belinda's mare.

Still, she was as accomplished as her brother and was up in the saddle a moment later.

After they'd set a steady walking pace, they rode in silence for a long while, each of them turning their faces up to soak in the sun and draw in lung-fuls of fresh air. Once Ballymore was far behind them, Belinda released a long exhale that sounded a great deal like a sigh of relief.

"That place does feel cloying at times."

"The castle?"

"Yes. I do love it, or at least I did as a child. But it doesn't feel like home anymore."

"No? Then where is home?"

"Anywhere Guy is." She offered Evie a beaming smile. "We've not yet been married a year, and I don't like to be away from him. But Aunt Oona convinced me that Alex's bride-to-be would soon arrive at Ballymore, and we should all come and welcome her."

Evie understood determination, especially when one was desperate. But their aunt had assumed a great deal about Lady Waverly's intentions—and Alex's—without truly understanding either of them.

"I wonder if that still might be true." Belinda said the words quietly.

But when Evie glanced over at her, she returned a grin of pure mischief.

"Your aunt can't wait for me to be gone, and now you're playing matchmaker."

"I don't think whatever's between you and my brother requires any machinations."

Belinda had led her in a different direction than Alex had, and they approached a thicket of bushes and trees with a little stream running through them.

"There's a river nearby, but I remember the three of us playing in this stream," she told Evie. "Well, two of us. Alex usually took himself off a ways after making sure we were safe and read a book."

Evie could envision it, and she realized he must have understood her when he stumbled upon her attempting to find a private reading nook in the garden.

While Evie mused, Belinda had dismounted and walked her horse to the stream, where it sniffed about and took a drink. Evie got down from Jane and drew her over too.

"I suppose I didn't realize he was such a reader."

"Oh yes, always has been. He needs quiet more than I or Rupert do. Something about reading allowed him to quiet his mind."

"I understand that completely."

"I thought you might." Belinda crouched down and swept her fingers through the water. "Alex tells me you're a writer like my Guy."

"Is your husband a writer?"

"Oh yes, did Alex not tell you? He's a reporter for *The Illustrated London News*."

"Goodness. How did you two meet?" Evie took a moment to digest the fact that a duke's sister had married a journalist.

"I was in London visiting a friend, and he was interviewing some wealthy businessman at the Metropole. Our eyes met, and we couldn't stop looking at each other." She laughed and then stared at the water, her gaze wistful as she recounted the moment. "When my friend excused herself, he approached. Rather bold of him, I admit. And we just . . . talked. I found talking to him was almost as good as looking at him."

Evie nibbled her lip, and the moments she'd spent with Alex tumbled through her mind, each full of life and color, like the pieces in a kaleidoscope.

Belinda leaned closer. "And kissing him was better still," she whispered and then let out a throaty laugh. "And my aunt disapproved, of course, and said we'd live in poverty. Money is tighter than either of us would like, but we make do, and we're happy."

"What did Alex say?"

Belinda stood and patted her horse's neck, then drew her fingers through its raven mane. "He made practical arguments much the same as Aunt Oona's. And then he relented because he wished for my happiness above all else."

"I'm glad you're happy, Belinda."

"I want the same for my brother," she said earnestly. "And for you, Evelyn. Don't you want to grab happiness with both hands if you can?"

Evie wanted Alex. There was no point in denying that to herself, though until hearing of Belinda's story, she'd struggled to see any future where their two lives could come together in any harmonious way.

Now she wondered if any of that mattered. She'd

become so used to planning for the future, down to the tiniest detail, so that anything that couldn't be scheduled and organized felt like chaos. But with Alex, she felt a sense of harmony. When they were together, everything felt right.

Inside, she felt suddenly lighter, as if something in her heart was unlocking, opening up to possibilities.

Chapter Sixteen

The Equestrian Society luncheon had gone better than Alex could have hoped. In the end, twenty-five guests attended, since each had been invited to bring a companion who might share their interests in equestrian sports or the welfare of Ireland's native breeds, and many had chosen to do so.

Even with a higher guest count than anticipated, Mrs. Frain and all of the staff had outdone themselves, especially considering that a gathering larger than family members and occasional visits by neighbors such as the Raymonds had not been hosted at Ballymore in years.

And the event had given Alex an opportunity to speak to a few of the guests about his hopes for Ballymore. One wealthy landowner who kept an impressive stable in County Clare had all but entered an order for any horses bred off the Connemara ponies his mother had acquired. Others expressed interest in Alex's ideas for developing Irish thoroughbreds too.

"We should find a time to discuss your plans for

Ballymore in more detail." Sir Reginald Booth, a Dublin merchant who'd built up a stable of thoroughbreds over the years, had donated generously to the Equestrian Society and seemed intrigued by Alex's hopes to build up breeding and veterinary facilities at the castle.

"That would be grand, Sir Reginald. You're welcome here, of course, but I'd be happy to come to Dublin."

"Or London," he said full of eagerness. "You'll attend the horse show next year?"

"I should." All of Alex's hopes for next year, next month, next week, felt suspended—a bit like his heart—until he and Evie could have the discussion she'd promised would come as soon as the luncheon wrapped up.

"Very good," Sir Reginald said with a decisive nod, as if they'd made plans and penciled them in on a calendar. "I'll be off, then." He waved to take in the table in the great hall. "Well done, Rennick."

Alex offered the merchant a nod of leave-taking and immediately began eyeing the stairwell, hopeful he might see Evie on her way down. There hadn't been an hour that passed when he hadn't found himself looking for her or wishing for her presence. Everything about the day had her mark on it.

Anna had informed him that Evie had gone out to ride with Bel, just as she'd suggested she might. He was happy the two had gotten out to enjoy the fine weather. But now, as the last of the guests made their way toward Ballymore's front drive and rain clouds had swept in to dim the sun's glow, he suspected they'd returned or soon would.

He was vibrating with impatience to find her, talk to her. Tell her all that he felt and hoped.

A footman approached at a quick clip, his brow furrowed.

"Something amiss?" Alex asked the young man.

A maid had already been sent to the great hall by Mullins, who'd positioned himself in the foyer to escort guests out, to retrieve a cane one guest had forgotten.

"Messenger brought a note for you, Your Grace." The young man held out a partly crumpled missive in his gloved hand.

"Where was the messenger sent from?" Alex asked as he unfolded the note, but before the young man could offer a reply, he had his answer. The note was short and to the point.

> *Master Byrne has taken a terrible fall but will not allow the doctor to come.*
>
> *Thought perhaps you could persuade him.*
>
> —*Elva McBride*

Mrs. McBride had once worked at Ballymore, and though she was beyond working years, she occasionally took in mending or did cooking and tidying for Aurelius.

"See that my horse is saddled. I'll depart immediately." The older man had been more of a mentor and father to him than his own had ever been. *A terrible fall* had his gut clenching. Mrs. McBride wouldn't be one to exaggerate, and the fact that she'd been able to get the message off at all without Aurelius stopping her told Alex that the older man wasn't himself.

He bounded up the stairs and couldn't help himself from stopping to rap on Evie's door. When no answer came, he headed to his own suite, shucked the suit he'd worn to luncheon, and put on his usual riding gear.

On his way back downstairs, he encountered Anna coming up.

"The ladies aren't back yet?"

"Not yet, Your Grace."

He stalled on the stairs and told the maid quietly, "Tell Miss Graves that I've gone to check on Mr. Byrne, who's had an accident. Hopefully, I'll be back before nightfall."

"I'll tell her, Your Grace."

"Thank you." Alex raced through the conservatory and out into the stable yard, anxious for Byrne and eager to beat the coming rain. One could never be sure if the skies this time of year meant to simply pour down drizzle or put on a proper storm.

And, most of all, he wanted to get back and see Evie.

By the time Evie and Belinda approached the castle, she could still see blue sky through the clouds, but a soft drizzle had begun. Nothing like the previous storms since her visit began, but enough of a dousing that they were both chilled and eager to get inside by the fire.

Though Evie would forego the fire if she could catch a moment alone with Alex.

Not only was she eager to hear about how the event went—and hoped he'd have reports of generous donations—but she was ready for the talk they'd been putting off. Well, in truth, *she* had been putting off.

"I'm sure it all went fine," Belinda told her as the stable hand took her horse and she waited for Evie to dismount.

"Oh, I think so too."

"You have an anxious look about you, but maybe that's for another reason." Belinda's knowing smile was matched with an equally knowing wink.

Evie suspected the things she most wanted to tell Alex would have to wait until the rest of the household had gone to sleep and he'd come to her room as had become his habit. But just hearing that his Equestrian Society had fared well would tide her over.

She gave Jane a pat and thanked her for the ride

before the stable lad led her back to have her tack removed.

Inside the conservatory, the staff had cleared off every surface, though some of the extra chairs they'd set out still remained. In the great hall, two maids were still working to tidy the area. Anna was one of the two, and she set down the dishes in her arms and approached Evie the moment she spotted her.

"May I speak to you, Miss Graves?"

"Of course."

"I'll head up and get out of these wet clothes," Belinda told Evie. "But promise I'll see you at dinner tonight. No more trays in your room."

"Promise." When she'd gone, she and Anna stepped aside for as much privacy as one could find in the open high-ceilinged room.

"His Grace gave me a message to convey to you, miss."

"Is he not here?" Evie glanced toward the stairs, certain she'd find him changing out of formal clothes or up in his study.

"No, miss. That's just it. He was called away. Mr. Byrne has had an accident, he said, and he was going to see to him."

"Oh no. I hope he's all right."

"His Grace said he hoped to be back by nightfall."

Evie glanced at the sky through the long-arched windows at the far end of the hall. Since she and Belinda had come inside, the sky had already begun to darken.

"Sherlock is a fast horse, miss. I'm sure he'll be all right."

"Thank you, Anna." An involuntary shiver raced down her back, not so much for the cold but worry for Mr. Byrne, and Alex too. "I must change out of these wet clothes."

"Tea sent to your room, miss?"

"That would be lovely."

"I can have a tub sent up too."

Evie chuckled. "You can read a lady's mind, Anna."

Within little more than half an hour, two maids had filled the sitting tub in the suite's dressing room. Evie washed quickly with the lavender soap they'd provided but couldn't make herself linger in the deliciously warm water.

Worry for Alex and Mr. Byrne had her out of the tub and rushing through the process of dressing to the point that she discovered her bodice buttons were misaligned.

"You're being silly," she whispered at herself in the cheval mirror.

There was little she could do but wait, though she couldn't help but notice that the rain that had been but a soft shower on the ride back was now a steady rush blown by occasional gusts. But though sunset would not come for a while, the sky had already grown dark. She imagined those narrow lanes on the approach to Mr. Byrne's and how difficult it was to see in this kind of downpour.

Settling onto what had become her favorite chair by the fire, Evie pulled her pile of story pages onto her lap and flipped to the last few she'd penned. None of what she'd written struck a chord, or perhaps her mind was too distracted to focus on the words.

She replayed her conversation with Belinda and considered the revelation that she had married for love and damn the consequences, much as Evie's parents had. And if Evie herself married for love?

Her first worry was Sybil. She'd saved a tidy sum from her wages over the last few years, enough to pay for the first year of medical college. But only the first.

Evie wondered, not for the first time, if she could earn money from her writing. It had long been a dream that she might find a publisher for her work. Alex would support her in that, she felt certain. But would she earn enough?

And if she made a life with Alex, she understood he'd wish it to be in Ireland. That felt right. Indeed, beyond her feelings for Alex, she'd come to adore the lush Galway landscape with a sort of awestruck admiration.

Sybil was the main thing she'd miss about London. But the journey between the west of Ireland and London, while tiring, was short and economical enough that it wouldn't be a barrier to visits.

She reached up to clutch at the pendant her father

had given to her. When she was nervous, she had a habit of running her fingertip over and over the raised design. One side of the ancient coin depicted the goddess Artemis in profile, a laurel crown in her hair; the other depicted her standing with a quiver across her shoulder.

The huntress. A goddess of action. As a girl, she'd looked for some symbolic meaning in the gift. That her papa was encouraging her to pursue her goals and dreams with Artemis's brand of fearlessness. Indeed, he had encouraged her to pursue her dreams of publishing her work, just as he'd encouraged Sybil's interest in science and medicine.

What would he make of her now? Only willing to do anything if she had an elaborate plan arranged beforehand?

An idea took hold. An impulsive, probably impractical idea, but she couldn't sit still. Rain no longer pattered against the windowpanes. There'd been a break, and she intended to take advantage of it.

Evie gathered her cloak, gloves, and hat and left her bedchamber. But before she could make it to the stairwell, she heard footsteps behind her.

"Are you running away from Ballymore, Miss Graves?"

"Lord Rupert, do you lie in wait for me to leave my room?"

"I like to think it's just my good luck." He

reached out and tapped the brim of the hat in her hands. "What's this all about, then? You can't be thinking of going out in this drizzle."

"It's stopped for the moment."

He twisted his mouth as if in contemplation. "That seems a very optimistic perspective. There's a sort of zing in the air that comes before an electrical storm. Don't you feel it?"

"No." She did feel a fizz of energy, but it was mostly her own anxiety and a need to get going.

"So where are you off to, then?"

Evie urged her mind to fabricate something reasonable, something to allay his suspicions and put him at ease. But fibbing had never been her skill.

"I'm going to see to Mr. Byrne. Apparently, he's had an accident."

Rupert crossed his arms and managed to almost look serious for a moment. "You're going after Alex."

"Yes, that too."

"He's probably on his way back by now."

"That's very unlikely. It took us over an hour to even get to Mr. Byrne's."

"In a pony cart. He'll be on Sherlock or one of the faster horses, I'm sure of it." He took a step closer. "Now, put all that away, and come down to dinner. We can all huddle by the fire, and I'll tell you embarrassing childhood stories about Alexander."

Evie nodded. "Perhaps you're right. I'll see you down in the drawing room before dinner."

It was a dismissal, but Lord Rupert didn't seem entirely willing to accept it. Arms still crossed, he assessed her as if looking for something hidden in her expression, her eyes.

"He will be back soon, and it's best we wait for him to tell us of Byrne's condition."

"Yes, I understand."

He relented, uncrossing his arms and turning to head toward the stairwell. "See you downstairs, Miss Graves."

Evie reentered her room, closed the door, and leaned her back against the panel. She kept her gaze focused on the windowpane. Still no sign of the rain, but the daylight was sinking into the horizon, and it *would* be too late to depart if she didn't go now.

She couldn't even fully explain the urgency she felt, only that she knew what she wanted now, and she didn't wish to wait a single moment to grasp it with both hands. To tell Alex what she felt, how she'd made up her mind, and that fear and hesitation weren't holding her back anymore.

Opening her door, she moved slowly, then peeked her head out to ensure Rupert had gone and the hallway was empty. Rather than taking the main stairway, she headed to the end of the long hall and took the servants' stairs. They deposited her in an area off the great hall that led down to the kitchens. She debated trying to make her way unseen through the hall and decided it was likely impossible. Either Rupert or Belinda or their aunt would be in the drawing room.

Instead, she entered the kitchen and beelined for the door that led out to the stables and garden. Mrs. Frain was too busy with dinner preparations to notice her. Only a maid glanced up but then immediately returned to her work.

She hoped she'd find the stable lad who always helped her with Jane, and she did. He sat in the tack room, bent over his task of polishing a saddle.

"Jack, would you help me?"

"Of course, miss. How can I help?"

"Would you ready Jane Eyre for me?"

His first response was to stare upward, as if he could see the darkening sky though the roof of the stables.

"Storm's coming, miss."

"When, do you think?"

"Soon, but it's hard to say. By nightfall, perhaps."

"Then I have no time to lose." The young man hesitated to tell her no, but she sensed that he wished to. "Please, Jack."

He searched her eyes, and perhaps he saw her determination or simply that she wouldn't be dissuaded, and he finally nodded and headed off to get the mare from her stall.

Only a few minutes later, he led the horse out, already saddled and bridled.

Evie stroked the horse's nose. "It will be all right, Jane. We'll be there soon enough."

"You're all right on your own?" He glanced back at the stables. "I could accompany you, miss, if you're not. Just need to ask Mr. Skerret."

Skerret was one of Alex's closest advisers and seemed to be an efficient and loyal one. Evie suspected he wouldn't take kindly to her impulsive plan and might thwart her entirely.

Evie mounted the horse while Jack held the saddle steady. She was getting better at it every time.

"I've a bad feeling about this, miss."

Evie looked up. If the clouds planned to pour, they still held back, and there was just enough dusk light left that she felt certain they could make good time.

"It will be fine, Jack." She glanced toward the stables where she saw a few other hands going about their work. "I'll not ask you to lie, but I'd appreciate you not telling anyone I've gone until I'm on my way."

He clenched his jaw but finally gave her one swift nod.

Evie took the reins and led Jane toward the lane that would take them to the road. Once they were on the path that led to Mr. Byrne's home, she nudged the horse into a canter and then a gallop.

As they traveled, the rain still held off, and Jane maintained her smooth gallop, allowing them to make good time. After a while, visibility lowered as night doused the daylight. Evie slowed Jane when she noticed a glimmer in the distance.

The source of light came closer, and then Evie heard hoofbeats and saw two horses running toward them, pulling a small, enclosed carriage with a lantern on its side.

Evie pulled Jane to the far side of the lane, though there wasn't much clearance even then.

As the horses approached, another sound overtook the rhythmic pounding of their hooves. A rumble that rolled across the sky. A moment later, a jagged line of light flashed in the distance.

Evie felt the change in Jane immediately. Her gait became uneven, and Evie bounced in the saddle. Between the oncoming carriage, and the worsening weather, she couldn't blame the animal. Leaning forward, she patted her neck.

"It will be all right, girl. We'll let them pass and then not much farther."

Evie pulled Jane off the road, into the tall grass at the side, and then almost pitched over the pony's head when Jane was forced to step down into a ravine. They stayed there, half-hidden in the foliage on the side of the road until the carriage trundled past.

Then she led Jane back up the rise and onto the road. She sensed the same hesitation as she had after the lightning. Jane's canter was less even, and she hesitated before moving into a gallop again. But she did, and they made what felt like good time.

"Can't be much farther," she shouted against the breeze.

Perhaps a quarter hour later, Evie felt the first drops of rain slap her skin. Within seconds, those drops turned to a downpour. Jane didn't slow, but Evie's visibility worsened quickly. She swiped the rain from her eyes. The brim of her hat was no defense. In fact, at her nape, it only served to pour the cold water down the neck of her coat.

She tugged at the ribbons under her chin and cast the hat aside, letting the wind take it. Bending lower in the saddle, she squinted and thought she saw the glow of light again. This one was wider, on the left side of the lane like Mr. Byrne's house, but still a ways off in the distance.

"I think that's it, girl!"

Evie shivered as a gust of rain caught them sideways, and she was thankful they'd made it this far. She'd reach Alex soon, touch him, and tell him the truth from her heart.

Thunder came again, a long approach from the distance, as if giants were marching toward them. When the sound rolled over them, Jane skittered almost to a stop, slowing them to an uneven canter. When lightning cracked the sky, she left the road and then turned, as if she was determined to take them back the way they'd come.

"No, Jane," Evie called, tugging the reins to redirect the horse back onto the road.

Jane turned back for a moment, then stopped and edged again in the direction they'd come. Evie tried to correct her, and the horse responded by taking them off the road into the tall grass once more. Evie couldn't even be sure of their direction now, but they were off course, and her pulse jumped in her veins, fearful Jane might stumble over a rock or get them lost entirely.

The ground seemed to give out below them. Jane stepped down into a depression, but Evie wasn't prepared. Instinctively, Jane turned hard, then stopped sharp. Evie's foot slid from the stirrup as her body pitched to the side. The ground rushed up, and when she landed, pain shot through her shoulder, her hip, her head. She sat up and swiped at the rain in her eyes. And felt warmth. Her fingers came away wet and dark, and she reached up to find a gash at her temple. She hissed at the pain.

Jane had come around behind her, lowered her head, and nudged her back. Whether in apology or concern, Evie didn't know, but she was glad the mare wasn't injured.

"We must go," she mumbled and tried to stand. Dizziness swept in the moment she tried. Reaching down, she lifted her skirt and found a dry patch of petticoat. Pulling at the fabric, she attempted to rip off a strip to stanch the bleeding that seemed to be rushing down her face, pooling at her neck.

Another moment to catch her breath and then she'd go.

Jane took a few steps toward the road and then came back to stand near Evie.

The rain was slowing, and they didn't have far to go.

Chapter Seventeen

"What are you doing there, boy?" Byrne growled the words from his bed.

Alex glanced over to make sure the injured man wasn't moving too much. "Stay still, or I'll be over to hold you down myself."

"Ach, you and that McBride woman have been sent to this earth to torment me."

Alex continued working on the second letter he was penning, ignoring the older man's grousing. He hoped Mrs. McBride would appear soon with some of her herbal tea that she promised would allow the man a bit of pain relief and sound sleep.

The best course, Alex suspected, was to get Byrne moved to a facility where he could be examined. There was an infirmary in Clifden and several excellent hospitals in Dublin, but he was loath to move the man so far. He feared he might have a concussion and that a rib or two might be broken.

"You listening to me, Rennick?" he wheezed, wincing in pain as he shifted on his bed.

Alex closed his eyes and let out an exasperated chuckle. "Have I any other choice?"

"Then tell me. What are you doing at my desk?"

"Writing letters."

"What the hell for?"

One was to the local doctor that Alex had called in last year when Rupert had fallen ill, and another was to a medical man who'd come to the Equestrian Society luncheon. He'd studied medicine and mostly practiced now on animals, but he occasionally made sick calls for those in the local village. He hoped one or both men might be available to come and examine Byrne.

"You're an intelligent man, Aurelius. You know that you need medical care, and I'm seeking it for you."

"Blood and bollocks. I've no need of a bonesetter or some quack who'll drain me of the little blood I have left in my body."

And that was another concern. Alex had no real idea of how long Byrne had lain in the field after his fall or how much blood he'd lost from the gash on his leg. That injury, at least, Alex had been able to examine, clean, and rebandage. Byrne also had bruising on his chest, though he insisted he'd broken ribs in the past and that wasn't the case now.

The bloody man and his hobbies were likely to be the death of him. But not yet. Alex had studied enough of human biology to know that, though Byrne had lost blood, his body was still full of it. He also knew that both of the medical men he was contacting would look askance at bleeding a patient as a main form of treatment for someone who'd had a fall.

"You underestimate me, Aurelius, if you think I'd invite *some quack* to visit you. I'm calling in Dr. Bailey and McClary, a gentleman I met this afternoon."

Byrne scoffed. "Then you can recommend him highly after an hour's acquaintance, can you?" The accident had done nothing to stem the old man's surly nature, that was for certain.

"He seems an intelligent and thoroughly *modern* medical man. Plus, he offered a generous donation to the Equestrian Society."

"You're calling in a horse doctor?"

"Good grief, are you trying to shout down the rafters, Mr. Byrne?" Mrs. McBride entered the room with a fully laden tray, her temperate tone and the even clip of her boots seeming to give Byrne a moment's pause.

"Forgive me, Elva. Pain makes me peevish."

"Does it, now?" She set the tray on a table and immediately uncovered a cup filled with some steaming herbal brew of her own design. "And here I thought you were a rapscallion every day of the week."

"You needn't be harsh, lady."

"Drink this, and I promise to say at least one sweet thing to you." She lifted the overlarge cup to his lips.

They'd stabilized his injured leg and propped

him up with pillows, so that he could lean back and rest but also take food and drink.

"I shall hold you to that, woman." Byrne eyed the steaming brew, then gingerly sipped. He winced at the taste, but Mrs. McBride urged him to take more, and he did. After a few more drinks, he cocked an eyebrow at his housekeeper. "Go on, then."

"Your balloon is a most impressive contraption, even if it is far too dangerous for a man of your years."

Byrne shot Alex a rueful grimace. "Did you hear that, Rennick? A backhanded compliment if I've ever heard one."

"I heard. And I mostly agree."

Byrne pointed at each of them in turn. "Don't you two go taking up against me. That device is nearly perfect in its design. The failure was mine and mine alone."

He referred to a hot-air balloon, his latest obsession that he'd taken to with the same passion he'd taken to horses, according to Mrs. McBride. Alex had heard tales of the contrivance, even seen photographs and sketches that Aurelius had excitedly shown him on his visits. But it had always seemed a bit of a pipe dream. Collecting all of the various parts of the device had taken time. During Alex's last visit, before the time with Evie, Byrne had only acquired a basket and some rubber hoses that would be used to transfer hydrogen gas into the balloon. The balloon, he'd proudly informed Alex, was being stitched in Paris by a famed aeronaut turned balloon maker.

Apparently, he'd acquired all the requisite pieces and tried his first test flight earlier in the day. They didn't know—and Aurelius wasn't certain—how far he'd fallen. But it had been enough to knock him unconscious, gash his leg on a rock in the field, and bruise various other parts of his body. Alex worried there might be internal injuries too, yet he didn't feel qualified to examine him and make a definite determination.

Once Mrs. McBride had finished getting Aurelius to drink the tea, she applied a poultice to his head, and then came to confer with Alex.

"Is there someone who can deliver these?" He offered up the letters he'd written. "Both men live quite close."

"There's a neighbor boy who takes messages for me." She took the folded notes. "I'll go now. Will you stay with him while I'm gone?"

Alex glanced at the clock. "Of course. But I would like to get back within the hour."

"Won't take me nearly that long. He's just down the lane." Mrs. McBride donned her cloak and was on her way.

Byrne settled back against the pillows with a groan and then a sigh. The lady's tea always soothed him.

Alex returned to the desk and turned the chair

so that he was near the fire and had a view of his friend, and his mind went immediately to Evie.

Would she be worried about his absence? He hoped Anna had been able to convey his message. Most of all, he hoped that she and Belinda had returned to the castle safely. The rain had been off-and-on, but the thunder had been fierce not long ago. He calmed himself by insisting she was likely tucked up by the fire in her room or down in the drawing room with his family.

He tried not to count the ticks of the clock and the minutes that would get him back to Evie. Luckily, he didn't have long to wait.

The front door opened, and Mrs. McBride appeared a moment later, walking slowly so as not to disturb Byrne, who'd begun to snore softly. "The young man's on his way to deliver the letters," she whispered. "Luckily the rain has let up." She said this even as fresh droplets clung to her cloak. "I think the worst of it is over."

"Then I should depart without delay. You'll be all right to stand watch overnight?"

"Of course, Your Grace. There's a cot in the spare room, and it will do quite nicely."

"I'll fetch it for you."

"No, no," she said and stalled him with a hand on his arm. "Thank you for coming and convincing him to get a doctor in to take a look."

"I'll return in the morning and relieve you of duty."

"That sounds fine, Your Grace. Now, off with you to see your young lady."

Alex put on his coat, hat, and gloves and then turned back to Mrs. McBride. "How did you know there's a young lady?"

She met his gaze and returned a warm, knowing smile. "You've got that smitten look about you." She glanced back at Byrne. "And Aurelius told me you'd come to see him with a beauty on your arm."

"That she is."

"Then don't you keep her waiting."

"Thank you." Alex smiled and headed out to Byrne's stable, where Sherlock had been given a bit to eat and drink when they arrived over an hour past. Alex had come out to place a blanket over him a bit later, hoping to keep him dry and warm.

"I'm afraid we're heading out into it again, but then you can stay put for a while."

As they rode out, Alex breathed a sigh of relief that the rain had stopped. Even better, a few clouds had scattered, allowing moonlight to guide his way, though he and Sherlock hardly needed it. Both man and beast knew the road home by heart.

Sherlock never wanted any pace but speed, and Alex was happy to give the horse his head. Within half an hour, he noticed landmarks—a craggy outcrop of rocks, a curve in the hedgerow—that told him they would soon be on the approach to the castle.

Then movement on the road ahead caught his eye, and as they drew closer, he could see that it was a horse. Riderless but saddled, its reins trailing in the wind behind it. He recognized the horse as they approached. Jane. But she was missing her rider.

Alex's heart seized as if enclosed in a tightening fist. And he knew—somehow, he knew with utter certainty—that Evie had fallen and needed his help.

He slowed Sherlock and then wheeled the stallion around to head back the way they'd come, but he had to do what his mount liked least: move slowly. Scanning each side of the road, he willed the wind to clear more clouds away so that the moon could light the shapes he spied in the darkness.

"Where is she? Let's find her, Sherlock."

The stallion tugged his head and tried to skip into a canter, but Alex slowed him again.

"Slowly, boy." Standing water in ravines along the road reflected the light, but none of the foliage looked disturbed. They kept on. At one spot, some of the tall grass had bent, and he pulled Sherlock off the road, jumping down to examine the area more closely.

He walked on, letting the stallion keep to the road as he walked alongside. Jane followed along too, and Alex willed her to understand his desperation and give him some idea of where to find her fallen rider. A tall hedgerow lined the other side of the road, so if Jane had bucked Evie off out of fright at the lightning or thunder, he suspected it was in this direction.

Sherlock stomped his hind foot, and Alex reached out to soothe him. As he turned, something glinted in the periphery of his vision. He snapped his head toward the spot but saw nothing. It was far too late in the season for glowworms, so he stepped toward the spot slowly and saw it. Evie's gold pendant lay snagged on a tall spear of grass.

Alex crouched to retrieve it and then stood to scan the area nearby.

He spotted her, dropped Sherlock's reins, and broke into a run. She wasn't far off the road, and he fell to his knees at her side.

"Evie, love." He turned her face and ran his fingers down to her neck.

The steady bounce of her pulse against his fingers allowed him to breathe again. He scooped under her knees and upper back and lifted her from the ground.

She moaned, and when she settled her head against his shoulder, he noticed the darkness on her collar and matted hair.

"We're going to get you home, sweetheart. Hold onto me until then."

Sherlock, bless the beast, hadn't moved, despite having his reins to himself. He and Jane looked on as he approached.

Alex settled Evie onto the saddle sideways as best he could, then swung up behind her and gathered her more snuggly into his arms. He draped her legs across his thigh and adjusted her head so it was tucked against his shoulder.

"So cold," she murmured.

Alex had never been so glad to hear another's voice in his life. "I'll keep you warm, beauty." Lifting his overcoat, he wrapped her in with him as best he could and then nudged Sherlock back toward Ballymore. Jane trailed behind them.

"We can't run. Let's just take it steady, boy."

For once, Sherlock didn't demand speed, and though they took a slower pace, the lane toward the castle soon came into view.

"Almost there," he whispered to Evie.

She'd laid a hand against his chest and gripped his shirt in response.

As the stables came into view, Alex saw movement. Skerret rushed forward, lantern in hand. Jack wasn't far behind him, and surprisingly, Rupert followed him out.

All three men came up to the road to greet them.

"I've got her," Alex called. "Just need to get her inside and warmed up."

"What can I do?" Rupert asked first.

"Go inside and ask the staff to bring warm water and bandaging to her room."

"Bandaging?"

"Just go, brother."

Alex dismounted carefully, and Skerret approached to help hold Evie in place and then lift her off the stallion's back and into Alex's arms.

Jack raced ahead as he crossed the lawn, opening the conservatory door.

Bel and Aunt Oona entered the conservatory as soon as they heard his footsteps, both wearing matching expressions of worry.

"Bel, come with me. We have to get her out of these clothes and into something dry."

"I've already laid something out for her," she said as she followed him up the stairs.

In Evie's room, Anna stood at the ready with towels, a large basin of water, and bandaging.

He'd glimpsed the blood in the darkness, but the sight of it in the lamplight made his gut churn.

"She's mostly conscious," he told Anna and his sister.

"But far too cold." Bel turned to him once he'd laid Evie on her bed. "Let us get her into something warm."

Alex shook his head. He couldn't even contemplate leaving her. "I'll turn my back, but I'm not leaving." He did as he said he would while the two ladies worked to undress Evie.

Evie hissed, and he glanced back to see Anna cleaning her wound. Since Belinda had her wrapped in a simple robe and neither of the ladies could argue for delicacy, he approached the bed.

"May I see?" he asked.

Anna lifted the cloth she was using to clean the gash. It was small, and there was minimal swelling. But as she cleaned the cut, the bleeding started again.

Alex folded bandages into a strip to stanch the bleeding and then used longer strips to wrap around the crown of her head and hold the other in place.

Anna took away the soiled bandages, and Bel hovered near the door.

"I'll see about getting her some tea."

"Thank you," Alex told her.

Evie's pale skin and flushed cheeks worried him. He settled on the edge of her bed and laid a hand gently on her forehead, careful to avoid her wound. She was overly warm, possibly feverish.

He stood to ring for cold water, and Evie's hand came down on his, holding him in place.

"Don't go," she breathed, her voice raw and raspy.

"I'm not going anywhere, sweetheart." He leaned toward her, stroking his fingers through the hair at her shoulder. "Where does it hurt?"

"Mostly my head," she whispered. "I'm thirsty."

"Bel's bringing tea."

"Water?"

Alex reached for a carafe and cup on her bedside table and poured some for her. She tried to bend her elbows to arch up, but the one she'd fallen on made her wince.

"I can help." Alex scooped his palm under her nape and helped her lift her head to sip at the water.

After she finished, she lay back and let out a sigh of relief.

"May I see your arm?"

"It's just sore," she murmured.

Alex examined her arm tenderly, noting that she had some mobility but bending it caused her enough pain that he suspected she'd fallen on the joint and may have sprained it.

He'd check again in the morning when he could make a better assessment in the daylight.

Bel entered a moment later, carrying a tea tray herself.

"You're awake," she said to Evie quietly as she filled a teacup.

"I am." Evie attempted a smile.

"How are you feeling?" Bel asked brightly, though her tone belied the worried crimp between her brows.

"Cold, mostly. Sore."

"We'll get another blanket." Bel bustled back out of the room and returned a moment later with a quilt that she stretched out over Evie.

"I'll stoke the fire," Anna said from the doorway.

"You'll ring for us if there's anything else she needs?" Bel asked.

"Of course," Alex told them.

Evie closed her eyes once they'd gone and seemed to drift off. Alex released her hand gently and moved a chair from near the fire, close enough to the bed that he could hold her hand.

Everything in him wanted to crawl into bed with her and wrap her in his arms. And in his head, he couldn't help chastising himself for leaving, for not protecting her better.

He sat at her side, stroking her hair, willing her to be all right.

After a while, the fire began to wane, and he let her go long enough to stoke it back into flame.

"Alex."

"I'm here, love. Right here."

"I'm sorry," she murmured. "I wanted to see you."

"I'm not moving from this spot tonight, so you can see me whenever you wish."

"Here." She patted the stretch of bed beside her.

"I don't want to hurt you."

"All the pain is on the other side," she told him with a lopsided smile. "And I'm certain having you beside me would help."

"That," he told her as he bent to pull off his boots, "is the only inducement I require."

He moved gingerly, gently, trying not to jostle her with his bulk. Soon he was next to her, their bodies pressed together, and he slid his hand under the blanket. She wrapped her hand around his and held both against her chest.

As they lay in the quiet, he felt her soft skin against his, the beat of her heart beneath his hand, and experienced the first measure of peace he'd felt since waking next to her that morning.

He closed his eyes and let exhaustion take him.

Chapter Eighteen

Jane carried Evie swift and true, and as Mr. Byrne's home came into view, she leaped from the pony, burst through the door, and launched herself into Alex's open arms. He'd wrapped her in the heat of his embrace, then cupped her face. "I'm glad you're here, Miss Graves."

All the love she felt for him was there, reflected in his eyes, and so she declared herself too. Right in front of Mr. Byrne, who seemed to have an inkling of what was between them from the first moment they'd crossed his threshold.

She couldn't just make it three words, of course. Though she felt none of the worry that usually brought on her bursts of rambling, she felt a writer's need to spell out her feelings as fully as possible.

Alex listened patiently. He was a patient man.

Still, as she spoke, thunder rolled over her words, obscuring them. Glancing over her shoulder, she noticed she'd forgotten to close the door, and the wind whipped inside. So hard it pushed her bodily, out of Alex's arms, off her feet.

She fell and grasped for something to hold onto.

"I fell," she heard herself say, and then came awake to pain. Her head, the whole left side of her body, and worst of all, her ankle. Even the bed-clothes felt like a heavy weight pushing at the pain. She tried flexing her foot to create some space under the blanket and sucked in a cry.

"I'm here," Alex told her, shifting beside her.

She closed her eyes and soaked in how comforting it felt to have him next to her. At least one side of her body felt good, but then he sat up and got off the bed, taking all his heat with him.

"Tell me how you feel," he said softly as he crossed the room and dipped a cloth in the water basin.

"Like I fell off a horse, landed in a ditch, hit my head on a rock, and lay there getting chilled to the bone."

He turned back and flashed a quick smile. "For a writer, that was a very plain summation."

She narrowed an eye at him. "I'll try for poetry when my head doesn't feel ten sizes too big."

"I shall look forward to it." He returned and gently smoothed back the hair on her forehead, then laid the cool cloth against her skin.

She sighed in relief.

"You have a fever, sweetheart." He sat on a chair next to her and laid two fingers against her neck. "But we'll get it down. Don't worry."

Evie swallowed a shiver of fear and told him quietly, "My mother died of a fever after Sybil's birth. For a while, it seemed all had gone well, and then she fell ill."

"You're not dying of this fever," he whispered. "I've sent for a competent doctor. Your color is already better than it was last night, and your pulse is strong."

Evie reached for his hand, and he gripped hers tightly. "I hate to say this, but I think I may have twisted my ankle."

"Well, let's have a look." He released her hand and stood, going around to the end of the bed and throwing the bedcovers up so that they still mostly kept her warm.

Even in her miserable state, the feel of his hand against her bare leg sent a ripple of warmth up to her belly. He touched her tenderly, as if fearful he'd cause her more pain. Though the truth was that the more he touched her, the better she felt.

"It's swollen. Can you move it at all?"

She did and winced, biting her lower lip to keep from protesting. "A bit."

"That is a good sign. Hopefully just a sprain. I'll wrap it, and we can elevate it a bit to help with the swelling."

"You're very good at all this."

"I did contemplate being a doctor, remember. As second son, I thought I had my options."

"What happened to your older brother?"

He stared at her, not as if the topic bothered him too greatly but as if he had something to say but held it back. And somehow, she knew.

"A fever?"

He lowered the blanket, tenting the fabric around her ankle so that its weight didn't bear down on her leg. Then he came around to sit on the bed beside her.

"Not the same situation in any regard," he said as he took her hand and lifted it to his mouth, kissing one knuckle and then the next. "He was at a Scottish hunting lodge." He kissed another knuckle. "He downplayed the fever until it was serious, and his companions were useless and did not get him proper care." He kissed the fourth knuckle and then nipped gently at the skin of her thumb. "You will be doted on, given herbal concoctions and cool compresses, and you will be better in no time."

He lowered her hand but kept hold of it.

Evie drew in a long breath and let it out on a sigh. "I'm sorry about your brother."

"I'm sorry about your mother."

"Heavens," she exclaimed, turning to him. "I forgot to ask about Mr. Byrne. How is he? And Jane. Did she make it back all right?"

"Byrne will be all right. He took a fall too, though I suspect from a much greater height. He has a dangerous hobby now and won't be dissuaded. I'm sure that doesn't surprise you."

"Not in the least, but he has someone to care for him?"

"A housekeeper. I did intend to relieve her this morning, but I'll send one of the staff."

"And Jane?"

"I encountered her on the road, heading back to Ballymore. When Sherlock and I came upon her, she was headed toward home. That's how I knew you'd fallen." He squeezed her hand. "I'm sorry she bolted."

"She was frightened of the storm, and I don't blame her. And I think I told her to go home. I can't remember. I got so dizzy." Evie had only vague memories of the fall, but she remembered the cold and the blood on her fingertips. "I'm sorry," she told Alex. "I was impulsive and shouldn't have gone out with her. I just had the overwhelming urge to get to you."

"Why?" he asked in a husky rumble, his brows lifted in question.

He had every reason to be angry with her for her recklessness, but she could sense that he wasn't. All she felt from him was what he'd given her from the night they'd met: kindness and a sense that she intrigued him, mattered to him.

Evie reached for his face, running her fingers along the stubbled edge of his jaw. He turned to press his lips to her fingers.

"I need to tell you something."

"Tell me," he urged, bending over her, one hand braced against the headboard.

"Alexander!" The shriek broke the moment. Evie was surprised it hadn't broken any glass in the room.

His aunt stood on the threshold, her mouth agape, eyes wide.

"The maid told me you slept in her room." She strode in and gripped his arm as if she meant to bodily remove him from Evie's bedside.

Alex shrugged out of her grip. "Aunt Oona, go downstairs, and I'll speak with you presently."

She scoffed and took a breath as if intending to unleash some diatribe, but he stayed her with a gesture of his hand. "No," he said before she could get a word out. "Evie is unwell and in pain, and I'll not have you disturb her. I'll speak with you downstairs."

His aunt huffed for a moment, letting out little half bursts of pent-up frustration, but she eventually relented, pivoted on her heel, and stomped back down the hall.

Alex turned back to Evie, leaning near her again, one hand clasped in hers, the other cupping her cheek. "I want to hear it," he told her fiercely. "Whatever you came to tell me last night. I want every word exactly as you intended, but let me talk to her first."

"Of course." Evie instinctively attempted to nod her head, and it pulsed with such pain that she closed her eyes instead.

"I'll send Anna up with willow bark and ginger tea. Should help with the pain and the fever."

"Go so you can come back to me," she told him with a smile.

He took the cloth from her head, went across to the basin to refresh it, and came back to gently replace it.

"Back soon." He bent and kissed her cheek like she was the most delicate porcelain, and then he departed.

IN THE DOWNSTAIRS drawing room, Alex found more family than he'd bargained for. All of them were assembled. Aunt Oona sat on the settee, still steaming, her arms across her chest. Bel sat on a chair, looking tired and worried. He'd awoken a few times during the night to feel Evie's forehead, and once he'd caught his sister coming in to check on her too. Rupert stood near the mantel, full of nervous energy, as if unsure what to do with himself.

Alex decided to start with what mattered to him most. "Evie has a fever and possibly a sprained ankle, but she'll be all right."

Rupert let out a sigh of relief at almost the same moment Bel did. Aunt Oona stared at him questioningly, as if waiting for him to give her leave to heap on whatever admonitions she'd intended upstairs.

"Is there anything I can do?" Rupert asked, almost beseechingly.

"There is," Alex told him. "Aurelius Byrne took a fall from his hot-air balloon. I suspect it wasn't too far off the ground, but far enough that I fear internal injuries. I've sent for two doctors to examine him and sent a note this morning for one of them to visit Evie too. Would you go and sit with him? His housekeeper needs to be relieved for a bit."

"Of course. I'll go now."

"Thank you, brother." Alex nodded at Rupert. "But let's have this out before anyone leaves the room. I don't want any further misunderstandings or antics." He shot a look at his aunt.

"I could go to help Mr. Byrne too," Bel offered.

"I think you might be more help here. Time spent with you will raise Evie's spirits."

She smiled at that. "Then I'll go up as soon as we're finished here."

Alex sucked in a breath, braced himself, and turned to his aunt. "Say what you must, Aunt Oona."

"I'm very glad to hear the girl will be all right. Anyone can see she's a lady of mettle."

It was the most complimentary commentary she'd offered about Evie, but Alex wasn't appeased.

"But?"

She returned an exasperated stare, as if she thought he was being obtuse. "We have a scandal on our hands, Alexander. You slept in that girl's room last night, in her bed, according to one of the maids I spoke to."

"Yes, I did."

Aunt Oona huffed. "And that's all you have to say for yourself? *Yes, I've ruined the young lady sent by a countess to assist me with a luncheon?*"

"Evie is not ruined. She's . . ." *Everything.* That was the word that came to mind. She meant everything to him. Nothing else compared. Not his goals, or his duties, or the expectations that others put on him. She mattered most, and he could not fathom the days of his life marching on without her being a part of each and every one of them.

And, ironically, the damned accident that he'd wish away to Hades if he could, that he'd undo if he could, gave him hope that she felt the same. Certainly, she had not come out in the dark with a storm on the horizon, desperate to get to him, to tell him that she didn't quite feel the same.

"Alexander?"

"Evie is an extraordinary young woman. Determined, intelligent, kind, and there is no other lady I will consider or be pressed to marry."

"You cannot marry her," his aunt spluttered. "She's a *secretary.*"

Alex rolled his eyes. "Good God, Aunt Oona, stop being such a snob. Your father, my grandfather, was a farmer."

"And a titan of the oil industry."

"I believe you've destroyed your own argument. You judge her for her means of employment, and yet judging anyone by a title, *whatever it may be,* is shortsighted to say the least." Alex drew in a breath to calm himself. He was fighting the urge to send his aunt from Ballymore altogether, and he knew his worry for Evie, and Byrne, had frayed at his sense of equanimity.

"So you'll marry the girl," she said with cool resignation.

"If I'm lucky, yes. If she'll have me, yes."

Aunt Oona shuddered and closed her eyes. "Your marriage could have saved us, Alexander. Now you condemn us to poverty."

Bel scoffed and edged forward on her chair to face their aunt. "You speak of poverty a great deal for a lady who's never experienced it."

"She speaks of marriage a great deal for a lady who never married," Rupert put in.

"Beckham and I are not living in poverty, as you so direly predicted, Aunt Oona. We make ends meet, and I'm learning to type," she said with a surprisingly proud smile. She looked at Alex and then Rupert. "I know it may not sound like much, but it allows me to bring in a few extra pounds and assist him when he must work at home on a story."

"I suppose I need to take up some profession," Rupert mulled quietly. "Though I've considered investing the rest of Grandpapa's gift, and that might do me while I ponder my fate."

Their mother's father had gifted each of them a

tidy sum in his will. Alex knew Bel had used part of hers to buy the modest Half Moon Street home she shared with her husband. Rupert had gambled some of his, but it sounded like he might be reconsidering his spendthrift ways. Alex, unfortunately, had sunk some of his into repairing the estate and paying Estings's staff, but he'd also reserved a decent portion to build up the stables at Ballymore.

"So that's your plan, children? To spend your only inheritance on mere survival and take up some profession, even if it's as grubby as being a typist, or a *secretary*?"

Bel let out a peal of laughter. "I enjoy the typewriter. Perhaps Evelyn enjoys being a secretary. No," she said pensively. "She enjoys her writing, and perhaps she'll earn by way of her pen as Guy does. Might you try not taking such a pessimistic view, Aunt Oona?"

Alex's mind raced, images flashing as if some part of his mind was replaying a dozen memories and predicting a dozen futures. Then the very practical worry for Evie and Byrne broke through all the noise.

Perhaps Evelyn enjoys being a secretary finally made its way into his thoughts, and he chewed on it, wondering if it was true. She certainly seemed to take pride in her work, but perhaps he'd been presumptuous to assume it would be something she'd willingly give up so that they could make a life together.

And London. Would she wish to give up living there, since her sister was so close?

As he puzzled through his thoughts and his family sat in tense silence, Aunt Oona stewing, a maid entered the drawing room.

"Pardon, Your Grace, but a Dr. Faherty has arrived. Shall I send him up to Miss Graves?"

"Faherty?"

"I sent for him," Aunt Oona said. "Served as a doctor to me several years ago."

"I've sent for a doctor," Alex said firmly. "No one will see her until he does." He feared whoever his aunt had invited was old-fashioned in his methods. He'd seen his mother worsen under the care of such a doctor, who saw bleeding as the main line of treatment.

"Shouldn't we let someone look at her immediately?" Rupert sounded genuinely concerned.

Perhaps he was right. Alex could oversee this man as he examined Evie, and he had no notion when Bailey, the doctor he'd sent for, might arrive.

"Very well." Alex turned back to the maid. "Have him wait in the great hall. I'll escort him up."

"Yes, Your Grace."

"Now," Alex said to the room, letting his gaze meet his sister's and brother's and then fall on his aunt, who still held a granite scowl on her face. "I do not know how long Evie will need to convalesce, but while she does, there is to be nothing done to upset her. More to the point, she's to be treated with respect. Hell, more than that, treat her as you'd treat my duchess."

His aunt's brows both shot up at that statement, and it gave Alex an odd sense of satisfaction.

"She will be," he said determinedly. "I hope she will be."

The questions about her employment and her sister now weighed on his mind. But he still believed anything could be overcome if they were together.

"I've already had a telegram sent to Lady Waverly," Aunt Oona said quietly.

Alex nodded and tried to conceal his surprise. It was the first helpful thing she'd done in . . . well, a good long while.

"Thank you, Aunt Oona. We should probably try to reach her sister too." Then another thought struck. "What exactly did you tell Lady Waverly?"

"Do not worry. I did not tell her of your *amour* with her secretary. Only that Miss Graves had fallen ill and would need time to recover."

"Wouldn't it be ironic if that actually brought her here?" Rupert mused.

Alex didn't think it would. However much Lady Waverly cared for Evie, he suspected she still viewed her as staff. But they'd deal with it if she did come.

"Right, is everyone clear, then?"

Bel nodded eagerly. Rupert gave one sharp nod.

Their aunt stared back at him. "Have I any choice in the matter?"

"No," the three siblings said in a single harmonious response.

"Now, I'll go up with Faherty. Rupert, you'll see to Byrne. Bel, perhaps you can come up when the doctor has gone. After being poked and prodded, I suspect Evie will be grateful for some cheering."

Without waiting for more assent than nods, Alex exited the drawing room, greeted the doctor, and led the man up to Evie.

She smiled when he entered the room, then frowned and pulled up the collar of her gown when she noticed the stranger behind him.

"Miss Graves, this is Dr. Faherty." Alex drew close to her, ahead of the older man. "Are you all right with him examining you?"

She nodded but didn't look entirely pleased with the idea.

"For modesty's sake, I'd ask you to step out, Your Grace."

"No, I won't be stepping out, Dr. Faherty. Unless Miss Graves wishes for me to."

"I do not wish for the duke to leave."

Faherty eyed each of them in turn and then set his bag on the table near her bed. He went through the physical examination, and Evie proved able to extend and bend her elbow and even seemed to have a bit more mobility in her ankle than earlier.

"Anna brought me tea and a poultice that seemed to help," she explained to the aged doctor.

"Mmm-hmm" was the only reply he offered.

After he'd assessed her, Faherty settled into the chair Alex had occupied earlier.

"You're a healthy young lady," he said as he tucked away his stethoscope and snapped his bag closed. "The fever is the greatest worry, but it seems to be diminishing based on what the maid who admitted me conveyed. Your color is good, your heart sounds strong, and I suspect with rest you will improve in no time."

"My ankle?"

"Twisted rather than severely sprained. Certainly not broken. You may begin attempting to put weight on it whenever you're able. Since the swelling reduced so readily, it seems to be healing well."

"Then perhaps I don't have to remain abed at all," she said hopefully, her gaze flicking to Alex. "I'd like to see Jane."

"I still recommend rest, young miss, as much as you can get. Have this Jane come visit you."

Evie chuckled, and the doctor's thick white brows jumped on his forehead.

"Jane is Miss Graves's favorite horse," Alex explained.

"Ah," Faherty said. "The one who tipped you into a puddle?"

"She didn't mean to," Evie said defensively.

Faherty twisted in the chair to address Alex.

"You've lucked into finding yourself a true horse-woman, Your Grace."

Alex grinned at the doctor and then at Evie. She was a great deal more than that, and he knew exactly how lucky he was to have found her.

Chapter Nineteen

Two days later, Evie stood in front of the mirror in her chamber and assessed the day dress she'd selected. It was an emerald one that she'd always thought made her eyes seem greener.

Anna, who'd become a friend and was as close to a lady's maid as she'd ever had in her life, had arranged her hair far more prettily than she could have done herself.

"Will it do?" Evie asked her, as the girl pushed in a final pin near her nape.

"You look lovely, and it's good to see you up and about."

"That's what I'm most excited to show him, but we must be quick, or he'll be back in here before I can impress him properly."

Alex had gone back to his room as he'd begun doing in the mornings to wash and change from the clothes he'd worn while sitting, or preferably lying, with her overnight. Evie still sported some bruises on her hip and arm, but they bothered her less and less. She'd been up on her feet shortly after the doctor had departed two days ago, but she'd only truly begun feeling her ankle was sound and would fully support her today.

"I think that's done for your hair. I'd say you're ready."

Evie swung back to face Anna. "Thank you. As usual, you've worked wonders."

She headed down the hall, favoring her ankle a bit, more anxious that it would twinge than in actual pain. But the fever had gone, and she felt more herself than she had in days.

Alex had been patient, tender, loyally staying by her side as she recovered. And he'd never pushed for the momentous conversation they'd promised to have as soon as the charity luncheon was over. The conversation she'd been so determined to have the night of her fall.

She was determined that they have it today. Now, if he was in his room.

Anna had confirmed which door was his, and she'd seemed a little surprised that Evie didn't already know. She'd never had reason to go to his room. He'd always come to hers.

Now, outside the polished panels, she hesitated, practicing what she'd say. Impulsivity had dropped her straight into misfortune. She wanted this to be right.

She knocked twice and heard his familiar footfalls as he crossed to the door and opened it.

His first reaction was the flash of pleasure that came into his eyes whenever he looked at her. Then a smile, and finally shock.

"Evie." He reached out, one hand on her hip, the other on her arm as if to stop her from toppling over. "You're all right?"

Evie lifted her arms and wrapped them around his neck. "I am very well indeed."

"Oh," he murmured in the low tone that made her toes curl.

She glanced past him into the dark cavern of his room. "Are you going to invite me in?"

"Of course." He swept an arm around her waist, and he turned as if she needed help the way she had in the last couple of days.

Evie could walk on her own, but she liked his nearness.

"Goodness, this room is very different than mine." The walls were papered in a rich maroon, and the long drapes were an even deeper shade, like the darkest mulled wine. Even the furnishings were darker. Perhaps rosewood or mahogany.

"It was my father's suite," he said tightly.

"Yes, of course." He would be expected to take the ducal suite, whether it was to his taste or not.

"I'd always thought I'd make changes one day, but it seemed low on the list of necessary expenses."

He looked down at her, and she felt that same

flutter in her stomach as she had the first time they'd met.

"I thought it far past time that we have that talk."

"Shall we sit?" He pointed to two chairs arranged before the fire, though they were very different than the comfortable, overstuffed lounging chairs in her room. These were leather wingbacks with broad armrests. Like little thrones.

Evie walked toward them, and Alex kept a hand at her lower back.

"Your ankle is much better, I see."

"I'm all but fully mended."

Once they were by the fire, he waited for Evie to sit. She did, the soreness in her hip only giving her the slightest of protests.

Though she'd imagined what she'd say to him and how, memories of the night of her fall intruded now. The urgency she'd felt, the power of her certainty.

And the loveliest part was that she could see in his gaze, in the tenderness of his expression, that he knew what she'd come to say. It wasn't going to be a revelation but a confirmation.

"What I wanted to tell you that night—" She longed to rush on and overexplain. Instead, she said the only words that mattered. "I love you."

His handsome face creased in a beaming smile, and he leaned forward, taking her hands, kissing one and then the other. "I love you too, beauty, but I suspect you already had an inkling."

"I had guessed."

He chuckled and then turned serious. "Shall I get down on one knee?"

Her heart caught in her throat, and her head spun like a top. And before she could answer, he did. He lowered to one knee in front of her.

"Marry me, Evie." His storm-blue eyes were clear, his voice deep and unwavering. "Marry me, and we will figure everything else out from there."

When she hesitated, a shadow of worry tightened his expression.

Evie reached for his shoulders and pulled him in for a kiss.

He wrapped his arms around her, and she gave into the hunger that had been building in her for days.

"Yes," she whispered when she pulled back, breathless. "I want to be yours."

She felt a shiver run through him. "Thank you," he told her, then pulled her toward him, up out of her chair and onto his lap as he settled into his chair.

"You needn't thank me," she teased before running her lips along the edge of his jaw. "We both have much to be grateful for, but—"

"Good God, not a *but*."

Evie laughed and cupped his face. "The figuring out everything else is all I meant. Even you acknowledged it. This isn't"—she searched for a word that would not mar the moment—"simple."

"Then let's unravel the complicated bits together."

"Yes, let's." He understood and wasn't going to be cross that she worried about all the details that needed to be untangled.

His mouth tipped in a cheeky grin. "I know your practical bent, Miss Graves, and your problem-solving skills."

"*Problems* sounds too dire. I'd say these are merely—"

"*Challenges.*"

"Exactly." Evie liked that characterization. Challenges could be met and overcome.

"The challenge of one of us living in London," he offered.

"And one of us in Ireland," she added. "For now. I know you'll wish to live here."

"Where do you wish to live, Evie?"

She nuzzled his cheek. For her, there was no question of the answer, but she adored that he cared what she preferred. "Wherever you are," she whispered against his skin.

He kissed her the moment she got the answer out.

A knock on the door stalled their discussion, and Alex glared at whoever stood on the other side.

"We could ignore them," he whispered.

"You should see who it is." Evie rose from his lap and returned to her own chair.

Alex opened the door and said, as if in warning, "Aunt Oona."

Evie sat up a bit straighter in her chair.

"There's a visitor for Miss Graves, and yet she is not in her room." His aunt squared her gaze on Evie. "Somehow, I knew where I'd find her."

Evie stood, curious and confused. "A visitor for me?"

"Waiting in your room for you, Miss Graves."

Evie stood and crossed to the door, glancing at Alex before she stepped into the hall, past his aunt, and headed to her bedchamber.

Her heartbeat sped. She knew who it was. Her sister trailed the combined scents of lavender and carbolic wherever she went.

"Sybil."

She pivoted to face Evie and then rushed into her arms.

"My God, I was so worried, and here you are up and looking fresh as a spring day."

Tears came quickly. Evie didn't try to hold them back. She hadn't seen Sybil in too many months, even before her departure from London. Arching back, she took her sister's face between her hands.

"You're not missing class for this, are you?"

Sybil laughed. "You worry about that when you were injured? Did you think I could receive such a telegram and not come?"

Evie slid a lock of blond hair back behind her

sister's ear. "I've missed you, Sybbie. And I'm fine, as you see."

Sybil stepped away from her, held her at arm's length, and examined her from head to toe. She narrowed in immediately on the healing cut near her temple that was mostly hidden by wisps of hair.

"The cut looks well, and you look . . . happy. Almost exceedingly so."

Evie heard Alex approach, and Sybil looked toward the doorway.

"Well, that explains quite a bit."

"Sybil, this is Alexander." Almost as an after-thought and to her own chagrin, after years of dealing with nobles, she added, "The Duke of Rennick."

"Sybil Graves, Your Grace. Thank you for tak-ing such good care of my sister. She usually hates being doted upon, but perhaps she made an excep-tion for you."

"Doting on your sister was my pleasure."

Evie blushed and felt the heat to the tips of her ears.

"Yes, well, I came to ensure she was receiving excellent care, and clearly she has." She turned back to face Evie. "Now we can head back to Lon-don together."

Evie saw the expression on Alex's face turn from the joy of their engagement to something like mis-erable realization.

"Sybil, there's a great deal I must tell you."

"We'll have plenty of time to chat on our return journey." She let out a weary sigh. "Though I can't say I look forward to making that trek again tomorrow."

"Tomorrow?" Alex said a bit too loudly.

Evie turned to him, even reached out a hand and laid it on his chest. "I should speak to her alone for a bit."

"Of course." He bent and pressed a warm kiss to her cheek. "Pleasure to meet you, Miss Graves."

When he'd gone and Evie turned back to her sister, Sybil faced her with one hand planted on each hip.

"I read the attraction between you two immediately, but can you explain why he feels so free to kiss you?" Sybil demanded.

"Yes, I can." Evie swallowed hard. "We're to be married."

Sybil tipped her head as if Evie's words confused her. "You've known him little more than a week." She stepped forward and reached for Evie's hand, turning it palm up and lifting the cuff of her dress. "There is the scar you received when you climbed into a briar bush to rescue me when I was four. So I suppose you truly are my practical, logical sister."

Evie clasped her hand over Sybil's where she still held her wrist. "If I think about it too long, it doesn't make sense. Even to me. So I focus instead on what I feel."

"Like the characters in your stories."

"Perhaps, but this isn't fiction. What I feel for him is real, and I know he feels the same. I never thought I'd have this."

"Have what?"

"Love, romance, a future that was anything else but being a noblewoman's secretary."

Sybil slipped her hand from Evie's and pressed a hand to her own neck. One of her contemplative gestures. She turned toward the long window that looked out on Ballymore's garden.

"And you're going to live here in this half castle half country house? You're going to be a duchess?" She spoke as she faced the window. "Is there no estate?"

"There is one in Wiltshire, but apparently it's let. Or was and probably will be again." Evie approached to stand beside her sister. "And yes, I think we would live here. The horses are very important to him, and I can write anywhere."

Sybil smiled at that. "I've always thought you should have more time for your writing and try to publish. It's what you love most."

"That's not entirely true," Evie teased. She leaned toward Sybil. "You come above writing, and now so does Alexander."

Sybil twisted her lips. "Does he support you in your literary endeavors?"

"We haven't discussed it at length, but, yes, I feel certain he will."

"Will I ever get to see you?" Sybil's voice softened. She rarely showed any bit of vulnerability, and when she did, every protective instinct Evie possessed responded.

"Of course you will. London is not so very far."

"Perhaps I could find work in a Dublin hospital." She sounded dubious even as she suggested it. "But I do feel a call to those without means, and London is likely the best place for that."

"I will come to visit you, no matter where you are. And you mustn't worry about your tuition. My savings will cover your first year and a bit of your second. I'll secure the rest, by one means or another."

Sybil turned to her. "Evie, I've never assumed you'd pay all of my tuition. I've been saving too. I tutor here and there, and I've applied for a scholarship, and perhaps I'll get it. Still waiting to hear."

Eyeing the closed bedchamber door as if she suspected Alex lurked beyond it, Sybil added, "And I will support whatever choices make you happy." Worry lingered in her tone, a quiver that wasn't compatible with Sybil's usual confidence. "You're all I have of family, and I won't allow us to lose touch."

"Nor would I. Ever." Evie pulled Sybil into a hug, and she held on tightly for a moment before releasing her.

"We should still return to London as soon

as we can." Sybil swiped at a tear that had slid down her cheek. "The sooner you settle things with Lady Waverly, the sooner you can begin a life with your duke."

ALEX CROSSED THE great hall, his mind whirling. Out of habit, he continued into the drawing room. Its door always stood half-open, and the flicker of firelight drew him.

Mindlessly, since his mind was too busy trying to sift the significant moments that had just passed, he approached the drinks cart and poured himself a small snifter of whiskey.

At the same moment that he turned to the fire, Rupert entered the room.

"There you are," he said. "I've just returned from my daily visit to Byrne. He's improving more and more every day." He let out a scoffing laugh. "Even with his arm in a sling, the man wants to climb back into that bloody basket and hurl himself into the sky."

"I'm glad he's improving," Alex said before sipping at the amber fire in his glass.

Rupert fell silent for a moment, watching him warily. "It's early to be imbibing. Especially for you who rarely partakes at all."

"Join me, why don't you?"

"Don't mind if I do." He sauntered over, poured himself twice as much as Alex had, and knocked half of it back in one gulp. "What are we celebrating?"

"I asked Evie to marry me, and she said *yes*." A sweet, fierce rush of joy grounded him in that moment.

"That's bloody marvelous, man." Rupert patted him twice on the back, then he tipped his head around to assess Alex's expression. "So why do you look so uncertain?"

"Because she's likely returning to London tomorrow."

"Bloody hell, that's a shame." He patted him again, this time more softly. "But surely you had to know she'd return at some point."

"I avoided the thought."

Rupert chuckled. "That does sound a bit like you."

"What the hell does that mean?"

Rupert raised both hands. "I only meant that you tend to . . . put things off if you don't wish to face them."

"That doesn't sound like a good character quality."

His brother shrugged. "It can be. Some things should be forestalled. Marriage, for instance."

"So I linger over decisions, except with Evie apparently, and I avoid what I don't wish to face. What else?" Alex threw back the rest of his whiskey and was suddenly eager for the truth about how his brother viewed him.

"You've sidelined your own goals for years, though I understand you had to when you inherited. But I can see that you're not going to do that anymore." Rupert poured himself more whiskey and joined Alex by the fire. "She'll come back, you know. Miss Graves does not strike me as the sort of lady who agrees to an offer of marriage and then reneges."

Alex realized he wasn't as practical as he'd often thought himself, for though he acknowledged that Rupert was right—Evie was always going to return to London at some point—the prospect of spending even a day away from her struck him as the wrong way to begin their future together.

"Give her time to prepare," Rupert urged. "Quit her job, collect her things, and come back to Ballymore unencumbered by complications."

Not complications, Alex thought to himself. *Challenges*, they'd decided. And, of course, Rupert was right. Evie was fully capable of resolving matters with Lady Waverly and packing her belongings. But he still hated the notion of saying goodbye to her, even for a short separation.

"I know you're right." He rarely gave Rupert enough credit for being thoughtful and understanding.

"Or . . ." Rupert said as if pondering some great dilemma. He sipped from his glass and stared at the fire and, maddeningly, said no more.

"Or?" Alex prompted.

"Or you could do what a completely besotted, desperate fool of a man would do."

Alex checked both boxes in his mind. Yes, utterly *besotted*. And yes, with Evie gone, feeling *desperate* seemed to hover in his near future.

"Which is?"

"You could follow her back to London."

Chapter Twenty

Four days later

$\mathcal{E}$vie felt odd standing on Lady Waverly's doorstep again.

Indeed, being in London again felt strange too, as if her senses had forgotten how to take in all the sounds and scents and busyness. She already missed the endless varieties of green surrounding Ballymore.

Alex would be in the city on the morrow if his travel plans came off as intended. Still, bidding him goodbye in Galway and then Sybil at King's Cross station had been too much parting for Evie.

Now it was time for another. Though this one would be less emotional. Employees left their posts every day in this city.

She lifted the lion's head door knocker and rapped twice.

A footman, Jeremy, opened the door to her formally and then recognized her. "Ah, Miss Graves."

He stood aside to let her enter.

"Heard you took a tumble, but you look as if

you're recovered and are ready to take on a dozen balls and soirees."

Evie chuckled. "I feel much better." Though the prospect of planning a dozen anything held much less appeal than it would have a week and a half ago.

"Where is her ladyship?"

The young man scoffed. "See there. That's the sort of question others ask you." He glanced toward the front drawing room. The door had been pulled shut. "Taking tea with one of her friends. Gives you time to get upstairs and rest for a bit before you see her."

He went out and wrangled her traveling case inside. Then he lifted the luggage and climbed the stairs to her room with Evie following behind.

A few minutes later, she stood alone in the bedroom decorated with simple elegance that she'd slept in for three years. Like standing on Waverly House's doorstep, like the fog and bustle of the city, the room felt odd. Nothing here had changed, but of course, she had.

In a fundamental way, she had altered during her time in Ireland. Found a rightness there with Alex that she'd never felt here.

Someone rapped on her door and then opened it.

Josie, one of the maids, popped her head in. "Good to see you back, Evie. Her ladyship wants you in the drawing room."

"Has her guest departed?" She'd only walked in but ten minutes ago.

"Dunno. Lizzie took in a fresh pot of tea when Lady W rang the bell. Her ladyship asked if you'd returned and then sent for you."

"Thank you, Josie. I'll go down directly."

Evie removed her gloves and the fitted coat she'd traveled in and laid them on her bed. Then she smoothed her hair in the small mirror above the wash basin.

Tears welled up, surprising her. She swiped them away.

She missed Alex, missed the feel of his hand in hers or simply knowing he was near.

"Soon enough," she told her reflection.

Of course, she had to settle things with Lady Waverly. She owed it to both of them to close off this chapter of her life properly so that she could write the next one with a clear conscience and, hopefully, her former employer's goodwill intact.

Downstairs, she found the drawing-room door shut and wondered if there'd been some mistake. Usually, when the countess called for someone, the door to wherever she was stood open a crack, an indication that she was alone and ready to receive a visit.

There were no other servants about to ask, so Evie rapped on the gilded door.

"Come in," Lady Waverly called.

Evie stepped into the sumptuous pink and cream room, and a cold shiver scuttled down her spine.

Lady Waverly wasn't alone.

She sat in her favorite damask chair, and the Duchess of Vyne sat on the settee. The duchess who was friends with Alex's aunt. Both ladies assessed her coolly, and Evie realized in that moment that they knew. Probably via Oona McQuillan, they knew details of her trip to Ireland that she would have preferred to share in her own way, if given the chance.

"Come in, Evelyn," Lady Waverly told her in the imperious tone she almost always employed with other staff but rarely with Evie. "It seems there is much to discuss."

As soon as she closed the door behind her, Chessie let out a whine. He was the only one in the room who seemed genuinely pleased to see her. He'd scooted to the front edge of Lady Waverly's chair, where he was tucked in beside her. But her ladyship rested a hand on his back, and he knew jumping down to greet Evie would be seen as a great offense.

Evie told herself to get plenty of walks in with the little man before she departed.

Though Lady Waverly did not direct her where to sit, Evie chose the stuffed chair nearest the door.

"You had quite an adventure in Ireland, Miss Graves." The Duchess of Vyne's tone was shockingly warm, almost friendly.

Evie sensed a snare had been set and both ladies were waiting for her to stumble into it.

"The trip was a success from my perspective.

I went to assist with a charity luncheon, and we ended up pulling in five times the number of attendees originally invited. Donations were seven times what the duke expected, and the Equestrian Society will now move forward with several initiatives its core members have been discussing for years." Evie took a breath. During her recitation, she'd noticed that both ladies considered cutting in, but she'd plowed ahead with her ramble.

Every word of it was true. Despite everything else, she was proud that the event had been a success.

"Congratulations, Miss Graves." The duchess tapped her cane, and Evie didn't know if she intended it as a stand-in for applause or a determination that they move on.

"I knew you would be of great help to Rennick, Evelyn," Lady Waverly said evenly. "That is, of course, why I sent you."

"And to see Ireland, you said."

"Yes." She returned a tight smile. "Though, in seeing Ireland, I understand you were injured. Thus, your extra days there."

"Only two."

"But I suspect you know that's not the matter that the Duchess of Vyne came to inform me about."

Evie shifted her gaze from one noblewoman to the other, unsure what gossip had been shared.

Unsure how much Alex's aunt could have conveyed in the last few days.

Quite a lot, she decided.

"The duke has asked me to marry him, and I have accepted." Even speaking the words made Evie a little breathless, made her heart feel twice its size in her chest. She felt a smile tickle at the edges of her mouth and glanced down at the carpet, but she couldn't stop herself.

The joy was uncontainable.

Then she looked up. The two noblewomen gaped at her. The duchess's mouth slightly ajar, the countess's brows disappearing into her hairline.

Ah, so that part they did *not* know.

"I beg your pardon?" Lady Waverly said. "You mean to tell me that Rennick set out to marry me and chose you instead?"

Evie thought the characterization inaccurate but also didn't want to offend Lady Waverly.

"I think it's more accurate to say that his aunt steered him toward you," the duchess mused. "Whereas *he* showed favor to Miss Graves quite on his own."

Lady Waverly flicked a glance at the duchess. "Regardless of how it transpired, such behavior is not at all what I would have expected of you, Miss Graves. You were sent in a professional capacity."

"And I fulfilled those duties, my lady."

"And a good deal more, it seems."

Evie felt her color rise, and her hackles rose

too. She stood and considered turning on her heel and walking out the door. For good. Her clothes could be sent to her. The only things she truly prized among her belongings were her books and her notebooks filled with her writing.

Chessie tilted his head and let out a little yip.

It was as if the little dog was reminding her: she wasn't a coward, and she wasn't ashamed of any choice she'd made.

"I am sorry that this news is unexpected, my lady. And it will necessitate me leaving your employment. But I won't be chastised for falling in love. I didn't intend it. I didn't expect it. Yet I certainly will take it as the gift it is."

The duchess dipped her head, and Evie thought she detected the hint of a smile. Not so for Lady Waverly, who stared at Evie in stony silence.

"You will give two weeks' notice." It wasn't a question.

"One week, my lady." This had been a point of contention with Alex. They both wished to start their lives together without delay, but she knew there were things she could do to prepare the countess for Evie's departure.

And though she hadn't said as much to Lady Waverly, she didn't intend to reside at Waverly House for the full week.

"Then you won't have much time to help me find your replacement."

"I will do what I can. Though I am sure many

would be thrilled to serve you as your secretary. If you haven't replaced me within a week's time, you surely will quickly thereafter." Evie felt no responsibility to serve as finder for the countess. The city was full of well-qualified candidates in search of work.

"We have a great deal to do in a week." Lady Waverly's voice had softened. She didn't sound pleased, just resigned. Even a bit sad. "I've left my recent invitations and a few notes about upcoming events on your desk. Have a look, and we'll meet to discuss them in the morning."

The dismissal felt like they'd fallen back into the natural pattern of their relationship. Though Evie suspected the countess was holding a great deal back because of her visitor's presence.

"Very good, my lady."

To Evie's surprise, the duchess moved to stand, leaning on her cane to leverage herself off the settee.

"I'll be going too, Katharine. Thank you for tea, and, of course, I'll see you at Lady Billington's luncheon next week."

Evie held the door for the duchess, and the older woman sailed out, sending a footman into action to retrieve her coat and accessories.

When they entered the foyer, the duchess turned to her.

"I offer you congratulations, Miss Graves. I

meant to offer you a higher post than secretary, thinking it might put you in position to mingle with the nobles you only send invitations to for Katharine, and here you've gone and snagged yourself a duke." She leaned a bit closer. "Rennick hasn't a very heavy purse if the rumors about his father are true, but you're an enterprising sort, and perhaps he can be too."

"Thank you, Your Grace." Evie was genuinely touched. Though she struggled to understand why someone who was an intimate of Alex's aunt could see the situation in such a sympathetic way.

The duchess busied herself slipping her gloves on, and Evie took her coat from the footman and helped her into the garment.

"Come and see me when you have the time. We'll speak of how you might be introduced to society as the Duchess of Rennick."

"Oh, I don't—"

"You have been a noblewoman's secretary for years, girl. Thus, you know how such delicate matters must be treated. To some, this will be seen as a scandal. To others, a bit of a fascination."

The *girl* still rankled, but Evie sensed the duchess's desire to aid her was sincere.

"Your kindness is appreciated, Your Grace."

The duchess waved her hand. "Not only kindness for you, my dear. Oona has been a friend since we were girls, and though she may have preferred an heiress, Rennick did not. Dukes choose as they please." She winked at that.

THE NEXT AFTERNOON, Evie rolled her wrist, trying to ease out the tension in her hand. She'd been working on a set of invitations for nearly an hour.

Chessie lay at her feet, his chin occasionally resting atop her foot. He liked to be her companion while she worked but usually from the comfort of his favorite chair. His nearness now made her wonder if the pug sensed somehow that she would be leaving soon.

"I'm going to miss you, boy."

He yawned widely at that, and Evie chuckled.

"Perhaps we can meet in the square if Josie takes to walking you. At least until I return to Ireland."

Alex promised that they could visit London whenever Evie wished to see Sybil, and until her week's notice to Lady Waverly was up, he would stay at Rennick House just a few blocks away from where she now sat.

He warned her that the house was only partially furnished and was usually let, but Evie hardly cared about such matters. Both of them wanted to make their home in Ireland, but both acknowledged that plan had to wait until matters were settled in London.

Lady Waverly had not spoken to Evie in the morning as she'd indicated yesterday. Evie wasn't certain if she was simply indisposed or still too cross to wish to see her.

Either way, Evie had plenty to keep her busy. Clearly, Lady Waverly had no foreknowledge that Evie would depart soon after her return from Ireland. The notes she'd left for Evie—half a dozen scraps, as if she'd torn pieces of paper into puzzle pieces—lay scattered across her desk. The first thing Evie had done was organize them by priority, and that was when she'd discovered the countess's plans for the enormous winter soiree in a month's time.

Evie would do all she could in a week, but some work would most certainly fall to her successor.

The clock struck four, which was usually the time when she'd begin doing her final tasks for the day. Today, she decided she could work a bit later. There was so much to catch up on, and despite Lady Waverly's less than warm attitude yesterday, Evie wanted to leave knowing she'd done the best she could for her.

What seemed only minutes later, the clock chimed the five-o'clock hour.

Mrs. Robards appeared in her periphery, and Evie sat up to stretch her neck and back. She hadn't sat hunched over in such concentrated work since writing out invitations in her room at Ballymore.

"Thought you might need a restorative. You've been working nonstop for hours, miss. Not even a walk for Mr. Chester."

At his name, the pug stood and stretched his front paws, his hind in the air.

"Sorry about that, Chessie." Evie smiled at the housekeeper. "And thank you, Mrs. Robards. I'm just trying to catch up."

"Aye, I can see that." She surveyed the piles Evie had created on her desktop. "Her ladyship was quite lost without you."

A pang of guilt tried to work its way into Evie's chest, but Mrs. Robards would have none of it.

"But she'll find another secretary, and you've found a much more appealing position, it seems."

Evie couldn't disagree.

"Our Miss Graves, a duchess. What a change for you."

"I don't know that I'll be a grand duchess in the sense of the Duchess of Vyne."

"No, I doubt you will, and why would you? You must be your own sort. And the Duchess of Vyne was not always her high and mighty self, you know."

"I suppose not." Evie tried to imagine the elderly noblewoman as a girl and suspected she was a bit of a spitfire.

"You do know, don't you?"

"Know what?"

"The Duchess of Vyne was her husband's governess before she became his bride. Came in to care for his children after his first wife passed." Mrs. Robards stepped closer. "Was a right scandal, it was," she added quietly. "None would invite her to their soirees or balls. So she was enterprising and threw her own. And look at her now."

"I don't know that I'll be throwing lavish balls." Evie knew she could pull off organizing such events, but if they spent most of their time in Galway, they'd rarely take part in the Season. "Maybe if we're ever in London."

Evie and Alex had not yet overcome all of the *challenges* they knew they'd face, but the chief solace was knowing they'd face them together.

"A ball is the best way to make the connections one needs to get on among this sort. And you know how to put on a good ball as well as any noblewoman worth her salt."

"That I do," Evie acknowledged. Maybe they would host a few events in London, if only as an opportunity for Alex to speak of his causes and discover others who might be willing to support them.

Josie appeared at the door.

"What is it?" Mrs. Robards asked warily. As housekeeper, she was the one the maids came to when something was amiss.

"A message for Miss Graves."

Josie approached and handed her a folded piece of paper. Nothing formal. It looked as if it had been scribbled hastily and folded just as quickly.

"Who delivered this?"

Josie's eyes widened, and she shrugged. "Just a man."

She and Mrs. Robards exchanged a look.

"We'll leave you to it, miss," Mrs. Robards announced and then escorted Josie from the room.

Evie unfolded the note.

Meet me in the garden. Bring matches. Love,
A xx

Evie sprang up from her chair, rushed out of the study, and found Josie waiting for her in the hall.

She handed her a box of matches.

"Thank you," Evie told her and then beelined for the door that led to Lady Waverly's back garden.

He looked magnificent in the late-afternoon light. He looked magnificent full stop.

Evie walked toward him at the same time he spotted her and began walking toward her. He wrapped her in his arms, lifted her off the ground, and buried his face against her neck.

"I've missed you," he said, his breath hot against her skin.

"And I you." Evie turned her head, and he took her mouth. The kiss was searing, bone-melting. She forgot what time it was, where they were, everything but him.

When they pulled apart, both breathless, both smiling like lovesick fools, Evie reached up and cupped his face.

"Why the matches?" she asked him. "What are we burning down?"

He laughed. "I see how your mind works. Just to light the lanterns."

They weren't lit this time of year, nor this time of day. Evie didn't know if their glow could even be appreciated in late afternoon. Still, she pulled a match from the box, struck it, and lit a few of the lanterns nearby before the flame reached her fingertip.

"There," Alex said, his hand at her back. "That reminds me of the night that changed my life forever."

"It was a fateful evening."

"Did you know it?" he asked softly. "You . . . departed swiftly, as if you were cross or had thought better about knowing me."

"I was a bit cross," Evie admitted. "For a moment, standing with you, talking to you, I imagined what life might have been. The things I'd given up any chance at when my father died and I had to provide for Sybil and me."

He swallowed hard and cradled her cheek in his palm. "You *thought* you'd given up that chance, but you hadn't."

Evie slipped an arm inside his coat, slinking it up his chest until she found the reassuring beat of his heart.

"I'd decided I couldn't change my circumstances, so I didn't dare to hope."

"I understand that feeling. I gave up on hoping too. Gave up on pursuing those things that matter to me most."

"But not anymore?"

"Not anymore." He stroked a hand up her back, pulling her closer. "You don't mind having a horse-obsessed, entrepreneurial husband, do you?"

"Not if you don't mind a wife who publishes romantic stories and is good at organizing."

He flashed a beaming smile. "Sounds perfect to me."

"Then I think we should. Marry, that is."

Alex chuckled, and Evie couldn't help but follow suit.

"Somehow," he said, cocking his head to the side as he studied her expression, "I had thought that was decided."

"I just wanted to make sure you hadn't changed your mind."

"In the last twenty-four hours."

"Well, I did leave you alone with your aunt, and I know she meddles occasionally."

"Daily."

"Well, I didn't want to be rude."

Alex bent and kissed her nose, then her cheek, then her forehead, and finally reached up to gently stroke the spot where her wound had healed.

"Nothing could keep me from you, Evie. Not waiting a week while you finish out your job. Not slow trains or clogged carriageways. Not the opinions of every single lord and lady in London or even Queen Victoria herself on her velvet throne.

Not even the machinations of a whirlwind like Oona McQuillan."

"Nothing could keep me from you either."

"I'm very glad to hear it." He kissed her, a quick, sweet taste. "You are my love, and I am yours."

"I wish we could start immediately." Now that she had him in her arms, Evie couldn't imagine letting him go again.

"We've already started, sweetheart. What's between us began the moment I stumbled over you in this garden and kept you from smashing a glowworm."

Evie laughed and buried her face in his chest, breathing in his scent, savoring the delicious warmth of his embrace.

"After this, no more nights apart if we can help it," she told him when she lifted her gaze to his again.

"Agreed."

"We're in this together. All the challenges."

"All the pleasures," he said with a seductive grin.

"Forever?"

"Forever, love."

Epilogue

Nine months later
June 1897
Ballymore Castle

Alex woke as the first glimmer of dawn lightened the horizon beyond their bedchamber window. With a satisfied yawn, eyes closed, he reached for his wife. And found only warm bedsheets under his palm.

He opened his eyes and frowned.

Evie did occasionally wake early or stay up late when she was working on a story. While on the deadline for her first published work—which was now in her London publisher's hands and would soon be bound and on sale by month's end—Alex had sometimes found her asleep at her desk in the guest room they'd converted into her office. He'd carry her back to bed and insist she compensate by sleeping in late the next day.

Today, he had a sneaking suspicion what had lured his wife from bed early. Evie had fallen in love—as had everyone at Ballymore—with the newest resident of Ballymore's stable.

Alex got out of bed and washed quickly, then donned his clothes.

Downstairs, he went straight for the kitchen. Mrs. Frain and the kitchen staff were up earliest, but he spied a light on in Mrs. Wilde's office too.

There was one other matter that might have caused Evie enough anxiety to rise early.

He knocked at the frame of Mrs. Wilde's open door, and the older woman immediately stood from her desk.

"Your Grace, is anything amiss?"

"Not at all. Simply looking for the duchess. Is everything set for our guests' arrival?"

"Indeed. I was just making a final list to make sure we've forgotten nothing. We may need to order in additional supplies for the kitchen."

"Whatever we need, you have my permission to place the order." Between rents from the London town house and Estings, as well as income from Evelyn's first published book, and the sale of several of Ballymore's horses, their finances were secure if not terribly flush.

They were expecting the imminent arrival of the Duchess of Vyne and Sybil. The duchess had taken an interest in Sybil's aspirations, and she'd become a champion and sponsor of both Graves sisters' efforts. She contributed to Sybil's tuition and introduced her to nobles with an interest in medicine, and she'd rallied the ladies of her literary society around the sale of Evie's first book.

Evie and the duchess had formed a close bond too. They corresponded frequently, and Alex and Evie had stayed with her on their last visit to London, since Rennick House was let.

"Her Grace is in the stables, I think," Mrs. Wilde said with a knowing smile. "None of us can seem to stay away from him."

So his instinct had been right. "The most adored colt in Ireland, I think."

"In Galway, at least," she agreed with a chuckle. "Shall I have a maid prepare some tea to take out to her, Your Grace?"

"Thank you, yes."

In no time at all, a maid had assembled a small basket with tea in a bottle and sturdy mugs rather than the delicate cups they normally used at breakfast.

Alex gathered the basket, grabbed a shawl of Evie's that she'd left on a chair in the conservatory, and made his way out to the stables. Shades of pink and gold and vivid orange lit up the sky, and though he expected a warm summer day, there was a cool, refreshing breeze this early in the morning.

He heard Evie's voice as his boots crunched the gravel near the stable. Though he couldn't make out her words, he recognized the cadence. She was reading. It was what she'd taken to doing with Brigid, one of the horses who'd come to them the previous year. They'd bred her with a thoroughbred, and throughout the tall regal ebony mare's pregnancy, Evie had taken to reading to her. Usually, from her own manuscript. She told Alex that reading it aloud helped her understand her story and where there might be gaps or inconsistencies she'd need to fix.

Brigid had been spellbound, calmed by Evie's voice and presence. Of course, Alex understood and had often come down to the stables, even when Evie didn't notice his presence, to listen.

Now she continued the tradition with Brigid and her foal. The colt was the same raven-black as his mother, and he had just begun to reveal his spirit. The little thing was full of wild energy, but he had a sweet nature too.

The combination had charmed everyone at Ballymore, and he'd lured nearly everyone out to the stables for visits. Even Aunt Oona.

When Alex rounded the corner, Evie immediately lifted her head and shot him a soft smile.

"Good morning, love," he told her as he brought the basket over and grabbed a low stool to sit beside her. She sat on a similar one, though she'd padded the seat with a blanket.

Alex settled the shawl around her shoulders.

"Good morning, husband." She glanced down at the basket. "If there's hot tea in there, I'll love you forever."

Alex chuckled. "I thought that was already a given."

"True, but tea is always appreciated."

Alex lifted the bottle of tea and spied a few freshly baked items the maid had included too. "I see some scones as well."

"Yes, please."

He filled both cups with tea and offered her a scone with a napkin the maid had tucked in the basket.

When she set her book down to take both, he realized she hadn't been reading her manuscript. Her book was to be bound in indigo and the volume on her lap was a distinct yellow shade. He recognized it was one of her recent favorites.

"Ah yes," Alex said as he took the volume into his hands. "Mr. Stoker's *Dracula*."

"I love the tale so much, and Brigid and the little man seem to as well. I might finish before Sybbie and Georgina get here."

"Mrs. Wilde assures me that everything will be ready for their arrival."

Evie glanced at him. "There are some aspects she doesn't know about yet. In Georgina's letter that arrived yesterday, she said she's reached out to some ladies in Dublin and thinks we should host a literary luncheon."

"That sounds like a grand idea."

"There will be a good deal of planning in a very short space of time."

"Your specialty, my love."

She smiled at that. "I'm still more comfortable with planning than hosting."

"But you're good at both."

They'd hosted a few largish dinners at Ballymore, and when they'd visited London, they'd accepted invitations to several social gatherings. Neither of them felt wholly at ease with the social whirl. But together, they'd found a balance between the work that truly mattered to them and making connections as Duke and Duchess of Rennick with those who supported or were interested in their endeavors.

"You know, we should probably decide on a name for him." Alex pointed through the slats in the stall door to the pretty little colt watching them interestedly.

"Well," Evie said, reaching over to pat the cover of her book, "if we're to follow in your mother's tradition, we should name him after a favorite literary character."

"No." Alex glanced at the black-eyed colt. "You're not thinking of naming him Dracula, are you?"

"Why not? It's a popular book by an Irish author. Seems perfect to me."

Brigid chose that moment to stick her nose over the stall door and heave her head up and down as if in agreement.

"I supposed I'm outvoted."

Evie leaned toward him, clasped his hand, and pressed a warm, sweet kiss to his cheek as if in compensation.

"I promise," she whispered, nuzzling his jaw,

"that you can have much more say the next time we choose a name."

"Thank you, sweetheart." Alex swept a lock of hair behind Evie's ear and kissed her properly. Then he bent to look down the line of stalls. "You hear that, Ophelia? I get to pick your foal's name."

The mare gave no reply, but she wasn't due to foal for another ten months.

"Of course, that won't be until next year," he told Evie in faux grousing.

"Actually," she said quietly, "you won't have to wait that long."

Her eyes glinted, and her lips curved mischievously.

"Oh?" Alex said, not understanding.

Then she reached for his hand, lifted it for a kiss against the back of his knuckles, and then lowered it, flattening his palm against her belly.

"Oh," he said, understanding dawning.

His heart thrashed in his chest as he swept Evie into his arms.

She laughed, and he stood, taking her with him.

"When?" he asked her breathlessly.

"Dr. Bailey says about seven months."

"How did you see him without me knowing?" By mutual agreement, they spent as many of their days together as they could.

"You'd gone to visit Aurelius, and I wanted to be certain."

Alex cupped her face in his hands, his body vibrating with so much love, so much joy, he wasn't certain he could contain it. And soon he wouldn't have to. They'd have a babe to share their love with.

"You've made me so happy."

Evie beamed. "As you have made me."

He kissed her until he was breathless, then once more for good measure.

She laughed at his exuberance, but he couldn't contain any of it. Didn't even want to try.

"Do you think we should tell Sybil and Georgina immediately? Or wait until Bel and Rupert know?"

"We tell them. We tell everyone. I'm ready to climb to the top of the Twelve Bens and announce it to all of Ireland."

She laughed so hard that she gripped her side. "Well, then I suppose we shouldn't wait."

"Not with this kind of good news."

Evie wrapped her arms around his waist. "We have enough joy to share."

"We do, sweetheart." And more coming soon, he thought and felt giddy all over again. "Indeed we do."

Acknowledgments

Thank you to my editor, Sylvan Creekmore, for helping me make this book better, and thanks to everyone at Avon who worked on this story along the way to publication.

Celebrate the summer with more books selected by Bridgerton's

JULIA QUINN!

UNLADYLIKE LESSONS IN LOVE

"Sizzling romance with a splash of intrigue."
—Julia Quinn

The first in a dazzling romantic mystery series, a half-English, half-Indian society hostess must grapple with her past, prove a man's innocence, and face off against a handsome yet infuriating man who seems determined to hate her—or does he?

WE COULD BE SO GOOD

"A spectacularly talented writer!"
—Julia Quinn

Casey McQuiston meets *The Seven Husbands of Evelyn Hugo* in this mid-century rom-dram about a scrappy reporter and a newspaper mogul's son, perfect for *Newsies* shippers.

HOW TO TAME A WILD ROGUE

"I am in awe of her talent."
—Julia Quinn

In this next installment of *USA Today* bestselling author Julie Anne Long's charming Palace of Rogues series, an infamous privateer sees his limits put to the test when he finds himself holed up with a prickly female companion at the Grand Palace while waiting out a raging tempest.

DUKE SEEKS BRIDE

"Simply delightful!"
—Julia Quinn

Christy Carlyle takes readers to the breathtaking coast of Ireland where a pretty, young countess's secretary agrees to impersonate her mistress to help a duke appease his fortune-hunting family...until he falls for her instead.

Discover great authors, exclusive offers, and more at hc.com